# THE DEVIL'S WEB

Shadow Squadron #3

## By David Black

Published by David Black Books

Copyright © David Black 2014


ISBN – 13:-978-1499723489

ISBN – 10: 1499723482




Cover design: David Black Books




Join David on Twitter - @davidblack21


http://www.david-black.co.uk



Contact David Black Books on:

shadowsquadron@btinternet.com

Dedication:


To:


**Roy, Scott & Glenn**

## ABOUT THE AUTHOR

David Black and his main character Special Forces team leader Pat Farrell - are so close as to be synonymous. 'I served as a part-time SAS Special Forces soldier leading exactly this kind of bizarre double life,' says Black. Like his main character Pat Farrell, Black worked as a London taxi driver during a long tenure as a Territorial SAS member, ready to be called into action in times of national emergency. The principal difference is that the author is now retired from the army, while his fictional counterpart is left to contend with 'the real world'… with direct relevance to the grisly global horrors being perpetrated today.' 'David Black' is a pseudonym, used to protect the author's identity and the integrity of his former Regiment.

# Foreword:

## Central Afghanistan

At last, the time had come. It was the morning of departure from Afghanistan.

Years of stomach-churning adventure serving Queen and country, were almost over.

Sergeant Pat Farrell was leaving the regular SAS for good. In a matter of weeks, he would cease to be a legend. Soon, he would become just another faceless civilian looking for a new job, and a fresh take on life.

\* \* \* \* \*

Pat Farrell surfaced reluctantly from a deep sleep, waking with an anvil-pounding hangover…

Despite the misery of his arid mouth and throbbing head, Pat's waking thoughts skipped a beat from the previous night's raucous farewell party, refocusing abruptly as it had done for a long time, inexorably slipping back to his decision to quit the army. Doubt had stalked him for months, as he carefully considered his options.

Just weeks after his final tour of Iraq, the first cracks had begun to appear. Pat started wondering. Was he being stupid? Suffering nothing more than some addled crisis; or was there something darker haunting his increasingly troubled thoughts?

Pat had accumulated a basketful of vivid and unwelcome memories; ugly moments from operations around the globe which he'd tried his best to forget. Subtly at first, dark memories began to exploit a chink in his subconscious armour, and now, privately; they were hurting.

Unable to rid himself of the painful echoes which now eddied all too frequently through his dreams, the truth became painfully apparent. It was time to change things for the better. He knew he must act quickly, before, like a drowning man slipping beneath the waves for the last time; memories of darker times overwhelmed him.

For his own salvation, somehow he must banish the sweat-drenched nightmares which began to invade his dreams. They came occasionally at first, but now, as the tough, gruelling years within the regular SAS wore on, the nightmares were coming too often.

To Pat's mind, inside the tough world of the regular SAS Regiment, there were lifelong friendships made, and plenty of good times too. He'd grasp the life belt of their memories tightly, but now a new challenge beckoned. He had to find a way to ditch the painful baggage no sane man wanted to rattle around inside his head, like a battery of loose cannons.

Pat knew the option was always there to admit the weakness to himself and others, and see the Regiment's medical officer, who would refer him straight to some un-badged military psychiatrist. That was not Pat's way. No, he decided; he didn't trust trick-cyclists from the big green army; however well-qualified they were on paper.

After what he had achieved with the Regiment, the reward of a shrink's mind-numbing pills and a medical discharge were not options worth considering. To Pat's way of thinking, this was a deeply personal crisis, he decided, was best kept to himself. He came to a decision. He'd fight this private battle alone, and seek salvation in his own unique way…

Now, he didn't wonder anymore; his mind made up; the future was clear. The army had been Pat's life for the last fifteen years, but he knew what must be done. Whatever happened, he realised that to heal these hidden wounds, it was time to pull the plug on active service. Pat was certainly going to miss the Regiment and all the good things that went with it, but it was time to go….

\* \* \* \* \*

# Chapter One

Even within the SAS, rank has its privileges.

Sunshine beamed through the small open window in Pat's private bunk. A single brilliant shaft of light flooded into the cramped room where he lay. Last night, he was the guest of honour; now Pat was a wreck; a crumpled heap on a camp-bed. With eyes tight shut, his fingers searched blindly beneath it for a half-empty bottle of mineral water, which he vaguely remembered, and hoped, still lay somewhere on the wooden floor beneath him. Cursing when his hand found nothing, he gave up the search as his mind drifted slowly back through time. He was still struggling to make sense of it all; seeking absolution for his past and justification for his life-changing decision to quit the SAS.

Pat's mind wandered elsewhere as he lay back on his camp-bed; the grimace faded. With his arm resting across his eyes to shield them from the light, he smiled fondly as he remembered, as a schoolboy, watching his father return home every evening from a local engineering factory. It was always the same; young Pat would hear the gate squeak as his old dad pushed his bicycle slowly down the covered alley at the side of the house, then locked it up in the shed at the end of their tiny garden. Dog-tired and grey haired, the old man would shuffle into the house, hang his cycle-clips, cap and scarf on a coat hook in the narrow hall, flop onto their dog-eared sofa and settle down in front of the television. Mum would bring him tea and his supper on a tray. It had always happened like that for as long as Pat could remember. His dad was so set in his ways; it was a mystery to the teenager, who yearned in quiet moments for something he couldn't quite put his finger on. The old man was somehow safe and comfortable with the same dull routine. Even his dad's social life was routine. Having a few beers with his cronies at the Crown and Anchor on a Friday night, or simply blanking out the empty hours before bed with soaps and the occasional Arsenal football match on TV; perhaps adding a bit of gardening at weekends during the spring and summer to change the tedium of otherwise mundane and ordinary days off.

In just a few years' time, his dad would have nothing more than a handshake and a small pension to look forward to when he retired. Where, teenaged Pat wondered, had been the adventure and excitement in a life like that?

By the time Pat was close to finishing school, he began searching for a way out, anything to avoid the same predicable routine, which was all his old dad had ever known.

Pat wasn't blessed with a childhood vocation. He had never nurtured boyhood dreams of being a policeman, fireman or engine driver. Without a calling to break the cycle, he felt doomed to the inevitable apprenticeship and a grey existence that his dad had lived since he was Pat's tender age. The idea of sharing the same kind of existence appalled Pat, but to his relief one day, something happened, which saved him.

Before he was finally done with his studies, every day, Pat trudged through his dreary run-down estate towards St Mary's school. As he passed the last row of drab terraces and reached the main road of the local high street, Pat passed one particular advertising hoarding, which from its first day towering above him, couldn't help but catch his eye. In bold six-foot letters, it suggested his path to an exciting life filled with adventure was to - '*Join the Professionals.*'

Pat struggled to concentrate during his first lesson that morning; flames of excitement were kindled. Throughout the dreary geography lesson concentrating on the annual cereal production within the Nile delta, something smouldered as his heart raced at what might be.

With the idea firmly embedded, Pat wrestled with the momentous decision for the final month through exams, right up to the very last day at school. It was, he knew, his one chance to break the logjam of routine and humdrum monotony, which beckoned. This was the only way to shed a dull, humdrum life working in some grimy factory, and change his future forever.

The day after he finished at school, spirits soaring, Pat took the bus to Enfield town centre, and with his parent's blessing, signed on at the local recruiting office.

That evening when he told them, his friends thought he was completely insane to surrender the many freedoms of civilian life, but in his heart, Pat knew he was doing the right thing. Two weeks later, after tearful hugs from his dear old mum and dad, Pat finally settled down on a train from the railway terminus of St. Pancras. Very soon, he was heading out of London towards the rural town of Royston, deep in the Hertfordshire countryside. His joining instructions ordered him to Bassingbourne Training depot. The time had come, there was no going back. His mind set on a life of pure adventure, Pat was going to be a soldier.

* * * * *

Basic infantry training was tough on young men who had barely learnt to shave; a massive shock to every teenager who attempted it. To his surprise, despite the rigorous discipline and ridiculously early-morning wake-ups by laughing corporals announcing reveille by prowling through their block banging dustbin lids with pickaxe handles, Pat found he enjoyed every minute of it.

After fourteen weeks of relentless square-bashing, map-reading, fitness and small-arms instruction, Private Farrell successfully completed his basic training. After a short period of leave, Pat was posted to the British Army of the Rhine in West Germany, where he joined his regular battalion, as a fully trained infantry soldier.

In the months that followed, he kept his mouth shut and his eyes wide open, volunteering for every course, which came along. His potential was spotted; Pat quickly became the youngest non-commissioned officer in the battalion, after less than a year in Germany. Two tough tours of Northern Ireland followed where Pat, now nineteen, was blooded for the first time into the harsh and merciless realities of war.

Pat led his own eight-man patrol on the second tour. Once again, he experienced the massive adrenaline rush of urban riots, bombings and shootings. This tour was different, however; this time he had his own men's lives to consider.

At the back end of the tour, his call-sign was ambushed by a pair of Provisional IRA snipers, in a back-street of the staunchly republican Creggan estate in Londonderry. His patrol chased down and cornered one of the snipers. After a shouted warning, Pat shot the Provo gunman, as he tried to climb over a wall and escape. L/Corporal Farrell kept his head, safely extracting his men from the ensuing riot, without casualties. The other sniper got away, but Pat had no regrets. It was still early days in his military career, and Pat didn't lose any sleep over the incident. To his mind, the N. Ireland '*troubles*' were a war of sorts, and he had simply done the job he was paid for.

\* \* \* \* \*

After five years of infantry soldiering, Pat felt that he was sliding into another bottomless vortex of boredom. In the limited world of the infantry soldier, the same training and exercises were becoming repetitive and routine; Pat decided he had had enough. Civilian life beckoned but then, in the capricious ways of life; something happened one day, which changed Pat's life and everything that went with it, forever.

Always looking for fresh material, a recruiting squad from the crack 22nd SAS Regiment had visited his battalion, who by then had moved back from Germany and were stationed in the tedious garrison town of Colchester. The small Special Forces team's slick presentation of life within the regular SAS captured Pat's imagination. Having thought about it carefully, rather than leave the military, he applied for permission to try the rigorous SAS selection course in the Welsh mountains. Unaware of Pat's discontent, his Colonel reluctantly agreed, and Pat was given his chance.

Based in Hereford, the regular SAS selection process was long and gruelling; by far, the toughest challenge Pat ever undertook. By day and night, short of sleep and often hungry, the exhausted hopefuls navigated independently across the wild and unforgiving Black Mountains and Brecon Beacons of south Wales, fighting through ferocious weather, carrying ever heavier packs, and always anxiously watching the clock. Set distances increased each time they went out alone into the hills. If a recruit failed to make the bogey time set for each long march over towering mountains and across deep, rain swept valleys that seemed to go on forever, they were failed and summarily returned to their parent unit without even the offer of a second chance. It didn't help that the ever vigilant SAS instructors kept each day's timings a closely guarded secret; they simply graded each wrecked candidate's performance, on what they had achieved that day or night.

Years earlier, during Pat's initial infantry training, the Training NCOs gave the green young recruits boundless support, getting into their faces, yelling threats and encouragement in equal measure; forcing the recruits to experience the hard way what they could really achieve if they pushed themselves enough. It was a solid training system for inexperienced teenage lads on the cusp of manhood, but now, the seasoned SAS instructors just stood back in silence, observing their more mature and experienced charges; assessing every action and reaction during the intense selection process. The SAS Training Wing ethos was simple: candidates came up to scratch and made the grade, or they didn't. It was entirely up to the individual to pass, through their own resources, grit and self-determination.

Knowing they were being closely watched added a heavy psychological dimension to the remorseless physical demands heaped onto each man's exhausted shoulders. Pat Farrell saw other candidates broken by the course; they simply succumbed to its hardships, or convinced themselves that this tough life wasn't for them, because in their hearts, they knew they didn't belong. The subtle difference between Pat and most of the others was that Pat knew something they didn't. Pat had found his place in the universe; everything in Hereford was right; he knew he definitely belonged exactly where he was.

Pat prepared himself well for the challenge, both physically and mentally. Avoiding serious injury, he ignored a multitude of painful and inevitable blisters and got on with the selection process without complaint. He knew only too well that the whole point was to root out the unworthy, so he gritted his teeth, played the grey man and took everything they threw at him.

All through the long selection process, the many individual qualities the Regiment was looking for in prospective recruits were rigorously tested; it was, after all, entirely voluntary. No-one forced any of them to march out alone, day and night, battling the terrain and themselves, struggling on through the pain-barrier of physical and mental exhaustion over the rugged, unforgiving Welsh mountains.

During Pat's selection course, the initial intake dropped from seventy-eight regular volunteers to just six, who finally passed the first mountain stage of selection. To earn the coveted sandy beret adorned with the famous winged dagger cap badge, there was a sting in the tail.

When the mountain phase was over, Pat and the five remaining SAS recruits switched to hot, steaming jungle marches beneath the dense canopy, toiling through oppressive heat, in a living hell of latticed shadows and trailing vegetation. Surrounded by the hooting and howling of hidden birds and animals, they patrolled and survived for days on end through miles of the untamed wilderness.It was another test, of course. Of the remaining six, another man lost it in the claustrophobic green of the rainforest; he was cut during the weeks of jungle training in far-off Brunei.

The SAS knew their job, and maintained their standards accordingly. They chose who they wanted and binned the rest, without the slightest hint of compassion or mercy.

# Chapter Two

Sgt Pat Farrell unzipped his sleeping bag and stretched. It was time to change things and go. He stood by his decision, and there was an end to it.

Pat got up from his camp-bed and yawned. Ignoring the hangover, he slapped his hand on his flat, hard stomach, wrapped a towel around his waist and pulled on an ancient pair of flip-flops. Pat stepped outside and sauntered slowly across to the shower block. As always, the sun shone brightly over the vast Camp Bastion in Helmand Province, located in the barren inhospitable desert of Central Afghanistan. At the time, it was base-camp to nearly six thousand British soldiers.

He and the other members of his troop had been relieved from their latest ambush operation in the Namakzar Mountains by another Special Forces troop two days earlier, and were now enjoying a few days rest in the relatively safe confines of the newly-built and heavily fortified camp. After three weeks in the mountains, his boys were ready for a good break. Despite random mortar and rocket-propelled grenade attacks by the invisible Taliban, Camp Bastion was the best and safest respite in country, the British army had to offer in wild Afghanistan.

The shower's spray of tepid water helped, but Pat's head was still feeling the effects of the large number of beers he had consumed the night before with the rest of his men. They had been joined by a dozen pretty nurses, who had been cordially invited from the adjacent military field-hospital.

Alcohol was, of course, strictly forbidden to all service personnel stationed in Camp Bastion, but with the usual SAS disregard for the rules of the big green army; ten cases of beer had mysteriously appeared the night before. It was smuggled into the small, separate and highly secure Special Forces enclave that nestled secretly behind thick rolls of razor-wire, sandbags and concrete blast walls, deep within the bleak confines of the otherwise 'dry' Camp Bastion.

Pat knew it was going to be a good party, without any consequences, when the beer was delivered personally on a trolley by Rover Walsh, his own squadron Sgt Major. Everyone respected Rover, who had earned his nickname the hard way as a young trooper in Hereford, during a short and vicious bar-room fight with a gang of Hell's Angels, some years earlier.

'As it's your last night, Pat, the boss thought these might help to say goodbye,' growled Rover with a conspiratorial wink, as he began passing beers to Pat and the rest of his delighted Troop.

Feeling refreshed after his shave and shower, Pat walked casually back to his wooden single-story troop hut and got dressed in what would have got him locked-up at the Guard's depot in Surrey, but passed for a clean and tidy uniform within the SAS. As he set off towards the cook house in search of breakfast, Moggy Morris, the squadron's clerk hailed him,

'Hey Pat, the boss wants to see you.'

Pat's solid, easy-going temperament made him popular with the men in his squadron. Moggy fell into step beside Pat, as they walked towards the squadron office.

'Good piss-up last night, was it?' enquired Moggy, who had been on duty, and missed it.

'It had its moments,' laughed Pat, holding his head and wincing. He was expecting a private farewell chat with his Squadron commander, and assumed this was it. Major Humphrey Harcourt-Reed was sitting behind his desk, studying a map when Pat and Moggy entered his office. He looked more serious than Pat was expecting,

'Hallo Pat, I need to talk to you... The Yanks have got a big operation on, and I want you to take your boys back into the mountains, tonight.'

Pat stood in stunned silence as the Squadron commander outlined the current situation,

'You will be operating in the White Mountains, close to the border with Pakistan.'

Using a pen, he indicated the area on the map.

'Specifically, the op. is in the Pachir Wa Agam District, about fifty clicks west of the Khyber Pass.' Knowingly he added, 'its real bandit country up there; specifically, you're interested in the area known as the Tora Bora cave complex.' The hard-faced major looked up and stared intently at Pat, 'The Americans have received strong intelligence, suggesting Bin Laden himself is hiding somewhere inside it.'

Pat knew it was pointless arguing or complaining. Although his papers were in, the army still owned his soul for another five weeks. He stood hunched over the map and continued to listen to his Squadron commander in silence.

'The irony of this place is that after the Russians invaded Afghanistan, the CIA paid for the complex to be strengthened and expanded, for the Mujahedin to use as a secure base. Apparently, the Yanks spent millions fixing it up. It's got its own electricity supply, a fully fitted hospital, underground ammunition dumps, air filtration, and plenty of room for the guerrillas. Intelligence thinks there are currently somewhere around two thousand Taliban, Chechens, Arabs and Pakistani militants dug in up there. They have taken a real beating in the area lately, and have fallen back and taken refuge in the Tora Bora caves. The Americans think they are planning a last-stand up there. Intel says the complex is huge, and near enough impregnable, so a ground assault has been ruled out.'

Looking up from the map, the boss dropped his pen on the desk. He stared at Pat once again, 'The Americans plan to bomb the place back to the Stone Age; they are pulling out all the stops on this one. Apparently, their B52s are going to carpet bomb the whole area, and afterwards; their Marines and Special Forces are going to sift through what the bombers miss.'

Pat nodded. He had worked with the American Green Berets and Delta Force before. They were all good men; a bit too gung-ho sometimes, but their hearts were in the right place.

'We have been tasked to throw out a screen of observation points on the western edge of Tora Bora, and call in fast-jet air strikes on any hidden exits which we spot being used, both during and after the B52s drop their bombs.' He shrugged absently, 'there are bound to be some survivors, and your job is to help the fly boys nail anyone trying to escape.' Major Reed paused, then shrugged apologetically, 'I know you are supposed to be going home today Pat, but I've only just received a flash signal from SAS Group in Whitehall, ordering us to assist in this operation. You and your Troop are all I've got left, I'm afraid; everyone is already out on operations…' He shrugged, 'There simply is not anyone else available...'

\* \* \* \* \*

Pat thought about the initial briefing as he sat huddled against the icy wind in the observation point overlooking the massive ridge, inside which the networked cave complex lay hidden. He had received a further detailed briefing from his squadron's operational intelligence team when the boss had finished his brief. When it was over; Pat wandered back to the Troop hut to pass on the bad news to his men. There had been grumbles, but as usual, his Troop buckled down to the operation and diligently prepared during the last hours in Bastion for their own appointed tasks.

Pat studied his own maps carefully. He'd identified only four points on the adjacent mountains overlooking Tora Bora which would suit his purpose. Each one offered good concealment, and could be entered and exited clandestinely. The small SAS patrols wouldn't stand a chance if they were 'bumped' by the enemy in their isolated positions, so getting in and out quietly and unseen was imperative.

His troop was comprised of four, four-man patrols, including two men drafted in from the attached S.F. signals' troop, who replaced casualties taken during their last mission. What worried Pat was that they wanted him to observe a full nine kilometre arc; his patrols, due to the geographical layout of the mountains, could cover a front of no more than seven clicks. He had explained his plan later to his boss, and in conclusion, added his misgivings to Major Harcourt-Reed, who shrugged his shoulders and closed the briefing, saying,

'It's the usual deal; I'm afraid. Do miracles with what you've got.'

Hidden in the small, uncomfortable observation point, despite extra layers of clothing, Pat shivered as the icy wind seeped into his bones and thoroughly chilled him.

The SAS patrols inserted on foot during the previous night. They were flown into the area and were dropped off by a blacked-out RAF Puma helicopter, well short of the reverse slope of the ridge they were going to use during the mission. It started to snow as they patrolled through the dark, dangerous territory and began to climb the steep ridge, heavily burdened with five-day supplies of food, water and ammunition, plus other specialist equipment, specifically carried for the mission. The different routes taken by each patrol had been punishing, but the Regiment's rigorous selection and constant fitness training in the mountains of South Wales had once again proven its worth. Each four-man patrol was safely in position and ready, as dawn broke the next day.

In the dark hours before first light, each patrol had begun to build their own observation hide, carefully camouflaging it to blend into the surrounding rocky outcrops. With the practiced eye, which only comes with years of experience, each patrol commander was eventually satisfied that their O.P. would be completely invisible from the target ridge, on the other side of the lonely valley.

Talking, even in whispers was dangerous and used sparingly. Working together, the SAS men quietly readied the LTM (Laser Target Marker) devices, which would help the American fighter-bombers target their laser-guided bombs with pinpoint accuracy. The patrol's signaller established secure communications with Bastion, and a 'rest' area where patrol members could shelter, when not on observation duties, was set up in the crags, a few feet behind the concealed O.P.

As the sun began to rise, it cast a warm orange glow over the range of snow-capped mountains, spreading long shadows into the deep valleys which surrounded the distant peaks. The Tora Bora ridge loomed large in the powerful binoculars of each hidden O.P., as the SAS soldiers continually swept the snow-laden ridge lines and gullies, searching patiently for any sign of enemy movement and escape.

\* \* \* \*

The first wave of American B52 bombers began to release their payloads at precisely 11.00hrs., local time. There was no overhead roar from the massive aircraft's Pratt and Whitney engines; the Stratofortresses were flying at their optimum bombing height, over five and a half miles above their target. The only clue to their arrival was the pure white con-trails streaking lazily across the cloudless heavens in the freezing rarefied atmosphere,high above Tora Bora.

Laden with tons of iron bombs, squadrons of the ponderously heavy bombers took off, hours earlier, from the American airbase on the tiny atoll island of Diego Garcia in the Indian Ocean. Slowly gaining altitude, they flew 5,000 miles north across the empty Indian Ocean towards landlocked Afghanistan. As the heavy bombers crossed Pakistani airspace, and began their final run-in to Tora Bora, the bombardiers made small adjustments to their computerised global positioning bomb sights, as the B52's massive bomb-bay doors swung open.

A repeat of the Arc-Light bombing missions during the Vietnam conflict, a maelstrom of explosions pounded the cave complex, as each 500lb and 1,000lb unguided bomb buried into the ground and exploded. Under the shattering drumbeat of high-explosives, deep inside the complex, lights went out as ceilings and passageways collapsed in thick clouds of choking dust. The concussions continued; hundreds of Taliban and their allies were buried alive under the falling rocks.

Over the next three terrifying days and nights, refuelled and rearmed, the bombers returned time and again, giving the SAS observers a grandstand view of the destruction. The B52's bombs fell like rain; earthquake concussions repeatedly pounded the Tora Bora stronghold, and ultimately, obliterated it.

Beneath dense clouds of acrid smoke, the hardened underground complex, which had promised sanctuary became, instead, an airless and wretched tomb.

On the last day, twelve hours after the fireworks ended, Pat and his men received a coded signal to extract themselves, and rendezvous with the chopper which would fly them back to Bastion.

Later intelligence analysis concluded that Osama bin Laden had escaped the bombing by just a few hours, using one of the 'blind spot' paths, which led south, away from Tora Bora.

While the SAS patrols had built their observation points during their first freezing night in enemy territory, Osama bin Laden had silently slipped out of the Tora Bora cave complex, with his lieutenants, wives and children following. Tribal warlords were paid hefty bribes to provide guides to help them pick their way through the White Mountains using the secret smuggling trails, which crisscrossed the area. The guide's local knowledge proved invaluable; the fugitives avoided hunting allied patrols, and eventually escaped eastwards over the snow-capped mountains, to the sanctuary of Pakistan.

Days later in Bastion, Pat's discharge was confirmed. He flew back to the UK and joined non-military life. His metamorphosis from steely-eyed SAS soldier, to just another grey civilian looking for a job, began.

# Chapter Three

Part Two –

Afghanistan - Present day

There was movement across the arid land. Black undulating shadows crawled sinuously over the rugged slopes beneath a burning sun, high in the lawless crucible of the Waziristan Mountains of northwest Pakistan.

After hours of unremitting heat, engines growling as they followed the ancient smuggler's trail; two battered Toyota pickups finally completed the winding and punishing climb. Acknowledging the heavily-armed sentries, they slowed and stopped in a cloud of red dust in the centre of the isolated mud-walled compound.

There were already other vehicles waiting, parked silently beside the lonely building, where Al-Qaeda had arranged the secret rendezvous.

In the first pick-up, Usman Jawad, commander of the Taliban in Waziristan nodded curtly to his brother-in-law; his most trusted driver, before opening the passenger door. Ignoring the searing blast of heat, Jawad gripped his AK assault-rifle, turned and raised it towards his other vehicle, which overflowed with his fiercely loyal bodyguard. Each of them wore untidy beards and ammunition bandoliers overflowing robes; their soiled, messy garb topped with the Taliban's distinctive black turban. Words were un-necessary; the fierce mountain men understood their leader's gesture. Grasping their automatic weapons tightly, they jumped down from the back of their vehicle, before fanning out to the high wall around the isolated compound. They joined Jawad's advance-guard, who had arrived two days earlier and already established a strong defensive perimeter.

Satisfied with his security, the cruel-faced commander walked towards the smiling, bespectacled man waiting patiently for him in the shadow of the low building's open doorway. Acknowledging the respectful nod of his host, he took the proffered hand and shook it as he was hugged and welcomed by Zahira Khan, newly appointed head-facilitator and coordinator of Al-Qaeda operations in Pakistan. Jawad remembered him from long ago as a playmate of his childhood, and was, he had been reminded in the letter which had invited him to the meeting, distantly related to his host.

Family ties, however remote, counted for a great deal in the barren region; it was a powerful vouchsafe; an unspoken promise of shared blood and allegiance. It had been the only reason the Taliban leader had overcome his initial reservations, provided security, and accepted the invitation to this lonely spot, high in the mountain wilderness.

As the two robed men turned and entered the only room in the small building, steaming cups were lowered and muted conversation died away from those already seated on cushions arranged on the earth floor, laid around the carpeted walls of its gloomy interior.

Jawad recognised none of the silent men. Some, like him, were hook-nosed, robed and swarthy; others appeared to be lighter-skinned Arabs dressed in European T-shirts and jeans. There were two skinny black men sitting with their backs against the wall, who whispered to each other as they returned his searching stare.

The Taliban commander's suspicious nature kept him alive as a young Mujahedeen, during savage battles with the Russians in years long-past. His mistrustful instincts still protected him, fighting against the latest infidel invaders who had come to the graveyard of Afghanistan. The danger of assassination by a rival Taliban faction was also a constant threat which kept him alert, and permanently on his guard.

His cruel eyes narrowing, Jawad continued to regard each of the strangers in turn with a cold, mistrustful stare as he slowly raised the muzzle of his AK. Jawad's thumb brushed the weapon's safety-catch as his index finger curled around the assault-rifle's scratched and pitted trigger.

His host noticed the subtle movements and his guest's suspicious expression; instantly understanding the imminent peril of their meaning.

Framed by the sunlight streaming through the open doorway, cautiously, he stepped closer to his kinsman thrice removed. Gently taking the Taliban commander's elbow, he smiled reassuringly and spoke softly,

'Ah, dear cousin, be not concerned. You are here among the truest of friends.' Zahira Khan gestured around the gloomy room with a slow sweep of his hand, 'These are all your brothers in Islam; an Ummah of warriors bound together by our beloved Prophet, peace be upon him.' Khan expression suddenly became sombre. 'The blood of their peoples, shed in our war against the evil ones, adds to the glue which binds us all in our holy Jihad.'

Zahira Khan's expression turned sour as his mind filled with thoughts of the enemies of Islam. Hatred flared for the West and burned brightly. His welcoming smile returned quickly, however, as he gestured towards the last unoccupied cushion.

Khan said softly, 'Please cousin, sit down, and trust in our words... I ask you, most graciously, to prepare yourself to hear your own part in an operation of the very greatest importance.' Zahira Khan's eyes narrowed; his wolfish smile grew, 'it is my humble plan to avenge the death of our martyred leader, Osama bin Laden.'

Surprise replaced suspicion on the Taliban commander's face.

Ignoring his startled kinsman for a moment, the Al-Qaeda facilitator turned to the expectant faces staring up at him from around the room. Raising empty hands towards the roof, Khan cried aloud,

'We will bring raging hell down upon the infidels, and strike everlasting terror in the hearts of the vile un-believers, who dared to martyr our beloved leader Osama bin Laden, the greatest of Islamic crusaders...'

\* \* \* \* \*

In his plush air-conditioned office in Langley, Virginia, William Bradley, one of the assistant directors of the Central Intelligence Agency, stared intently at the images on the high-definition screen set up before him. Beside him, Jack Lumis, head of the C I A's Special Activities Division blew out a cloud of cigar smoke and smiled with satisfaction at the vivid results his drone was beaming back to Langley,

'Damn!' He exclaimed with poorly hidden pride, 'No matter how often I see them; I can never get used to such pin-sharp clarity coming out of my birds, from halfway around the world.' He turned away from the colour screen and looked at his companion, 'Can you, Bill?'

William Bradley shook his head in silence as he watched the two vehicles stop outside the lonely flat-roofed building. Men tumbled from the second truck, while just a single figure paused, then entered the isolated structure, from the first Toyota.

On the desk before him, the triangular conference speaker crackled momentarily as a remote voice broke the silence and enquired,

'Err… are you getting this OK, Jack?'

It was the voice of Henry Tallows, Jack Lumis' number two, who had flown out yesterday, and was now in Nevada, personally overseeing the deployment of the drone sortie, which all three men were currently focused on. Leaning forward, Lumis nodded absently,

'Yeah, Henry, we see everything you do.'

Bounced in real-time, via military satellites from northern Pakistan, the images were coming from high-definition video cameras carried in the nose of a high-flying drone aircraft. The live, streamed pictures were used by their operating pilots, based safely on the U.S. Creech Air Force complex near Indian Springs, hidden deep in the vast Nevada desert. The pilots remotely flew the unmanned MQ-1Predator drones, which constantly crisscrossed the jagged mountains of the Pakistani badlands, observing areas of interest for the CIA, gathering intelligence, and seeking valuable targets for their deadly Hellfire missiles.

The CIA deputy Director licked his lips. Shaking his head slowly, he sighed,

'I'd give my pension to hear what is being discussed at this meeting, Jack.'

His colleague nodded. With a snort of agreement, Lumis added,

'Hell, something sure has got them all riled up, and that's a fact.' He rubbed his chin, 'Let's face it, the Intel. paper-trail that got us this far has taken huge resources and months of surveillance and intelligence analysis, just to track this damned meeting. We've got Al-Qaeda, Hamas, Al-Shabaab, the Taliban and God alone knows who else down there; all having tea and a cosy little hubbub together.'

William Bradley had to agree. Like so many times before, despite billions of dollars the U.S. spent every year fighting Islamic terrorism on behalf of the free world, this time, they had simply got lucky. Tracking an Al-Qaeda courier after an unguarded slip on one of countless thousands of monitored cell phones in Pakistan; the Brit's at GCHQ in England had their suspicions aroused when they heard the name – Al-Amin. They shared their intelligence as evidence of something in the Al-Qaeda pipeline grew, and eventually led, through the shadowy world of intercepts and informants, to a newly appointed Al-Qaeda leader, one Zahira Khan.

Unsubstantiated intelligence linked him with the deadly four-day attack on the most affluent quarter within the densely populated Indian city of Mumbai. Showing no mercy, the terrorist murder squad roamed the streets seeking victims, ultimately claiming one hundred and sixty-six innocent civilians dead, and twice as many wounded. Ajmal Kasab, the sole survivor among the heavily-armed Lashkar-e-Taiba terrorists who attacked unprotected hotels, schools and churches subsequently confessed, was found guilty, and hanged in Yerwada Jail in Pune. His admissions under interrogation, before his trial and execution, pointed inexorably to Al-Qaeda. To the anger of the Indian government, he suggested duplicity by the ISI; Pakistan's Intelligence Agency, as being somehow complicit in the murderous attack.

\* \* \* \* \*

When the Indian's intelligence and suspicions were shared with the West, red flags began appearing in the U. S. Defence Committee meetings. The CIA was ordered to point its immensely powerful resources at the man, now known as Zahira Khan. Piece by piece, the trail leading to the current secret meeting of terrorist leaders was uncovered. The final location had only been gleaned hours before the arrival of Khan's first guest. There was time enough to divert a patrolling American drone, but not, unfortunately, enough time to mount a covert operation to bug the heavily guarded meeting place, and listen in on the terrorist gathering.

What, William Bradley wondered, could have brought so many high-value terrorist leaders together, to a damned goat farm in the middle of nowhere, at Zahira Khan's invitation? The CIA's sophisticated face recognition software identified and confirmed most of the high-ranking fugitives in turn. They were all wanted men, who belonged to different and unspeakably ruthless Islamic terror organisations. Between them, their bloody hands bombed, maimed and murdered everywhere from Bali to Jerusalem, and viciously attacked across Europe in the name of their twisted beliefs.

*Hell!* Bradley thought angrily. For that matter, they cast their dark shadow everywhere across the world, particularly after a recent spate of deadly attacks on U.S. and friendly embassies scattered around the globe.

All the men currently gathering together in Waziristan, he mused, shared two deadly connections. Each was a wanted Jihadist leader, and secondly; their respective organisations were, at least, in part, associated with the terrorist group responsible for the infamous and diabolical 9/11 attacks on the Pentagon, and the Twin Towers in New York. Al-Qaeda certainly appeared to be the key, but why, he wondered, were they holding such a dangerous meeting in northern Pakistan, and more importantly, what exactly were the bastards up to?

Jack Lumis lent forward and stubbed his smoking cigar into the ornate crystal ashtray sitting on Bradley's desk. Staring at the thin wisp of smoke, which rose from the crushed stub, he enquired,

'So what's the plan now, Bill? Whatever's going on, this meeting is clearly very important, but let's be honest. We've no idea what it's about.' He raised an inquisitive eyebrow, and then enquired,

'Do we go on observing, or take them down?'

William Bradley sucked his teeth while he considered the question, and his limited options. The President had authorised a highly successful, but controversial, cross-border assassination campaign, using missiles fired from the CIA's high-flying Predator and Reaper drones. The Pakistani government and their military leaders, despite a national outcry and subsequent riots, according to secret diplomatic exchanges, not only tacitly agreed to the drone strikes, but indeed, back in 2008 had requested that the Americans should increase them.

The biggest problem came with the inevitable collateral civilian casualties. Unsanctioned deaths had occurred too often, and only recently the provocative policy had hit the world's headlines once again, when a mountain wedding party on the Pakistan/Afghanistan border had been mistakenly attacked. The custom of firing into the air by the guests, in celebration, was mistaken for hostile action against the drone, tasked with monitoring the gathering. Missiles were launched; thirty-seven wedding guests died, and another eighty-three were wounded.

In Washington, the press and elected opponents of the shoot-to-kill policy up on the Hill had a field day. The CIA had, secretly, and immediately, launched their own campaign; lobbying to continue the aerial offensive, which was finally agreed at a midnight meeting in the Oval Office of the White House. As a result of the general furore, stringent new controls had been implemented. Authorisation now had to come direct from the Pentagon for every future strike, before it could be launched.

As the minutes ticked unhurriedly by, William Bradley, his mind finally made up, reached for the red telephone on his desk, and lifted it slowly from its cradle.

The whole purpose of the campaign, he had decided, was to disrupt future terrorist operations against the continental United States and her allies, and take out the command elements of their fanatical enemies wherever possible. Like his colleague, he had no idea what the current meeting was about in far-off and volatile Waziristan, which grazed the mountains of nearby Afghanistan. Whatever its purpose, he rationalised, given the personalities attending, he'd bet his career it must be something extremely serious, and therefore, almost certainly something highly dangerous to the U.S. A decisive strike now would cut the heads off many serpents, and the fireball hammer blows from the drone's supersonic missiles would certainly disrupt the meeting, and whatever was being discussed and planned in the far-off mountains.

Depressing the button bearing the legend *Pentagon*, Bradley said softly,

'This is William Bradley; calling from Langley… Put me through to General Harrison…'


The terrorist summit in the Waziristan Mountains was drawing to a close. There were appreciative gasps, feral grins and earnest grunts of approval as Zahira Khan outlined his murderous plan to his confederated audience. It was agreed; when the trap was fully set, the last stage of his plan would be a spectacular, world-headline grabbing attack; matching in the eyes of the West and Al-Qaeda supporters everywhere, the power and destruction of the hugely successful plot of 9/11.

Sensing their swelling approval, Khan had answered his guest's questions easily, and basked in the warmth of support and enthusiasm he received from everyone who spoke out at the terrorist Shura. Every guest had willingly accepted the plan and formally pledged their organisation's support, and now; to Al-Qaeda's Zahira Khan, his way was clear to launch the next phase of the deadly conspiracy. He smiled with self-satisfaction. All was well with forging the new brotherhood, which to his guest's mutual delight, he had aptly named: Al-Amin – *'The Faithful.'*

Their organisation's roles and operational details were encoded on individual and clearly labelled memory sticks. When, at last, he firmly embraced every conspirator in farewell; he handed one to each guest in turn, as they left the building.

'I'm sorry, Mr Bradley; the General is in a meeting…'

William Bradley glared at the telephone's handset, before jamming it back to his ear,

'I don't care if he's in a goddamned meeting with the Arch Angel Gabriel, son,' he snarled, 'get him on the horn, right *NOW!*'

Jack Lumis listened to the exchange in silence, and kept his eyes glued firmly to the screen. He understood the time-lag which the new protocols sometimes imposed, but there was nothing he could do about it; when careers hung in the balance, things had to be done by the book. William Bradley's neck would be on the block if something went wrong, and he was found to have acted without the proper authorisation.

Lumis' involuntary eavesdropping was deflected when he saw sudden movement on the screen. William Bradley was still distracted; he was tapping his pen and scowling intently at an ink stain on his blotter, while he waited impatiently to be put through.

'Hey Bill, looks like the meeting is breaking up.'

At that moment, Henry Tallows voice, calling from distant Nevada filled the Langley office. He sounded agitated,

'Ah, hey Jack, we've got movement in Waziristan. Are we cleared for a strike? What do you want me to do?'

Jack Lumis winced; raising his eyebrows, he stared anxiously across at his boss. Red faced; the deputy Director returned his stare, but held up his hand,

'No, not yet… *Wait!*'

On the screen before them, clouds of dust were beginning to rise. The first vehicles had begun to leave the compound. Lumis groaned. Like Henry Tallows, there was a new edge of anxiety in the CIA man's voice,

'But Bill, it's over; they're leaving…'

There was a distinct click from Bradley's handset. A gruff voice announced,

'*General Harrison…*'

With an audible sigh, the Deputy Director spoke rapidly,

'General, its William Bradley calling from Langley. We have an urgent situation here and need an emergency authorisation for a missile strike from one of our drones over northwestern Pakistan, close to the Afghan border.'

There was silence for several seconds. Then the General's reply came,

'Who is the target; exactly where and why is the strike required and are there civilians involved or at any collateral risk?'

With one eye on the screen, as he watched the third vehicle depart; Bradley answered quickly, 'No civilians, in a deserted region in the mountains of Waziristan, and a hat full of very senior Al-Qaeda linked operatives…All of them on our most-wanted list.'

There was silence again before General Harrison angrily spluttered his reply,

'Damn it, Bradley! Your people have been wrong before. Telling me this is another emergency, short-circuits the President's new rules of engagement… I will not…'

William Bradley could not spare a single moment more and begin a protracted argument with the General. He had tried to get official sanction, but was out of time. Abruptly, he interrupted the General in mid-sentence,

'I'm implementing the Fall-Staff protocol, General. I take full responsibility for the strike…'

This time the General's reply came swiftly,

'Very well, Bradley,' he said, '… but on your head be it.'

The General hung up, confident that the call was logged and recorded both at the Pentagon and Langley. His hands were now clean of the matter. In exceptional circumstances, the Fall-Staff protocol could be called, but exercising it placed sole responsibility on anyone so authorised who used it, should things go badly wrong.

As he replaced the handset, the Deputy Director shouted towards his conference phone,

'Still there, Henry?'

'*Yes Sir!*'

'You are formally authorised to launch the strike…'

Hidden in the restricted CIA area, in a remote corner of the Nevada air force base, Henry Tallows stared at his own screen. The first vehicle was now almost quarter of a mile from the walled compound, and in the still mountain air, its dust was badly obscuring the other vehicles which followed.

'Which vehicles shall I target, Mr Bradley? I've only got two missiles, and I can't identify who is in which.'

Inside his office in Langley, William Bradley clicked his tongue with profound frustration; he cursed himself for not arranging another drone to loiter over the target area in case it was needed. He could see exactly what Tallows could see, which now, because of the swirling dust kicked up behind the lead vehicle, wasn't much. Despite the air-conditioning, a thin bead of sweat trickled down the side of his forehead. Sometimes, a guess was the only trump card he could play. He stabbed at an answer, his voice betraying the pressure he was suddenly under,

'Go for the first and last vehicles, Tallows. *Nail them both!!*'

The conference phone crackled once again with Tallow's reply, then fell silent.

'*Roger that!*'

Jack Lumis squirmed uncomfortably in his seat. The risk was; he guessed, acceptable, but the outcome was far from certain. Raising one eyebrow, he whispered,

'Spray and pray, Bill?'

William Bradley nodded morosely. With more than a hint of irony, he replied slowly,

'Yeah, Jack, something like that…'

There was an agonising delay as the drone's pilot, sitting in his air-conditioned cubicle in front of Tallows, lined up on the leading vehicle with his aircraft's on-board laser target marker. The picture from Waziristan shuddered suddenly, as the first Hellfire missile surged from beneath the drone's starboard wing. Sensors in the missile's nose-cone quickly identified and locked onto the illumination of the brilliant laser spot reflecting off the fleeting vehicle far below. At almost twice the speed of sound, the missile raced from the heavens towards its target. Like a streak of lightning, with a final roar, it hit squarely in the middle of the target pick-up, and exploded with a brilliant orange flash and a thunderous roar. From both Nevada and Langley, the CIA men watched the silent spectacle of the vehicle disintegrating in fire, smoke and metal-rending chaos.

Unfazed by the destruction, the pilot calmly switched the laser marker to the rear vehicle, and shortly afterwards; the drone's wings and fuselage shuddered once more…

Far below, as tangled metal rained down around them, the other vehicles swerved and stopped with a screech of brakes. The occupants immediately realised the danger they were in. Jumping from their vehicles, they ran pall-mall in all directions, desperately seeking cover. The first pick-up had contained a few guards and the guide who was ordered to lead the convoy back to the remote mountain village, where it was planned they would spend the coming night. The driver was a local man, well versed in the lonely trails which crossed the mountains. Concentrating on the rock-strewn track ahead, he didn't hear the final hissing whoosh of one hundred and nine pounds of supersonic missile, and didn't feel the heat and blast of its twenty-pound, tank-killing high-explosive warhead. One moment he was driving along the track, the next, he simply vanished in the massive explosion; his pulverised remains spread across hundreds of metres of surrounding wilderness.

The last vehicle, filled with Taliban commander Noor Usman Jawad's cut-throat bodyguards, fared no better. In the sudden confusion of the initial strike, and the concussion of the massive blast, vital seconds were lost in a swirl of stunned confusion. Even as the first bodyguard leapt from the vehicle, the red dot of the drone's laser sparkled and flashed between them. Someone had noticed the dancing sprite and frantically screamed a warning, but it was too late. Fifteen battle-hardened Taliban were blown to pieces in a blinding instant, sent in search of paradise by a fiery streak from the sky, which had, until moments before, been stencilled with the legend: *Manufactured in the U.S.A.*

Beneath thick palls of oily black smoke, shocked and dazed, Al-Qaeda's operations planner, Zahira Khan, stood up and brushed dust from his robes. Blood ran from cuts to his forehead and cheeks, caused when his vehicles' windscreen had imploded; blown to jagged shards by the first concussion. Ears still ringing, he noticed the black turbaned Taliban commander striding unsteadily towards him. He was also bleeding, and alone.

'Your men, cousin?'

Glancing back at the burning, pounded wreckage at the other end of the convoy, Jawad slowly shook his head. His face sour, he spat,

'They are gone…' Jawad's shoulders hunched into a shrug. His eyes matched the cold indifference of the gesture, 'it is of little matter cousin; I have many more….'

# Chapter Four

Six months later

The man's breath clouding white around him, hooded eyes narrowed as he slowly lowered the binoculars. Watching from his concealed vantage point, surrounded by silent dripping forest and swirls of morning mist, a thin smile of satisfaction spread beneath the woollen scarf he wore tightly wrapped around the lower part of his face. Everything, he thought, foretold in the training camp, was coming true.

A violent shiver coursed through his body; prompted this time not by the cold, dank atmosphere of the forest; the involuntary shudder was fuelled by a sudden avalanche of adrenaline and anticipation, which surged through his veins, making his heart beat even faster. Excited by what he spied far below, the watcher firmly depressed the send button of the small two-way radio he held tightly in his other hand. His voice betraying his rush of sudden excitement, he lifted the device to his mouth and spoke rapidly in Arabic,

'It is time, Youssef. Get ready; they are coming…'

Beneath grey, sombre skies, the Range Rover growled through the grand chateau's ornate iron gates. In minutes, clearing the estate's acres of dense and private forest, the gleaming vehicle would join the coastal trunk road which hugged the sinuous Normandy coastline. In less than ten minutes, the sleek 4 x 4 would arrive at its destination; the privately owned Angelopoulos stud farm, located just outside the sleepy fishing village of Almar St. Clair.

Having received a terse acknowledgment from the crackling handset, his job done, the watcher slipped his binoculars and radio into the back pannier. He climbed easily into the saddle of the motorbike. Flicking the starter peddle with his foot, he kicked down hard to start its engine. It coughed on the first attempt, and then suddenly roared into life in the cold morning air as he kicked again. The watcher gripped the clutch lever tightly and clicked down on the gear peddle. Through a mixture of swirling mist and blue exhaust smoke, the observer turned the trail bike away from the chateau and accelerated slowly into the shadow-filled gloom of the firebreak behind him. Keeping the revs low, concealed from all directions by tall standing pines, the trail bike quickly disappeared into the depths of the dripping forest. The watcher was heading towards the rendezvous point, where shortly; he would join the others.

Unaware he was being observed, behind dark tinted windows, the Rover's muscular driver glanced up into the rear-view mirror and stared for a moment at his brooding teenage passenger, who slouched silently with a velvet covered riding hat and leather crop across her thin knees. To the driver's mind, despite the camouflage of her expensive Chanel makeup, the girl sitting behind him remained painfully plain and ordinary. Christina Angelopoulos' beautifully matched Calevo riding outfit screamed money, but her complexion, he decided, was awful; her sallow features ravaged both by a faint shadow of facial hair and by chronic acne, which had plagued her since the onset of puberty. To the casual observer, he thought, who might pass her by on the sidewalk of some chic, bistro-lined Parisian street; the girl would not have drawn a second glance; just another unremarkable round-shouldered adolescent who quickly faded like smoke into the dull mass of Parisians busily going about their business. Looks, however, were deceiving, he thought knowingly; they hid her secret well. Her lifeless hair and pockmarked face betrayed nothing of the vast fortune she would one day inherit from her father; one of the richest and most powerful shipping magnets in Greece.

Flicking his eyes back to the road ahead, her burly driver absently winced and dropped a broad hand away from the steering wheel. He reached inside his jacket and adjusted the position of the heavy 7.62mm Tokarev pistol he habitually wore concealed in a shoulder holster while engaged on escort duties.

His powerful torso and broad shoulders were chiselled by years of entertaining the crowds on the tough European circuit of the professional wrestler. Crooked far-eastern betting dictated most bouts were choreographed and their results fixed, but ultimately, it had proved dangerous employment. One particularly bad landing, and the spinal injury that ensued, had forced an abrupt career change. Now, he led a different life, guarding and chauffeuring members of the absurdly rich and usually arrogant Angelopoulos family. A smug smile of satisfaction played momentarily across his lips. Young or old, they all felt safe with him, wherever they holidayed, like now in France, and chose to leave the walled security of their opulent palace, high up on the wooded hill.

His gun felt bulky and uncomfortable; he'd never got used to wearing it. Hunched over the Rover's steering wheel, the butt of the Russian-made pistol always dug spitefully into his rib cage during driving duties. Given the sleepy nature of the provincial Bayeux region, the temptation often lingered to leave it behind, but he knew instant dismissal awaited, if he was caught without it. Withdrawing his hand from beneath his jacket with a mildly frustrated sigh, he rubbed the stubble on his chin. After all, he thought, he did not need the gun. His massive strength was all he required to protect the sulking girl, in the unlikely event of something bad happening on his watch.

Scowling, as she stared vacantly at the leafy blur of forest sweeping by, Christina didn't notice her driver's furtive glance, or the smile that followed. Wrapped in her own thoughts, she was consumed by a massive teenage sulk after the angry telephone exchange she had just had with her father. He was so unreasonable; she concluded morosely. She didn't mean to interrupt his stupid business meeting in Geneva, when she telephoned him on his private cell phone. She only called to ask him for a new horse.

As usual, he had treated her like a child and immediately brushed her perfectly reasonable request aside. Her father's voice sounded distinctly irritated as he snapped at her that cross-country horse-jumping was too dangerous. No, he declared angrily before abruptly hanging up; she must forget the idea and make-do by continuing to ride Socks, the Chantillez pony, he gave her six years earlier, in celebration of her tenth birthday.

It simply wasn't fair; the brooding girl fumed. She was grown up now and after all, she thought bitterly, Father owned every manicured acre of the sprawling stud farm where she would arrive shortly for her morning ride. The teenager snorted angrily to herself; she loved Socks of course, but it was time to move on. There were always plenty of fine horses bred specifically for point-to-point; they were all safe jumpers at the stud, and he could certainly afford to be generous towards his only daughter...

Her father, Christina pouted moodily to herself, was just a mean, selfish, old man.


The girl's bodyguard reacted quickly as he rounded a tight bend and saw the obstruction. Braking hard, he stopped the Range Rover just short of a rusting Peugeot van, which blocked the track ahead. Beneath the flaking paintwork of its raised bonnet, a leaning figure rummaged in the engine compartment, obviously intent on making a repair, oblivious to the Rover's arrival.

Still in her mood, but startled by the abrupt stop, the sulking girl looked up sharply. She demanded irritably,

'Why have we stopped, Claude?'

The ex-wrestler grunted as he half-turned towards his passenger,

'It's nothing, mademoiselle. Just some idiot broken down in front of us,' his wide shoulders shrugged. 'Probably a local poacher or some damned fool stealing wood for their fire.' Claude depressed the interior handle and shouldered his driver's door open, 'don't worry; I'll soon deal with it.'

Intent on pushing the broken-down van off the track, the bodyguard left his engine idling and stepped down from the Rover. Claude glanced around the otherwise deserted forest track, then strode confidently towards the van's driver; whose head remained hidden within the engine compartment. Angrily, the bodyguard barked,

'Hey! You there! Get this filthy pile of scrap out of my way!'

The van's driver did not seem to hear. Temper rising, the bodyguard continued to close on the crippled vehicle. He snarled louder this time,

'I said, this is private property, you maggot!' Eyes flashing dangerously, there was more threat in his voice when he added, 'You're trespassing and have no right to be here.'

Now within a few metres of the van, the bodyguard stopped and grasped his clenched fist with his other hand. Grasping both broad hands together, he loudly cracked his knuckles. It had been his trademark, as he entered the ring before bouts in his previous life, and if things got physical now, which he secretly hoped they would; his opponent would feel a lot more than just an assault on his ears by the ex-wrestler's cracking joints.

The sounds he made had the required effect. The driver of the van suddenly tensed and straightened. He turned. The man's dark complexion and features, the bodyguard thought, were distinctly Arabic. He was dressed in nondescript jacket and jeans. In one grease-smeared hand he held a spanner; the other was concealed behind his back.

The van's driver said nothing. He stared silently at the bodyguard for a moment, and then the Arab's cold face smiled mirthlessly. The big man suddenly felt distracted and uncomfortable. Something cruel and terrible seemed to brush his very soul as he returned the hypnotic stare of those burning coal-black eyes. In a blur, the van driver's hand suddenly flashed from behind his back. He pointed something yellow and faintly reminiscent of a gun towards the big ex-wrestler's chest. It all seemed to happen in slow motion. Startled, Claude had no chance to react, or reach for his concealed pistol.

Trailing micro-thin silver wires behind them, two barbed electrodes flashed through the cold morning air as the van's driver fired. The stun gun's darts bit deeply into the bodyguard's chest; simultaneously, sixty-five thousand volts of savage, paralysing electricity surged unopposed through the ex-wrestler's muscle-bound body.

Like a frozen statue, stunned and paralysed, Claude fell helplessly and heavily forward onto the track. Throwing his head back, a cry of triumph escaped his swarthy assailant's mouth,

'*Allahu Akbar!*'

The cry declared victory of sorts, but it was a signal too. The back doors of the old van burst open; two more Arabs leapt from the confines of the rusting vehicle and dashed straight to the rear doors of the Range Rover. The bewildered girl screamed with fear and panic as they wrenched open both passenger doors; she was dragged from the vehicle, slapped hard and thrown violently onto the cold ground. One of her attackers knocked the wind from her lungs as he knelt on her back. He grasped Cristina's flailing hands; securing them tightly with a length of cord. At the same time, the other man stuffed a dirty wad of cloth into the girl's open mouth, effectively stifling her piercing screams.

Eyes bulging with undiluted terror, she was quickly lifted up, carried unceremoniously by her kidnappers, and dumped heavily onto the cold ribbed steel floor in the back of the old van.

Less than a minute had passed since the Range Rover had stopped. The two men danced triumphantly around their leader, whooping with unbridled excitement. Their mission had gone like clockwork, just as their leader had promised.

Hidden by jagged mountains, deep within the remote Pakistan tribal homelands, their Taliban controlled training camp had provided safe haven while they practiced relentlessly for this mission. They trained far from the prying eyes of the western invaders, and their deadly air power. Infidel spies had yet to locate the isolated camp. No drones had looked down from the skies and seen either men or vehicles, as they rehearsed the kidnap on the dry valley floor under the watchful eyes of Usman Jawad, and his battle-hardened Taliban. The four Arab men repeated the snatch time and again, until every facet of it had become second nature.

The Hamas leader snapped at them. He ordered them to calm themselves, get back to the van and guard the sobbing prisoner. Still grinning, they complied. Their leader, Youssef, dropped the bonnet of the van back into place and secured it. His sharp ears detected the approaching whine of the Yamaha's engine. Staring towards the source of the noise, he saw Mohammed speeding through the trees towards him. Moments later, the motorbike skidded to a halt beside him. Mohammed glanced first at the empty Range Rover, then at the groaning semi-conscious bodyguard who was still lying helplessly on the ground. Youssef pressed the Taser's trigger again, sending another long burst of agonising high-voltage current through the bodyguard's twitching body. Without a word to Mohammed, Youssef threw the Taser aside and reached into his jacket. Withdrawing a razor-sharp box-cutter from a pocket, he casually walked over to the groaning man and knelt down beside him.

Youssef was no stranger to death; it was his companion even as a child in the ragged refugee camp on the Gaza Strip. Hamas fighters noticed the thin orphan's hollow, emotionless stare. The men recognised the emptiness inside him. They searched the refugee camps, recruiting many boys like Youssef, to join their ranks of death. The religious and ideological grooming supplemented his military training during the teenage years which followed. They produced what he was now; a perfect, ruthless tool in their war against Israel, and their hated American and British allies.

In the damp air of the clearing, Youssef snatched up a handful of the bodyguard's hair, roughly yanking the powerless man's head to one side. His face impassive, Youssef lifted the knife and slashed down in one fluid movement, slicing deeply through the ex-wrestlers carotid and jugular arteries. As blood sprayed, to Youssef and his companions, this man's death was completely justified. It was a necessary and vivid lesson. When the body was found and the girl's family alerted, they must understand, absolutely, that life meant nothing to her captors. They must realise that not one whit of mercy would be shown towards the prisoner, if demands were not met in full, and their instructions carried out to the letter.

Youssef stood up and backed away from the rhythmic spray of arterial blood, which pooled a spreading stain around his victim. Having no further use for it, he casually dropped the bloody box-cutter beside the still twitching body. His face cold and expressionless, Youssef reached inside his jacket again and this time, withdrew a white envelope. Walking casually back to the idling Range Rover, he leaned in and propped it against the dashboard where it would be easily found. The bloody hand-print he left behind on the envelope was a nice extra touch, he thought, smiling to himself.

The envelope bore words scrawled in bold black ink:

*Christos Angelopoulos - read <u>before</u> you contact police.*

\* \* \* \* \*

Just hours after the body beside the abandoned Range Rover was discovered, Christos Angelopoulos' small executive jet touched down in a cloud of blue tyre smoke on the tarmac runway of Saint Aubin airport, a few kilometres outside Dieppe.

As the aircraft's engines lost power, and their high-pitched whine diminished, the plane turned off the single runway and taxied onto a private apron. When the captain cut the engines and signalled to his cabin staff to open the cabin door, grim faced, Christos Angelopoulos brushed aside the ingratiating smile of the young air hostess who had fed him whisky sours throughout the emergency flight from Geneva. Feeling the intense cold of the onshore breeze on his ruddy face, the billionaire climbed down the short flight of steps.

As he stepped down onto the concrete apron, a car left the shelter of the nearby hanger complex. It swept up to the Lear jet and stopped beside Angelopoulos. The passenger door opened; the billionaire immediately recognised his estate manager from the chateau, who emerged from the driver's seat. The Greek magnet's blood ran cold. In his employee's hand, the manager held what appeared to be a crumpled, bloodstained envelope. The man's face was ashen. Ignoring any of the usual pleasantries, Angelopoulos snapped,

'Well, is it true, Barreau? What happened? Has my daughter been kidnapped?'

Nervously, the estate manager nodded. He said sadly,

'Yes sir, I believe she has been…. One of my gardeners found Claude's body in the grounds, when he came to work earlier this morning. I immediately ordered the staff to search the area where it happened, but we found no sign of Miss Angelopoulos,' he looked despairingly at his feet for a moment, and then looked up again. The manager added almost apologetically,

'There was a lot of blood, Monsieur. Claude's throat was cut…'

The Greek billionaire's heart hammered in his barrel chest, but he dismissed the news of one of his bodyguard's murder with a wave of his hand. His cheeks flushed with growing anger, he glared at the estate manager, and snarled,

'What about the police? Have you called them?' he demanded, his voice rising.

Frowning and fearful, Marcel Barreau shook his head rapidly,

'No, Monsieur!' He thrust the envelope towards his employer, 'Err… we found this in the car. It must be from the kidnappers; it said not to…'

Angelopoulos looked down silently at Barreau's shaking hand. He snatched the proffered paper from it and stared at the bloody hand-print, and the message scrawled across it for several seconds. Exhaling loudly, he nodded and sighed,

'Yes, of course. You were quite right to wait,' He stuffed the envelope into his coat pocket and nodded towards the waiting car, 'Get me to the chateau quickly. I need time to think,' he patted the pocket containing the envelope, 'I'll read this on the way…'

# Chapter Five

In the bar of 'A' Squadron, 21 SAS, not everyone was happy. After a month of well-earned leave, several faces had surfaced once again in the most exclusive military watering-hole in London's fashionable Chelsea.

In a private corner, the three core members of the elite Shadow Squadron sat around a low table, heads down, deep in their usual conspiratorial conversation. Plans and solutions were often hatched quietly over a beer in the bar, on a strictly need-to-know basis. If conversation suddenly stopped when someone uninvited crashed a private gathering, the visitor generally took the hint of stares and sudden silence, shrugged and wandered away. If they didn't take the hint, a quietly hissed - *'Piss off! This is need-to-know,'* always got the message across.

This time, however, the subject of conversation was different.

'So that's it then; it's another bloody cover-up?' Spike Morris snorted angrily.

Pat Farrell nodded. There was that same resigned expression on his face; he habitually wore it when discussing any subject causing his young troopers dissatisfaction, ever since he had been recruited by his old regular Sgt Major, into the Territorial arm of the SAS.

'Yep, that's about the size of it, Spike.' Pat sighed softly, sitting straighter. 'Hey, look, you both know the drill, and should be well used to it by now. The government won't publicly admit anything to do with our trip into the Congo.'

The two troopers were silent for a moment, but neither had forgotten. When the RAF transport had returned the reserve SAS men and their civilian charges to UK soil, the press were waiting. As the reporters jostled with microphones and cameras, desperately trying to interview the rescued civilians, Pat and his team had quietly slipped away.

'But… but those bloody idiots announced in the press that we were going in, for God's sake. They damn near got us all killed,' spluttered trooper Danny Thomas, as he lifted a brimming beer glass to his lips. The smile lingered for a moment more on Pat's face, then his expression changed to a more serious look as he replied,

'Look Danny; after the casualties we inflicted on the rebels, the last thing the Foreign Office wanted, was to be caught with blood on their dainty public-school hands. Especially, remember, when it's someone else's war which officially anyway, we hadn't been invited to.' Pat took a long swig of his beer and swallowed, 'As we did them a big favour and nailed that murderous Mai-Mai bastard Ojukwu, the Congolese government are all smiles now and back on friendly terms with our lot.' Pat's smile changed from serious to sardonic, 'Don't forget, both of you, something which is vitally important to this or any other government; announcing firm action gets them votes, and makes them look good in the press,' with a knowing wink he added, 'And God knows; they need it at the moment.'

All three men knew it was going badly for the coalition government, halfway through their five-year term. The voting public were deeply jaded over the Economic Union, and the blank refusal to honour the promised membership referendum during the current term. Fresh pledges were made by the Prime Minister, but trust in the words of politicians had, to the Mother of Parliament's collective shame, been consigned by disillusioned voters, to long distant memory.

Gay marriage had been another issue, which left the public scratching their heads in bewilderment. With immigration controls in apparent tatters, and the nation's economy in dire straits, huge amounts of parliamentary time had been used up recently, debating the seemingly unimportant marriage rights of homosexuals. The Prime Minister's fixation on this issue made many old-guard supporters question his leadership; this wasn't part of announced policy, and to party official's surprise, had not appeared anywhere in their pre-election manifesto.

The current state of the country wasn't the only cause of the general gloom in the bar, however. The latest terrorist outrage in Woolwich left a big hole in everyone's heart. A young, unarmed British soldier had been barbarically murdered just outside his barracks by two rabid Islamic Jihadists. Inevitably, the three men's conversation turned to the outrage. Spike shook his head sadly; like most, he felt a soldier's kinship for the murdered drummer and his grieving family,

'I still can't get my head around it. We've come up against some pretty mean characters in the last eighteen months, most of them hell-bent on mass-murder, but never anything quite like this... I just don't understand why the government doesn't do more to catch these mad bastards, before they kick off in the first place, or sling out all those nutcase Muslim preachers who put them up to it in the first place?'

Their Sergeant remained silent for a moment. Pat slowly placed his empty glass on the table. He could sense the frustration oozing from of every pore of both troopers. Pat had heard the same thing from most of the passengers, who rode his taxi around the streets of London, during the previous weeks,

'Too much European Court of Human Rights interference and liberal thinking by our political masters stops all that from happening. Truth is, boys we are in deep shit. What some of these useless politicians just don't seem to understand, or fully grasp, is that we are fighting a covert world war with Al-Qaeda, their Islamist splinter groups, and every fundamentalist franchise with a chip on its shoulder against the Yanks, or us.'

'So what's the answer, Pat? We ain't going to talk them into giving up, are we?' asked Danny, who felt they were getting nowhere.

Pat shook his head, and shrugged.

Danny sniffed, 'So come on Pat, what's the regular SAS opinion? What's Hereford's take, and what's their solution?'

Pat's face was impassive, as he considered his reply,

'Well, it's basically the same as ours, simple really. These madmen just don't think like we do. You can't sit down and reason with religious fanatics strapped with explosives, or holding an AK47 to your head. In their minds, they are warriors, holding a first-class, open-ended ticket to paradise…. They really do believe that. As you've both already found out the hard way, none of them follow a word of the Geneva Convention, or what we would regard as the rules of war. They're perfectly happy to murder absolutely anyone who disagrees with them, or just happens to be in the wrong place, at the wrong time. Unarmed men, women and little children; it's all the same to their way of thinking. Suicide bombings and barbaric murders are carried out without the slightest remorse or conscience. That's the way they cash in their ticket to paradise. Their sole intention is to create absolute terror, and as much carnage as possible among their innocent victims.'

Pat stared at his empty glass as dark memories surged. These were good men, and deserved the truth. 'Look at the Spanish railway station bombings. Spain withdrew its troops from Afghanistan a week after that atrocity.' With a sigh, Pat continued, 'What you've both got to understand, my lucky lads, is that you can never ever change these nutter's minds or what they believe in.' Pat's head raised, and he stared at both young men in turn, 'There's only one option left. If they are unfortunate enough to stray into your gun sights, double-tap a couple of 9mm rounds into their head. Do what you've been trained to do… and kill them.'

There was silence at the table, as Pat's words sank in. It wasn't long before both troopers nodded their agreement. After the action they had seen, since the formation of Shadow Squadron, both knew Pat's chilling assessment was the truth of it. Spike broke the gloom of the moment. He looked up and said,

'Then it's just as well that we're all back down to Hereford tomorrow morning, to start the Troop's next anti-terrorist work-up, to cover the forthcoming G8 summit.'

Pat nodded,

'Yeah, be back here bright and early. We've got new equipment to train up on, and we're all a bit rusty on our assault drills.' He stood up and stretched. Sternly, he added, 'Right. I'm off for an early night. Don't be late, you two…'

Spike grinned,

'Yeah right, Pat. As if…'

# Chapter Six

The setting sun sparkled across the water, as its burning crescent slowly disappeared on the ocean's horizon. From the veranda of their beach-side chalet, recently retired Director of SAS, Brigadier Charles Lethbridge and his wife Edith, relaxed in comfortable wicker armchairs, surrounded by the warm evening atmosphere of the exclusive holiday resort, just a mile along the coast from the fishing village of Kalymnos, on the holiday island of Cyprus. The Brigadier turned his head and regarded the face he had married more than forty years ago. He smiled silently to himself. His dear wife's fine features held their beauty, despite the onset of time during their long and happy years together.

The holiday was a surprise; his devoted wife's reward for following him faithfully from posting to posting, having long since accepted their roving life together. Without complaint, like so many career military wives, she had never had a true home to call her own. The Brigadier knew she had stoically accepted her life as a soldier's wife, bearing long periods of separation during her husband's distinguished service career, which had constantly torn him away from her; often placing him in terrible danger in faraway lands. For years, she had overcome both fear and loneliness, while she prayed quietly and privately each night, for his safe return.

To their mutual regret, tomorrow would be their last day at the idyllic coastal resort. They would return to England, and at last settle in the delightful rose-strewn retirement cottage they chose together just outside Hove, in Sussex.

A local boy, dressed in the livery of the resort, walked up and coughed politely. With a slight bow, he enquired,

'Would you like another drink, sir… madam?'

Edith quickly shook her head, and placed a flat, well-manicured hand over her glass,

'No, thank you, Cristo,' She turned and looked lovingly towards her husband, 'I'm tired, Charles. Perhaps I've had a little too much sun today?' Smiling, she added, 'I think I'll go to bed; we've an early start tomorrow… You have another if you want one, but don't be too late, will you, dear?'

At peace with the world for the first time in many years, the ex-Brigadier smiled lovingly at his wife,

'One more snort then, and I'll call it a night and join you inside.'

As the Brigadier's wife stood up and left the veranda, Lethbridge turned to the waiting houseboy,

'Another whisky and soda, Cristo,' with a grin and conspiratorial wink beneath his bushy eyebrows, he added softly,

'Better make it a large one…'

\* \* \* \*

Lying asleep in their comfortable bed, Brigadier Lethbridge and his wife slumbered peacefully. Fans turned quietly, moving the still air and keeping their room pleasantly cool. Beyond their locked chalet door, the peaceful Mediterranean night was serenaded by crickets,which chirruped softly to each other in the darkness, beneath a black, star-studded sky.

Almost imperceptibly at first, the tranquillity was disturbed by nothing more than a soft whisper, a muffled burr which drifted from somewhere beyond the gentle waves, which broke on the resort's sandy beach.

Rocking on the gentle swell of a silent ocean, a dark smudge crept towards the sleeping shoreline, after a voyage of well over two hundred miles.

Closer now, the dhow's Syrian captain squinted into the darkness as he wiped his shining brow with the back of his hand. Usually, he used his old boat to fish the abundant waters off the coast of Syria, close to his home port of Lattakia, but when the dreaded Takfiri militants burst into his home one night, and threatened to kill his entire family if he didn't help them, only a man intent on suicide, he knew, would refuse their demands.

Seeing the phosphorescent line of low waves breaking on the flat beach ahead, the captain lent forward, grasped the throttle, and cut power to his ancient diesel engine. As sounds of the throbbing motor died away, the crowded boat coasted silently, until its wooden bow scraped the sand and shingle of the waterline. Gentle breakers slapped peeling paintwork as the boat came suddenly to a shuddering halt. There were whispered words aboard in the shadows, and then dark figures, clutching automatic weapons, rolled over both wooden sides and waded cautiously through the shallow water, until their naked feet touched the sandy beach. The last man off pulled on the rope and rammed the boat's anchor into the dry sand, tethering it securely to the beach.

Their sweating faces covered with loosely wrapped Shemagh head scarves, a dozen Takfiri guerrillas huddled down together on the sand. Straining their senses to the limit, they listened for the slightest hint of a police ambush. Somewhere far away, a dog barked, but the men ignored it. The slits of their eyes glittered in the starlight as they cast about, searching for the slightest hint of betrayal.

Satisfied that all was well, their leader stood up and silently beckoned his men to follow. Ignoring the dark outlines of abandoned tables and parasols, on his hand signal, they splintered into smaller groups, fanning out across the empty beach to search the nearby collection of smart single-storey chalets. They were looking for the sign. The message their leader had received said it would be a simple piece of white rag, tied to a veranda railing. In the darkness, the marker would identify the chalet which contained the prized hostage they had been ordered to capture, alive, and at any cost.

It took time to organise the sea-borne attack. A week earlier, a message reached the receptionist. He must send word to his comrades hiding in the mountains of his homeland, if anyone of importance came to stay. The man working at the beach-side resort was in hiding on Cyprus, he was wanted in Syria for terrorist crimes, and his face was too well known over there. Supporting himself by working on the holiday island was a good cover, until the heat died down at home, and it was safe to return.

Unaware of any imminent danger, recently retired SAS Brigadier Charles Lethbridge had scrupulously observed the security advice issued by the Foreign

Office to overseas travellers, and followed all their tourist security protocols. He'd diligently booked the holiday under his surname. When the couple arrived at the resort's reception office at the start of their holiday, however, the Takfiri man noticed the Brigadier's old rank still printed on his passport. Since the message arrived, there had been only dreary tourists, mainly English, German and French, arriving at the resort. All westerners were rich by the poverty-stricken standards of local Cypriots, but none, he knew, were what his comrades sought. When he arrived at reception, in the eyes of the agent, a British Brigadier, almost a General, had to be a prize beyond measure. Word was quickly dispatched by cell phone, that a victim worthy of the merciless Takfiri fighters, had arrived to stay at the Golden Cove resort.

Battered Russian-made AK assault-rifle held at the ready, creeping silently along the line of beachfront chalets, the guerrilla leader stopped suddenly and dropped quietly to one knee. Suspended across the wooden rail of the end chalet's veranda, hanging just yards away, bathed in the gentle moonlight had been the white cloth he sought. Beside it, suspended by a thin cord, was the resort's master key, which would unlock and soundlessly open any chalet door. Confident now that he had found the right building, the Takfiri leader pointed towards the sign, and then nodded to the man beside him to go back and gather the others.

When all twelve heavily-armed gunmen were crouched down and grouped around him, their leader pointed again at the marked rail, and the silent chalet behind it. He grinned broadly and eyes glittering anew, whispered triumphantly,

'*Allahu Akbar!*'

# Chapter Seven

Dropping his last fare close to Paddington station, Pat decided to call it a night. It hadn't been one of his best, and no matter how he tried trawling the streets in search of new fares; the shift had never picked up since he started at six o'clock the previous evening. The takings for the long hours he had put in were disappointing; barely adequate to cover his time and diesel. Life in civvy street, Pat had found to his cost, came with its own collection of problems. One way and another, it had been an expensive month, and to make matters worse; his mortgage payment was due in a few days' time, and he was still a little short.

Inside the darkened driver's cab, Pat glanced down at the luminous dial of his watch. It was well past one in the morning, and the streets around him were empty. Even the centre of the West End had been practically deserted when he found his last fare, which was pretty unusual for a Thursday. The radio was quiet, and on each rare occasion the dispatcher called a decent job over the net, he missed out, to a nearer taxi, which snatched the fare from under his nose. Tonight, even the ranks outside the best hotels were slow, and every job, when it finally came, had turned out to be a lemon. He'd had one earlier that evening, after fruitlessly burning fuel, cruising empty for more than thirty minutes. Taking refuge on the Chesterfield Hotel's rank on Charles Street, just off Berkley Square, Pat had been patiently waiting his turn for almost three-quarters of an hour. When he finally pulled onto poll position outside the plush hotel's entrance, he'd waited another boring ten minutes before a minor celebrity he recognised vaguely from the TV, stumbled up to his cab, obviously worse for wear,

'Palladium please, driver,' hiccupped the new passenger. Concentrating on focusing bloodshot eyes on the task of climbing aboard, the celeb failed to notice the irritation of his cabby's expression. Pat was definitely not impressed at the thought of a short, five-hundred-yard fare, after fifty minutes of waiting for something to make the shift worthwhile. The small c celeb apologised grudgingly as he awkwardly lurched into the back of the cab,

'Sorry, mate. I would have walked it… but I'm too pissed!'

The rules said he couldn't refuse the job, and there wasn't even a tip at the other end, Pat remembered bitterly. It couldn't be helped though, Pat thought with a resigned smile; that was just how things went sometimes if a shift turned bad. Better to call it a night, get some sleep, and start all over again the following evening. He'd learnt the hard way that driving a London taxi could be a deeply frustrating and stressful job, but there it was. Pat was grateful for the relief and the constant distraction of his reserve SAS Troop down in Chelsea. All the excitement his warrior spirit still craved, with the chance to return to the mundane when a job was over. The added bonus that kept Pat on track, was that in the last couple of years, there had been no more bad dreams when it was time to sleep. Most cabbies didn't have the benefit of the best of both worlds he thought; driving a hack was all they had to look forward to.

Pat switched off his radio, reached up then turned his yellow 'For Hire' sign off as well. Swinging the taxi around, giving the shift up as a thoroughly bad job, he headed for home.

Having ignored the occasional drunk weaving his way, Pat's cab growled past Harrow Road police station. He caught the next set of traffic lights still at green, and turned off into Fernhead Road. Pat's flat was halfway down the long road on the right, at the end of one of many lengthy Edwardian four-storey terraces. With the enormous pressure on the housing market in London, developers had moved in and converted virtually all the buildings in the area into flats and bedsits. As a result, parking down one of the side-streets near his own place was always a headache, particularly late at night. Everyone and his dog seemed to own a car in today's society. Parking had become a real pain ever since, to the utter dismay of local residents; Westminster Council splashed double yellow lines everywhere, making parking almost impossible. Pat had his own resident's parking permit, but to his constant annoyance, day and night, the bays were almost always full.

To his relief, with a late-night change of fortune, Pat got lucky while patrolling the darkened side streets in his search for a parking slot. A car pulled out suddenly in front of him. Seeing his chance, Pat slid smoothly into the vacant residence space. Gratefully, he killed the drumming diesel engine. For the briefest of moments, Pat luxuriated in the darkness and quiet of his silent, vibration-free cab.

Clutching his heavy cloth change bag, Pat climbed out of the silent taxi and stretched away hours of confinement. His nose wrinkled as he detected a faint whiff of cannabis in the air. '*Life in the big city*,' thought Pat ruefully to himself with a grin.

At the far end of the darkened side street, music was blaring. Bob Marley was giving it everything, cranking out *No Woman, No Cry* at full volume from an open upper-storey window, where lights blazed into the night.

Unseen, there were others watching along the darkened street; perhaps, the tallest thought with a smile, they'd get off the streets and crash the party when they were done...

Shrugging to himself, Pat turned away and headed towards his flat. Late at night, throughout the week, Westminster Council's anti-noise patrols were always busy. Like the rest of the capital, The Paddington - Maida Vale border was a cosmopolitan area. Loud birthday parties and raucous celebrations happened all too frequently, to the dismay of frantic neighbours', trying desperately to get small children to sleep. Someone began banging on the noisy building's communal front door. When it flew open, a serious row quickly erupted between revellers and, by the sound of it, an angry parent living next door. Pat grinned to himself. For once, it wasn't his problem, and he had no intention of getting involved.

It was odd, Pat thought, as he ambled up the deserted pavement, that despite living in a crowded city, teeming with people, without a current woman in his life, sometimes he still felt so isolated and alone.

As Pat neared the corner with Fernhead Road, there was movement among the shadows, just a few yards ahead. Someone stepped out of the darkness and blocked his path; something glinted dangerously in his hand.

'What's in the bag, man?'

Pat's body stiffened; forgetting the long night's fatigue. Like so many times before, his senses came instantly to full alert as two other young black men slouched from the same shadows and took up position behind the first.

His courage bolstered by the blade and his sniggering accomplices, the tallest hoody sliced his knife through the empty air towards Pat. Angrily; he demanded,

'Give me the bag and your money, you honky fucker, or I'm gonna carve you up.'

Pat's mind whirled as his eyes narrowed. When he'd begun to learn advanced unarmed combat in Hereford, years earlier, he never forgot what the instructor had said on the first of many lessons,

'Imagine you're faced with a wild bobcat attacking you. It's a fraction of your size and weight, but when it comes at you, it's a blur of teeth, claws and spitting fury. When you fight, there are no rules. Just be the bobcat and put your opponents down before they know what hit them.'

Leering at his victim, the first hooded thug stepped closer. Pat took a half-step sideways against the brick wall beside him. With his back safely covered, he crouched slightly to make himself appear small and vulnerable. A little too loud, feigning panic, Pat stuttered and lied,

'I…I don't want no trouble, lads. Relax, take it easy, I've… I've got a heart condition..."

As his terrified victim shrunk backwards in the gloom, feeling the buzz which came with every street robbery, the tallest thug swaggered forward, followed closely by the other two. It was a huge mistake; they would pay the price for their overconfidence. Unknowingly, all of them stepped into the deadly arc of Pat's fighting zone. Tonight, they picked the wrong man to rob.

His eyes widened momentarily with confusion, as the knife-wielding thug's cowering victim suddenly dropped his bag and explosively unwound with a roar. Pat's right hand had been down on his left hip, as if he was fumbling for his wallet. The thug and his small posse failed to notice their victim's fingers balling into a fist. His bicep locked against his forearm, Pat's crooked arm flashed out and upwards. With immense force, the tip of Pat's elbow connected with the lower edge of the nearest hoody's jaw with a loud crack. Dropping the knife, the thug flew backwards, his jaw shattered. Pat recovered in a split-second, slamming his balled right fist into the left-hand assailant's throat, with every ounce of weight and power Pat could muster. With a stifled cry merging quickly to a gurgling gasp, the second thug fell to his knees with shaking hands clawing at his flattened windpipe. He pitched forward heavily onto his face, raggedly gasping for air. The last assailant froze with horror as Pat spun towards him. Hypnotic eyes wide and blazing, Pat snarled like a crazed, rabid animal, as he kicked the stunned thug hard in the crotch. With a scream of pain, eyes bulging and clutching at his crushed testicles, the last attacker fell heavily to the ground. He remained curled in a foetal position, groaning with pain. Suddenly, the man's stomach heaved; he gagged and vomited noisily across the cold concrete pavement.

It took seconds; Pat was so focused on doing exactly what he had been trained to do, he barely registered the flash of blue lights sweeping across the parked cars and deserted street around him. With a screech of brakes and rubber, the area car slewed across the side road and stopped abruptly. Three burly police officers jumped out and rushed towards Pat. By chance, they had come from only a street away, responding to the reported disturbance outside the noisy party. They had seen the stark image of Pat's vicious kick, and the shape of a man falling to the ground, as they rounded the corner and their vehicle's headlights swept the scene.

Showing no signs of resistance, Pat compliantly raised his arms and was quickly restrained by two of the officers. Even before the youngest of them could reach for his handcuffs, eager to prove himself to his peers with excitement edging his voice, he declared loudly,

'I'm arresting you on suspicion of aggravated assault. You don't have to say anything, but anything you do…'

The reaction of the restrained man was instant,

'Hang on a minute, mate; this is all wrong. You don't understand what just happened.'

Pat stared coldly at him. To the young officer, fresh out of the Metropolitan Police Training College at Hendon, and just starting his two-year on-the-job probation, it was quickly becoming apparent that there was something distinctly strange going on here. Was it the piercing look in the man's steely eyes, or the fact that he was wearing an oval London taxi-driver medallion around his neck? Hasty over-reaction leading to ill-judged conclusions weren't how they'd taught him at the Met police Peel centre. Face flushing and suddenly unsure of himself, the young constable fell momentarily silent. As he glanced towards his more experienced colleagues for guidance, Pat looked down at the three semi-conscious hoodies groaning on the ground. The older, more seasoned police officers had already spotted the large knife laying in the gutter between them, and were trying their best to stifle growing amusement at their young colleague's botched first arrest. To make matters worse, their prisoner smiled innocently, and nodding towards the hoodies lying at his feet, said quietly,

I live over there at the end of the street, you see officer, and I know you're not going to 'believe this, but I'm the victim; I've just been mugged!'

# Chapter Eight

Behind tall perimeter fences topped with miles of rolled razor-wire, the euphemistically named: UK Government Communications Headquarters in Cheltenham, Gloucestershire performed the intelligence role of worldwide electronic eavesdropping, 24-hours a day.

Nestled deep within the newly-built doughnut-shaped building and the tight security surrounding it, immensely powerful super-computers, linked via Bude, Scarborough and Harrogate to British MI6 spy satellites, simultaneously scanned the HF and UHF frequencies used by foreign governments to transmit coded messages, sent to and from their ministries and embassies around the world. A different department specifically tasked to break the coding and security ciphers disentangled the secret messages, and then sent them to various intelligence department desks at MI6's London headquarters, on the banks of the River Thames, for further analysis.

Constant technological surveillance didn't stop at eavesdropping on foreign governments, however. With eye-watering levels of sophistication which remained highly classified, and the envy of intelligence agencies around the world, radiation given off by millions of mobile or landline telephone conversations, and email messages from anywhere around the world, were also intercepted and closely monitored.

Heavy demands were constantly made to the humming mainframe computer array, which was fondly referred to within the heavily guarded security cloisters of GCHQ, as *Mother*. It tirelessly scanned and searched telephone, telex and fax numbers, which MI6, Mi5 and other UK intelligence agencies were currently interested in. From millisecond to millisecond, the computer arrays simultaneously searched outspoken or written keywords and phrases in hundreds of languages and sub-dialects, which suggested individual recorded calls, should be elevated from routine traffic, through various stages of the complex vetting lattice to *Further Action Required*. On rare occasions, the electronically translated intelligence was upgraded to the highest level of all - *Operation Critical*.

The GCHQ duty officer was busy with his head-down, sifting and checking through the previous night's scan logs. A loud rapping on the glass door separating him from the main analysis suite made him start. Even before the duty officer had a chance to look up and say *'Come in'*, slightly breathless, one of his junior analysts burst in, carrying a red edged message flimsy,

'Sorry, Mr Curtis, but Mother has just intercepted something which I think you really should see immediately…'

Still startled and mildly irritated at having his train of thought interrupted, Alan Curtis sighed as he snatched the proffered message sheet from his assistant and read it.

When he'd finished, Curtis looked up with his mouth open, before two words softly escaped his lips,

*'Bloody hell!'*

\* \* \* \* \*

It was eleven o'clock. Sir Alex McLean was sitting in the M.C.C. Chairman's box at Lords, watching England's cricket team step onto the hallowed turf. Sir Alex was head of Britain's Secret Intelligence Service (MI6), and since boyhood days, had a passion for cricket.

It was the beginning of the final day of the crucial last Ashes test match, against England's old arch-rivals, the Australians. Sitting next to him was Cornelius Wilde, who was also an avid fan of English Cricket, and intent on enjoying C's invitation at the start of his annual leave. This was the first opportunity either man had had for months, to take quality time off work, and enjoy the beginning of the final test match, bathed in London's late-summer sunshine. It seemed to both to be the ideal way to relax, and forget the pressures of work.

They had long since finished deliberating on the round of coming analysis department promotions, and were now engrossed in discussing the finer points of Australia's spin bowling attack, when Sir Alex's bleeper suddenly went off. He eyed the device with angry dismay,

'*Damn!* Excuse me, Cornelius'.

Knowingly, his companion smiled and said quietly,

'Ah well! So much for a quiet day off, C'.

The original head of MI6, Captain Sir Mansfield Cumming RN, always signed himself as 'C'. When he formed the service in 1909, he inadvertently began the long tradition of the head of the service adopting the initial 'C', as his or her personal icon. Within MI6 parlance, C also stood for Sir Alex's unofficial title of 'Control'.

The current SIS Director excused himself and headed into the depths of the pavilion, to find seclusion where he could make a private call to MI6 headquarters at Vauxhall Cross. Finding an empty oak panelled corridor, lined with painted portraits of past England cricket captains, he took out his cell phone and pushed the speed dial key linked to the direct line to his number two, David Fishburn, at MI6 headquarters on the south bank of the Thames,

'Hallo David, Control here, what's the matter?'

David Fishburn was a career intelligence officer; he always tried to take as much pressure off his boss as possible, but not this time. A freshly read copy of the signal faxed over from GCHQ sat open on the desk in front of him,

'Sorry to trouble you, Sir, but there's a bit of a flap on, I'm afraid. I think you had better come back to the office.'

Sir Alex wouldn't ask questions on an unsecured line; he didn't need to. The phrase 'bit of a flap' was office code. It alerted C that something very serious had appeared on the worldwide operations' board, which required his immediate and personal attention.

With a terse, '*Very well*,' Sir Alex snapped the flip-lid of his phone shut. He strode back to the Chairman's box and alerted Cornelius. Moments later, both men were heading down the exterior fire escape at the back of the ancient pavilion towards the Director's car, which was parked securely and unobtrusively in the member's car-park.

\* \* \* \* \*

Besides the Afghan border, nestled in the barren southern foothills of the Hindu Kush, the unremarkable town of Kalat, in the Balochistan district of Pakistan, attracted little attention from the authorities. For centuries, it was one of many gateways for trade into Afghanistan. Since ancient times, local people have used its crowded bazaar as a hub of regional commerce. For centuries, poor, illiterate farmers bartered and haggled over prices, sitting beneath the welcome shade of haphazard stalls within the dusty and bustling market place. It was somewhere to drink hot sweetened tea while swapping gossip and news, and listen to suggestions from trusted friends, as to where the best prices for meagre harvests or scrawny flocks of sheep and goats might be found.

Zahira Khan had chosen Kalat as his headquarters for Al-Qaeda operations because he was born there; he knew only too well the town was perfectly unremarkable. His home and office were combined; hidden within a two-room apartment in a run-down, overcrowded tenement block beside the busy Kalat bazaar. It was easy to slip in and out of Pakistan without arousing the suspicion or interest of local customs officials and border police. Their attention was highly unlikely anyway, as they were generously bribed to look the other way, when it came to the affairs and movement of Zahira Khan. Local law enforcement pliability was not the only reason for picking the shabby tenement in the heart of Kalat. Khan chose the densely populated block for another reason. The lethal attack by the Americans, in the mountains only days earlier, had confirmed the wisdom of his original decision to hide away from discovery and the inevitable American drone strike, by surrounding himself with innocent women and children who he well knew, for political reasons, the Americans feared to slaughter. He often smiled at the thought. It was a weakness of his enemies; their strikes had become one of the best recruiters for the cause in recent years. The un-believers feared the bad press of unwanted civilian casualties, which all too often resulted as collateral deaths during their deadly air raids.

Should his presence be betrayed to the I.S.S., the Pakistani intelligence service, despite friends and supporters in high places, there was no automatic guarantee of immunity. Without time to make the usual threats or bribes, should he need to make an unscripted escape from Pakistan's government agents; he wasn't overly concerned. The sanctuary of the Afghan border laid just a few dusty streets away, beyond the often unguarded and always porous, border crossing.

The Al-Qaeda commander was gazing out of his window, staring absently across the bustling bazaar when his cell phone rang. Removing it from beneath his robe, he pressed the green button, held the device to his ear and said wearily,

'Yes?'

A distant voice spoke briefly in Arabic,

*"There is no God but Allah, and Muhammad is the Messenger of Allah.'*

There was a distinct and hollow click, as the caller abruptly hung up.

Zahira Khan smiled mirthlessly to himself as his stare returned thoughtfully to the stalls within the busy market place. He gazed longingly at a group of small boys playing in the dirt beside one of them. Waving his arms angrily, the stall-holder chased the hungry children away when they got too close to the tempting fruit he had just laid out to attract new customers.

The telephone message was the agreed code, which, without betraying its true meaning, confirmed the success of the kidnap operation in Cyprus. The Syrian fighters would proceed to the next phase as ordered; transporting their hostage to thepoorly guarded docks at Lattakia on the coast. There, the kidnappers would rendezvous with the docked Athens registered cargo ship called the Athena Express. Zahira Khan's orders were for the kidnappers to wait until nightfall, then quietly hand over their prisoner to his own men, who now made up its skeleton crew. An empty steel shipping container would be loaded aboard from the dock by crane. It would serve as their prisoner's dungeon during the next stage of the ship's voyage.

It was the second such message he had received from his network of operatives, since returning from Waziristan. The first also offered a passage from the Quran. Again, it would be utterly meaningless to anyone listening in, but the initial phrase confirmed the girls kidnap; the first vital stage of Zahira Khan's unfolding master plan.

His eyes narrowed as the cold, cruel smile returned to Khan's face. Momentarily, he imagined the confusion and fear in the Greek billionaire's voice, when the Greek had called, ringing the throw-away cell phone number printed on the bloody note left in the Range Rover. That had been the moment for Khan's agent in France to issue his demands for the girl's safe release. It was reported to Khan later the girl's father had tried desperately to negotiate; telling his daughter's kidnapper that his demands were quite impossible. Instead, he offered a huge payment in unmarked U.S. dollars or untraceable bearer bonds for the girl's safe return. His counter offer was immediately and firmly rejected. The girl would be repeatedly raped, then dismembered alive, her father was told, unless the kidnapper's demands were met, and their instructions followed to the letter. He was told that he may inform the local police of the kidnap and murder, but no mention of the note should be made, and nothing more said to them, on pain of the girl's brutal and excruciating death.

Sweating profusely during the call, his stomach churning, despite his wealth and power, the girl's father knew his position was utterly hopeless. As a hard-nosed, old-fashioned CEO, who dealt regularly and ruthlessly with new business opportunities, negotiation over deals and subsequent contracts was akin to a game of poker, where showing his hand too early was a mistake which could ultimately cost millions in lost revenue. This time, however, the deck was stacked against him. The vile, anonymous swine he was dealing with was holding every card.

There was nothing clever to be done, the Greek billionaire was beaten, and he knew it. His heart heavy, he accepted there was only one chance of seeing his little girl alive. Despite the fury boiling inside him, he acquiesced meekly and agreed to make the shipping arrangements demanded by the anonymous and heavily accented voice at the other end of the line.

Christos Angelopoulos didn't know it at the time; but his part in this complex operation had never been about money. It was all about Zahira Kahn using everything he had gained while planning and executing the suicide attacks on the Indian city of Mumbai, and the shopping complex in Nairobi, Kenya; it was all about thrusting Al-Qaeda back into the world's headlines, and extracting a terrible revenge for the death of his beloved leader.

Kahn's hand strayed to his beard; he stroked it thoughtfully. Two hostages successfully kidnapped, the ship secured and about to be loaded. The men already recruited and trained as suicide bombers were ready. All was progressing well.

Like a chess master moving his living pieces on a global board, Zahira Kahn was delighted that the operation was running so smoothly, and remained on schedule. Returning his attention to his cell phone once again, adding the English international 0440 prefix code, he dialled a Bradford number in England, which had been long since committed to memory.

After a few rings, a voice answered. The man's tone sounded distinctly suspicious,

'Hallo?'

Like the long telephone number he dialled, Zahira Khan knew what he must say by heart. It was time to send his own coded message. In just fourteen short days, devastating attacks on London would begin.

Kahn spoke softly and clearly into the phone's mouthpiece. In precise Arabic, he said,

*'He who obeys the Messenger, has indeed obeyed Allah.'*

The reply, from the cold, rain-sodden West Yorkshire city of Bradford came swiftly,

*'I understand….it shall be done!'*

# Chapter Nine

In the Troop room, buried deep within 'B' Block, Duke of York's Barracks, Pat checked his watch. There were only five minutes before the start of the evening's training, and several men were still missing. Running the Troop was entirely Pat's responsibility, but alarm bells had begun to ring after recently being called aside and having private words with several of his most experienced men.

More than one married member of the Troop was struggling to balance home life and the intense time commitment the Troop demanded. Married life and the Regiment were always tricky subjects to weave together; the high Territorial SAS divorce rate already proved that, beyond any doubt. Civilian jobs were safe and guaranteed, but some wives were beginning to complain; they found themselves abandoned all too often at weekends. Without their husbands in tow, children and family life were beginning to suffer. The single guys hadn't complained at all but this situation would quickly spiral into a serious issue in the life of the Troop, unless it was fixed. Pat had chewed over the problem for the last week, while he was busy plying the streets of London in his taxi. Bringing in non-SAS outsiders were out of the question.

There were good guys in HQ squadron who would jump at the chance; many were specialists in signals, intelligence and so on, but had not been through long months under the strict Training Wing regime, and had not passed the ultimate operational qualification of SAS Sabre squadron selection. No, Pat decided; this specialist role had to stay firmly locked in-house. Clearly, greater rotation with other members of 'A' Squadron was the key to maintaining their classified role of protecting London against terrorist attack. Almost every member of his parent territorial squadron was up for it; there would be no shortage of first-class volunteers to choose from, so manpower wasn't the problem. Getting replacements up to the required levels of CRW anti-terrorist training would be the main spanner in a smooth rotation of personnel, he thought. Pat knew his powers were limited, so he had to take this rapidly escalating situation upstairs. He had requested a conference with his Colonel, Adjutant and officer commanding Training Wing later that evening, to discuss the growing manpower situation. Between them, Pat was sure they could find and implement a solution, before things went critical.

The door opened, and two men entered the Troop room. With apologetic nods aimed at their sergeant, they quickly took their seats with the others. Satisfied everyone was at last present; Pat stood up,

'Right then, you lot, shut up and listen in…. ' Pat paused for a moment while his men settled; silence quickly filled the Troop room as he began,

'We'll cover admin notices at the end of the evening, lads, because time is tight tonight. The G8 summit meeting between the richest countries in the world kicks off in a couple of weeks, and I've got something important I want to run by you all. We've changed things round this evening, because there's a new idea being tried to increase our reaction times while we cover the G8, if there is a major incident in London where we are needed…Lights please, Don,' Pat ordered.

The lights quickly flicked off as Pat turned on the projector. The large screen in front of his men was suddenly filled with the image of a white, nondescript long-wheelbase high-topped van. Before anyone could make a quip, Pat explained,

'If there is an incident, and we are called out, our biggest delay is coming here to kit-up, before we can deploy. SAS Group in Whitehall has come up with an idea, which I think should work really well in certain circumstances, and more than halve our reaction times.'

There were a couple of appreciative whistles, and murmurs around the Troop. Pat ignored them, and continued,

'Our equipment, weapons and ammunition will be carried in this van. It will be driven straight to the incident by a duty member of the permanent staff.

When we get our individual calls, if we're given the location, we make our own way there, as fast as we possibly can.'

Immediately, Spike's hand shot into the air. Pat nodded,

'Yes, Spike?'

Spike's suspicion was obvious. Ever the pessimist, he sniffed and said wearily,

'What about the traffic, Pat? If we've got to make our own way through it, perhaps even in rush-hour across central London, how the hell are we supposed to get to an incident quickly, when we're stuck in a bloody traffic jam?'

Pat grinned. He tapped the side of his head with his finger,

'Already thought of that, thanks Spike.' He smiled, 'We've got a little treat for you all. Your own cars are going to be fitted with police two-tone horns, and concealed blue lights, same as undercover cop cars have. Met. Police Traffic Division instructors are going to give us some high-speed urban driver theory tonight, and we start hands-on training this Saturday…. Reckon that will cover it, then, Spike?'

Grinning broadly, Spike nodded enthusiastically. Who would know they were SAS anti-terrorist soldiers responding to a call, not simply plainclothes officers reacting to a shout over the police net?

Still grinning like a Cheshire cat, like the other men in the Troop, Spike was convinced. He mouthed a single, enthusiastic word to his mate, Danny, who was sitting beside him,

'*Wicked!*'

Suddenly, with a bang, the door burst open. Unannounced, the 'A' Squadron commander, Major Peter Howard, followed closely by their MI6 liaison officer, Cornelius Wilde strode in. With a nod to Pat from both men, Major Howard said,

'Sorry to interrupt you, Pat, but something has happened. I need to brief the entire troop immediately.'

Pat nodded. He saw the drawn look on both men's faces; Pat knew instantly that the sudden visit wasn't a social call. Pat stepped aside as the Major became the focal point of his audience. He began with the usual security warning, reserved for a serious and unfolding crisis,

'This briefing is top secret, gentlemen, and must not be discussed outside this room.'

Major Howard's hand slipped into a trouser pocket, and quickly withdrew it. He was holding a memory stick. He passed it to Pat, and said softly,

'Plug this into the projector will you, Pat? I'll give you a nod when I want you to play it.'

Intrigued, Pat nodded, 'Sure, OK boss...'

Major Howard returned his attention to the tough men of the Shadow Squadron troop,

'The Colonel and I have just had a briefing from Cornelius. A grave situation has arisen which we need to be informed about, but the news has been deemed by the government, for the time being anyway, to be strictly need-to-know. For the time being, they have ordered a media blackout.' Major Howard paused for a moment, and then continued,

'At approximately 02.00 hours this morning, a terrorist operation was carried out at the Sun Cove coastal resort on the Mediterranean island of Cyprus. According to the local civilian police, supported by our own military police from the island's Akrotiri RAF airbase, it was a well-planned, well-co-ordinated attack. One British citizen was kidnapped, and the man's wife was badly beaten, and left unconscious. Thankfully, although latest reports suggest her injuries are not life threatening, she's an emotional wreck, of course, but not in any immediate danger. She's now recovering under armed guard at our hospital at RAF Akrotiri.'

As Major Howard finished his opening, Pat gave him a silent thumbs-up. The projector was loaded and ready. Major Howard continued,

'Under normal circumstances, gentlemen, unless we were tasked to assist, we'd all have heard about this kidnap on the 9.00 o'clock news when the story is released to the press, but I'm sorry to say; I've been asked to brief you personally as this is a…. family matter.'

Every man in the briefing room noticed the grim expression on Major Howard's face as he uttered his next sentence.

'The victim in this kidnap, gentlemen, was our own Brigadier Lethbridge.'

There was stunned silence for a moment, then gasps of anger and surprise around the room.

The Troop and the rest of the squadron had dined the Brigadier out only weeks earlier, in true, informal SAS fashion, shortly before he officially retired. The black-tie evening had begun formally enough, with everyone on their best behaviour, but had descended into the usual alcohol fuelled riotous night, after the Brigadier had said his parting words, and the other speeches of congratulation and farewell were almost concluded.

Out of the candle lit darkness, tired of speeches, someone launched a bread roll at the Adjutant, as he began the final address. An old hand at Regimental dinners, he simply ducked the missile, and straight-faced, continued on as if nothing had happened, much to the amusement of the Brigadier, and the reserve SAS men crowded into 'B' block's drill hall, converted for the evening into a white-linen and regimental silverware dining room. Unable to resist the challenge, more projectiles followed, and the resulting bread roll fight ended with the Brigadier, Colonel and Adjutant making a valiant last-stand from behind the top table, protecting their honour, reputations and a full decanter of fine Port, which laughing uproariously, they shared and drained at the height of the lethal barrage.

It was the irrepressible SAS way, and had been a brilliant, typically irreverent send off, for a tough, much-admired man whom every dinner guest held in the highest esteem.

\* \* \* \* \*

The men's mood suddenly became sombre; there was shocked silence in the Troop's briefing room, as the Squadron commander's devastating news of the kidnap sank in. Having broken the story to them, Major Howard grimly handed over to Cornelius.

The MI6 analyst cleared his throat and began,

'Ah… As Major Howard has mentioned, this was clearly a deliberate, pre-planned attack. The Cypriot police were slow to react, and in the confusion, spent the first few critical hours treating the incident as a botched robbery, which gave the kidnappers enough time to make their escape.'

Cornelius sipped from a glass of water. Resisting the urge to grimace at its flat taste, he continued,

'We've been looking into the incident over at Vauxhall, and here is what we surmise so far.' Cornelius paused for a moment, and wiped his hand across his mouth. He needed something stronger than water. It was always the same when pressure to find answers consumed him. Cornelius was an alcoholic in recovery; his thirst constantly prowled around him like a hunting wolf. It was always there, staying hidden in the shadowy tree line, but never far away. It lurked just beyond his mind's visible horizon and constantly called out to him from the darkness: '*Go on, one vodka won't hurt…It will steady your nerves…*'

Everything rested on willpower; his future, marriage and job depended on it. Pat knew his secret, but kept it to himself. Resisting temptation was the only defence from slipping back to the dark days of addiction. He was almost lost everything when Pat had saved him the previous year. Struggling to shunt his inner turmoil aside, Cornelius breathed deeply and continued,

'The kidnap was initiated by a terror group based in Syria called the Takfiri. Our latest intelligence suggests they have forged close links with Al-Qaeda. The police in Cyprus have got their act together at last, and arrested a Syrian-born member of staff at the resort this morning. He is currently being questioned and is a strong lead, but we have nothing further from the Cypriot police yet. On a balance of probabilities, we think it likely that the Brigadier was snatched, and then taken aboard a fishing vessel,which used the best part of a four-hour head-start to disappear into a large fleet of fishing vessels heading back towards Syria. Because the time-lag delayed issuing an island-wide alert, the terrorists disappeared long before the Royal Navy could get a positive radar lock on the boat, or the RAF could put an aircraft into the air and track them down.' Cornelius paused again, and stared into the angry faces looking at him,

'Kidnapping foreign tourists is usually done for ransom by common bandits or pirates, but this time it's different… This is what we intercepted at GCHQ last night. It was addressed to the Prime Minister and all members of the British government.'

Cornelius turned and said,

'Run the clip, please, Pat.'

Pat lent forward and depressed a button. The projector splashed brilliant white light onto the whitewashed wall behind Cornelius. Immediately, the picture on the wall changed, replaced by an outline, the shadowy head and shoulders of a man, concealed in the folds of an Arab-style shemagh headdress. Whoever he was, further identification was impossible. In the gloom which surrounded him, the dark figure lifted a small recording device into the picture, and pressed the play button. The message it contained chilled the blood of the listening men.

'We are the soldiers of the Takfiri. We act under the orders of our Al-Qaeda brothers. We have captured your Brigadier Charles Lethbridge. He is now our prisoner. Any attempt by you to free him, will lead to his immediate death.'

The Arab holding the device pushed the pause button, and lowered it out of shot. A torch behind the dark figure suddenly flicked on. The brilliant beam illuminated a bound figure, lying on what appeared to be a boat's curved wooden floor. From the shadows, a hand grabbed the captive's hair, turning the groaning prisoner's head towards the camera. The torchlight displayed an ugly, bleeding wound on the side of the semi-conscious man's head, where the butt of an AK had struck him, while he slept. The blood didn't hide his identity, however. Every man in the Troop room instantly recognised the bloody face. It was the Brigadier.

The hand holding the recording device reappeared. It pressed the play button again,

'As you can see, our prisoner is still alive. He will remain so, until the day of his execution. He will be publicly beheaded, as part-payment of the debt of blood, which exists and must be paid. We are the soldiers of Islam who will avenge the martyrdom of our glorious leader, Osama bin Laden…. *Allahu Akbar!*'

The screen suddenly turned pure white again, as the message ended. Cornelius exhaled deeply and continued,

'So there we have it, gentlemen. Brigadier Lethbridge has been kidnapped as part of a plot to avenge Bin Laden's death…. Ah, lights, please.'

There were murmurs from the Troop, which died away as the lights flicked on and Cornelius spoke again,

'We have analysed the video, and have gleaned meagre intelligence from what you have just seen. Firstly, from the motion of the camera and quality of the picture, we believe the video was filmed using a cell phone camera, after the attack, aboard a boat. Once they'd finished filming, it would be a simple matter to email the video to wherever the group are based, and then upload and syndicate it across numerous terrorist web sites. We're currently trying to track down the location of the re-broadcast, but due to the current lack of diplomatic links between both governments; what with the civil war going on over there, our request to the Syrian government for assistance has so far been ignored.' With a shrug and a sigh he continued, 'We have also done some technical work on the voice you heard. Initial investigation of the accent suggests the speaker comes from the region of northern Pakistan; it's definitely not Syrian. We're still working on identifying the narrator's true identity, but unfortunately, that's going to take time…. Ah, any questions?'

A dozen hands shot skywards. Cornelius nodded first towards Spike.

'What can we do to help?' he demanded.

Cornelius shook his head, 'Nothing right now; I'm afraid. We can't rescue the Brigadier until we know exactly where he is. Hereford is on standby, of course, they will get first shot at a rescue, but without a location to assault, their hands are as tied as ours.' Cornelius looked towards Major Howard. He was done; there was nothing more to add.

Danny was next to ask a question,

'Does this have anything to do with the G8 meeting?'

Cornelius wiped his hand across his mouth. As his hand fell away, with tired resignation in his voice he said,

'There's always a possibility that there is a connection. We're certainly due another Al-Qaeda spectacular,' Cornelius stared hard at Danny. 'Over at Vauxhall, we're looking very, very carefully for a connection.'

Major Howard concluded the briefing when Cornelius had finished answering the other's question,

'We'll keep you informed when we know anything more, of course. The Prime Minister has given finding the Brigadier top priority, so for the time being, gentlemen; we just have to sit on our hands and wait…'

# Chapter Ten

Days passed, but there was no news of the Brigadier. Pat's men shared his deep frustration, but there was absolutely nothing he or Shadow Squadron could do.

The men assembled for their high-speed urban driver training early, on the following Saturday morning. The skies were grey and filled with clouds, threatening rain at any moment.

To maintain secrecy, arrangements had been made to carry out their high-speed urban driver training deep within the British army's Military Vehicles and Engineering Establishment on Chobham Lane, close to Chertsey in Surrey. Experimental armoured vehicles were usually proved and tested on the heavily wooded tracks surrounding the MVEE, but today, as the establishment was shut at weekends, it had been pressed into service and was hosting a handful of Metropolitan Police advanced diving instructors, Pat and his fifteen elite Special Forces troopers.

As the training started, it began to rain. Showers pulsed off and on as Pat's men were split into four groups of four, with a uniformed instructor and high-performance BMW police car attached to each. Spike noticed Danny's odd look when their instructor introduced himself. As they got into the back of the car, Spike whispered,

'What's the matter, Danny?'

Danny flicked his eyes and locked them with his friends. There was a strange glint in his best mate's eye… Spike knew instantly trouble was brewing; that look meant only one thing; Danny was up to something.

'Just my luck, I know this bloody copper,' hissed Danny. 'He works my borough in the East End.' Danny scowled, 'he's the bastard who did my sister Pauline for speeding last year, when my old mum was sick and Pauline was late leaving mum's place to pick up her kids from school.' Danny sniffed, 'he could have easily let her off with a warning, but the bastard nicked her instead…She got three points on her licence, and a two hundred quid fine.' Danny's eyes narrowed ominously as he added, 'so I owe him one...'

Danny was born and raised in London's tough East End. His dad owned a back-street garage in Shoreditch, and had more than a passing acquaintance with several local criminal gangs, and also, off and on, with the local law. Danny didn't like or trust the police; it was the way it worked on the tough streets of Shoreditch, where he had been brought up.

Spike nodded. He knew how his friend thought, and was instantly concerned,

'Look, don't do anything stupid, you idiot. Pat will do his nut!'

Danny smiled. Spreading his hands innocently, he muttered,

'Wouldn't dream of it my old son…' he sniffed as his eyes narrowed to slits, 'trust me!'

\* \* \* \* \*

The high-speed training drew to an end, after an adrenaline filled day. It was a blur of pounding rain, flashing blue lights, two-tone sirens, breakneck speed and tyre-screeching twists and turns through narrow streets with sheets of water lying across them. Each member of the reserve SAS crews had spent several hours driving with their foot to the floor, around the complex of roads surrounding the buildings which made up the deserted military vehicle establishment. It went against the grain to stamp on the accelerator in built-up areas, but that was what the instructors demanded. Constantly fighting for control, making sudden heart-pounding hand-brake turns and hard-core emergency stops sending pulses racing. Taking corners at three times the usual safe speed led to plenty of white knuckles grasping the wheel. It was fun, but took every ounce of concentration to master the techniques they were being taught.

Eventually, the instructors were satisfied and confident that every man they were training was competent to be let loose, in an emergency, onto the streets of London at breakneck speeds. Danny held back; he saw to it that he was last to drive. To his friend's amusement, he had made an obvious point of driving through every large filthy puddle he could find, much to the horror of the police sergeant sitting beside him. The wipers kept the windscreen clean, but the powerful car's smart chequered livery was splattered, stained and streaked with mud and filth when they finally arrived back in the main car park at the end of the session. Their traffic police instructor wasn't amused at all. Angrily, he said,

'Listen, you lot. I had to give up a bloody rest day to do this training session, and I'm responsible for the vehicle. This beamer is on my signature, and it's got to be returned to Traffic Division clean,' he glanced through the windscreen at the mud on the bonnet; then he turned and scowled at the grinning crew of would-be racing drivers, who clearly couldn't care less.

Glancing at his watch, he growled, 'Can't see I should sort it, and I've made sure there's twenty minutes left before training officially finishes.' A vein throbbed ominously on the side of his forehead as he snapped, 'You got the motor dirty,' he nodded towards the sign declaring - Vehicle Wash-Down Point – 'so you can bloody well go and clean it!'

There was mutinous silence among the group for a moment. Danny nudged Spike in the ribs with his elbow, and leant forward. Staring at the instructor, with head bowed and a contrite look creeping across his face, he declared,

'Fair enough, mate. You're right; it's our fault it's in such a mess.' Danny turned around and faced his friends. With a surreptitious wink, he declared, 'It won't take long to get it all shiny and new… come on boys, let's take the motor over to the wash-point, and get it cleaned up….'

Twenty minutes later, Pat called the assembled troop together for a quick de-brief. When he did the head count, he was four men missing, although their instructor was there. Pat wondered absently where Spike, Danny and the other two had got to, and where the last police interceptor had gone. Noticing their instructor had finished talking to the other police officers nearby, he wandered casually over to the huddle and enquired,

'What happened to the rest of my boys then?'

Sgt Dibcot sniffed with disdain,

'Look mate, I know your regiment isn't exactly famous for spit and polish, but your blokes made a real mess of my motor. It looked to me; they deliberately got it filthy.' With an arrogant grin towards the other instructors, he added, 'so I sent them off with their tails between their legs to clean it… It'll teach them a lesson not to mess with the Met.'

Pat nodded, but he growled silently to himself. He didn't like this muppet's attitude one little bit. Knowing who they were, somehow, he didn't think the missing crew would simply slink off with their heads bowed. Nevertheless, Pat kept a straight face; he shrugged and muttered, 'OK, fair enough….'

\* \* \* \* \*

*'Pat! Come quick, Danny's been hurt!'*

From the corner of a building, on the far side of the car-park, Spike frantically waved and shouted across to his sergeant. Eyes wide, he yelled,'

'Danny's not breathing, I think he's dead!'

Without a word, a cold knot growing in his stomach, Pat forgot about the de-brief, and broke into a flat run. His mind whirled as he sprinted towards the distraught trooper. It was well known that more men were killed in the Regiment due to training accidents, than on active service. Pat offered up a silent prayer that it wasn't so today.

Before Pat reached him, Spike turned and dashed back towards the wash-point, followed thirty yards behind by an untidy posse of running troopers and their traffic police instructors.

As the men ran from the car-park, none of them noticed the missing police car enter from the oppose side, and quietly park up beside the other three. The driver got out, locked the BMW, and placed the keys under the police car's windscreen wiper blade. Satisfied, he walked casually over to his own military Land-rover, opened the door, and climbed aboard.

Pat was first to reach the wash-point. He skidded to a halt on the wet ground beside Danny, who was lying unmoving, soaked to the skin beside a large, concrete lined deep-water submersion tank, used for checking the seals when experimental armoured vehicles deep-waded through water obstacles.

There were wet tyre tracks leading into the black, scummy water, but ominously, the other ramp leading out of the tank was dry. Bubbles of air and small globs on engine oil were bubbling up from the centre of the tank's oily surface.

One of the other four-man crew was frantically administering CPR to Danny.

'Jesus, what happened?' demanded Pat, as he took in the whole ghastly scene.

'Danny was ordered to clean the police car, and he drove it into the bay,' gasped Spike, his chest still heaving after his desperate dash. 'He didn't realise it was so deep, and the bloody motor sank straight under with him in it,' The anguish on his face was obvious, as he spluttered, 'He was down there for ages before he got out and floated to the surface… It wasn't his fault Pat, honest. Our instructor said there would be trouble if he didn't get it cleaned up straight away…'

With his colleagues, Sgt Dibcot arrived at the run, and heard what Spike had said. Colour drained from his face. With a horrified look, the traffic policeman gasped,

'Christ! I didn't tell him to bloody well drown himself!'

Pat's head snapped around. Seething with anger, he snarled at the distraught policeman,

'This is one of my best men. It's your bloody fault, you bastard! I'll have your job, and you're fucking pension, damn you!

Chalky Palmer, the trooper administering CPR, placed his ear against Danny's chest. Relief flooding his face, he turned to Pat and shouted excitedly,

'I've got a pulse Pat. I can hear his heart beating…'

Danny suddenly coughed, groaned and spat out a mouthful of scummy water. It splashed onto the soaking ground beside him.

Behind the huddle of men, one of the Troop's Land-rovers suddenly squealed to a halt.

Spike glared at the police instructor, glanced across at the idling Rover and then looked pleadingly at his sergeant. Desperately, he said,

'Danny's alive, but he's in bad shape Pat. We'd better get him straight to hospital.'

Pat nodded as one of the other policemen stepped forward,

'Look… We can do that.'

Pat glared at him and snapped,

'No thanks, you've done quite enough. We look after our own… we'll see to Danny.'

Four of Pat's men knelt down and gently lifted the unconscious trooper into the back of the Rover. As Spike climbed in to look after his friend, still seething, Pat scowled at Sgt Dibcot,

'You'd better get your story straight, mate. My trooper was following your orders, and you damn near killed him...'

Sgt Dibcot's mouth was open, but no words came. His earlier arrogance evaporated. The inevitable IPCC enquiry would show no mercy, and it would burn him; he was absolutely certain of that. His mind raced as his stomach churned. He'd not carried out a risk assessment on the wash-point, issued ambiguous orders outside his jurisdiction and failed to properly supervise trainees in his charge. In the politically correct world of the capital's policing nowadays; they'd hang him out to dry over this; that, he was convinced, was for sure.

As Pat climbed into the driver's seat in the Rover, he ordered the rest of his men back to Chelsea in the Troop's other vehicles. He called into the back,

'How is he doing, Spike?'

'Still breathing, Pat, but you'd better hurry,' came the urgent reply.

Pat slammed the gear stick forward and let the clutch slip. He knew time was of the essence. The golden hour, critical to Danny's survival, was quickly ebbing away.

The Land-rover surged forward in a shower of loose gravel. It careered around a building and sped back towards the car-park, and the main gate beyond. Despite his concern about Danny, Pat couldn't help but notice four police BMW's neatly parked to one side, as he flashed them by. A quizzical look flooded his face; something was wrong with the numbers… there should only be three, the other was somewhere behind him, still in the black depths of the submersion tank. Like everyone else, he had spied the convincing stream of bubbles, hadn't he? Leaching pockets of trapped air, which popped on the surface as they seeped from the sunken car confirmed the car's location, didn't they? The rainbow sheen of escaping oil added to his conviction that the car was certainly in there, and yet…?

Pat glanced in his rear-view mirror. To his surprise, Spike's look of concern for his mate had gone. Spike's lips were moving, and he was grinning broadly. Pat's mind cleared suddenly, he knew the two rogues in the back; and the mischief they were capable of. Pat was beginning to smell a particularly large rat,

'What are you two buggers up to?' Pat growled. 'Danny, you'd better be at death's door in the back, or there's going to be some very serious trouble for the both of you!'

Danny emitted an unconvincing groan.

'He's still very poorly, Pat,' said Spike, trying unsuccessfully to stifle a grin. Spike's diagnosis sounded as hollow as Danny's groan.

Pat pursed his lips. He said sternly,

'Right, that's enough. Danny, if you're not sitting up and taking notice by the time I count five, I'm going to bust you both out of the Troop as soon as we get back to Chelsea. ONE!... TWO! … THREE...FO…

Danny suddenly sat bolt upright, his eyes wide open. Spike fell backwards and crossed himself theatrically as he gasped,

'Bloody Hell, Pat, it's…it's a miracle!'

Their sergeant's eyes narrowed, 'Shut up, Spike,' Barked Pat angrily. 'Danny, I don't know what was going on back there, but whatever it was, you'd better explain yourself, and believe me, it had better be good…

\* \* \* \* \*

Pat listened in silence, as reluctantly, Danny explained his tale. When he had finished, Pat, suppressing the urge to laugh, kept his eyes on the road and remained silent for a moment as he thought about a suitable response. To Pat's way of thinking, it was nothing more than a well-executed prank. On balance, the Troop's training session had been highly successful, and no-one had actually been hurt. Danny's revenge was nothing more than a well-planned takedown of a particularly arrogant policeman's pride. Pat guessed the story would quickly circulate within the close-knit community of the Metropolitan Police. Dibcot had been out-witted and humiliated; within the tight-knit ranks of London's Traffic Division, he'd never live it down.

As Danny glanced nervously at Spike, Pat was drawing closer to a conclusion. Hands on the steering wheel and eyes still glued to the road ahead, Pat finally spoke in a voice which betrayed none of his earlier anger. Calmly, he said over his shoulder,

'OK, I hear all of that, but tell me something…. When I first got to the wash-down tank, I saw trapped air and oil bubbling up to the surface. If there was no car in there, how the hell did you get it all looking so real?'

Relieved at the change of tone in his sergeant's voice, Danny regained his usual self-confidence; he laughed,

'Oh, that? It was all camouflage and sleight of hand, Pat. I found an old oil drum half full of sump oil at the back of the wash-down when we first got there. I strapped a big lump of concrete to it, punched a small hole in the middle of the drum, and slung the whole lot into the deepest part of the tank.' Danny grinned, 'It sank like a stone and worked a treat, didn't it?'

Pat couldn't suppress his own grin any longer. The ruse worked on him, and everyone else. Being a Troop sergeant in the SAS was never an easy job, but there were points to be earned from this, and could only add to his men's confidence and bravado. There was no damage done, except to Dibcot's pride. Chances were the Traffic Division would be too embarrassed to mention it again through official channels. Miracles happened sometimes; they might even see the funny side. Pat decided he'd best have a quick, off-the-record chat with the Adjutant when he got back, but like countless other episodes of unscripted and unsanctioned skulduggery he had had to contend with during his tour of duty with the highly-tuned firecracker of the reserve SAS, the Adjutant would make it go away by quietly burying the whole episode. For now anyway, Pat decided to be lenient,

'All right Danny, you're off the hook, laddie, for now, but sometime in the future; you'll have to pay the piper for not clearing your plan with me first.'

Spike smirked. Pat saw it in the mirror and said sternly, 'I don't know what you are laughing at, young Spike, you were up to your neck in Danny's little scheme too, weren't you?'

Spike gulped, and remained quiet. Suitably ticked off, the two occupants in the back of the Rover sat in silence for several minutes, until Danny winked at his best mate, grinned, and piped up again,

'Pat?'

With a sigh, their sergeant snapped,

'Yes, Danny, what is it now?'

'Did you mean what you said, you know, when you thought I was dead…' There was mischief in the air; it filled the inside the Rover. Danny continued, 'About me being one of your best men?'

Pat saw Spike's head go down with a grin and a stifled snigger, as he stared into the rear-view mirror. In the frigid silence which followed, Danny gulped, and wished he'd stayed quiet. He knew he might have overstepped the line this time. In the mirror, ominously, his sergeant's eyes narrowed to slits. Unimpressed, Pat hissed dangerously between gritted teeth,

'I'd button it, Trooper Thomas, if I were you. Remember this sunshine, you both owe me now, and trust me; I won't forget.' With an angry snort, Pat

added, 'I'd listen to a few words of friendly advice if I were either of you two…
Don't push your bleeding luck!'

# Chapter Eleven

As best he could judge, it was the third day since he'd been lifted. At least, he thought grimly; his stomach was settling. The gut-wrenching nausea from his recent concussion seemed to be easing slowly, which was something. Brigadier Lethbridge opened his eyes and groaned softly. The bonds, which cut into his wrists and held his hands securely were as tight as ever. His head still throbbed like the devil, but the bleeding had stopped sometime before he had first regained consciousness.The hood over his head, which smelt of diesel oil and damp jute, kept him in permanent semi-darkness. He'd fallen heavily when he first tried to stand; he discovered he was shackled by his ankles, via a chain padlocked to a metal cargo ring, welded firmly to the container's steel floor.

Judging by the rhythmic sound and vibration of distant engines, and the slow rocking motion within his echoing cell, he was inside a steel shipping container, aboard, presumably, a cargo vessel, somewhere out at sea.

The Brigadier's intellect was straining to make sense of it all, but he knew he must do his best to work out what was going on. Clearly, he was a prisoner, but he had seen only one jailor through a tiny pinhole in his hood, since his kidnap. The door of the container had swung open last time he was lying on his side awake; the outline of a thin man with frizzy hair had been momentarily silhouetted against the doorway and the bright sunshine outside.

From the brief glimpse he had, the guard didn't appear to be carrying a weapon, which suggested to the Brigadier that the man was untroubled by discovery. It also suggested his jailor was a member of the ships complement, which led to the natural conclusion that the whole crew knew of their prisoner. For now, until he knew better, he must conclude that the Captain and officers were also complicit in his kidnap. The man had entered, shaken him, and partially lifted his hood. He gave the Brigadier a cup of tepid water to drink. It was a relief, but when the water was gone, the hood was firmly pulled down and his jailor left without a word, slamming the steel door with a loud bang. It sounded, from outside, like a bolt was slammed home immediately afterwards, and then there was only silence, save the rhythmic thrum of the massive marine engines somewhere below him.

Despite his confusion over what had actually happened, one question surged to the top of the list. It repeatedly invaded the Brigadier's thoughts. What had become of his dear wife during the kidnap? The question gnawed and grated in his belly; was she alive or dead? The Brigadier felt his gorge rise as he contemplated her fate. Poor Edith, what had become of her? Charles Lethbridge had no idea as to her fate, but either way; he thought grimly; he'd make them pay. The moment would come, but for now at least, escape was impossible, so he'd rest as much as he could while he recovered his strength and bearings. Any intelligence he could gather in the meantime could only be of help. He knew the Regiment would move heaven and earth to rescue him, but for now, he was on his own. Slowly, he began to make his assessment.

The atmosphere was warm in his steel dungeon. The Brigadier chewed his lip as he tried to deduce his location. If the ship had gone south through the Suez Canal, they'd be somewhere in the Red Sea or beyond it in the Gulf of Aden by now. From his previous experience, fighting years ago against the Ado; communist led insurgents in the Oman; it would now be unbearably hot in his steel box. To the Brigadier's considerable relief, however, where he lay wasn't an overheated sweat box. That probably meant, he reasoned, the ship was still sailing in the Mediterranean; west perhaps, towards the Atlantic? They were obviously taking him somewhere, for some purpose that for now anyway, didn't bear thinking about. None of his kidnappers had attempted to interrogate him so far, but someone had gone to a great deal of trouble to capture him. If they hadn't wanted him captured alive, one thing was for certain he thought grimly; he'd be dead already.

Behind the jute hood, concern fell away, and a smile crept across the Brigadier's bruised face. Apart from a buzzing headache, nothing appeared broken in his body, and he certainly wasn't beaten yet. His smile widened just a little. Let his civilian tee-shirt and shorts, and the clipped, blood-matted grey hair fool them for now; he thought. It was camouflage of a sort, and would serve him well. An opportunity for action was sure to come, but for now; he'd make the most of his situation, bad though it was. He'd exaggerate the head injury in the eyes of his captors and the pain it was causing him. Charles Lethbridge dug deep and recalled his Special Forces anti-capture training from long ago. It was best to play up and act the fearful, broken prisoner; he remembered. Anything which would relax his captors guard would help. He'd groan pitifully and exaggerate his distress next time his jailer fed or watered him, enough to be worthy of a Hollywood Oscar. Word would soon spread among the others. Unthreatening, he would lead them along, but in reality, he would be biding his time, until an opportunity presented where he could strike back at them, whoever the hell they were.

The Brigadier closed his eyes. Before sleep came, the wolfish grin returned behind the mask. He hadn't become Britain's most senior Special Forces soldier by being soft, and after all, he reasoned, he'd only just retired. If he couldn't make good his escape, he thought savagely, he'd stay focused to the very end, and do his absolute damnedest to take at least some of the bastards with him.

# Chapter Twelve

Friday prayers had come and gone in the small warehouse just off Vincent Street; recently converted into the eighth Greater Horton mosque, close to Bradford city's heart. It was surrounded in all directions by row upon row of cramped terraced houses, spreading like a dark stain across West Yorkshire's rolling Pennine foothills.

There was room for a thousand worshippers in the newly converted building. To the delight of the radical Tunisian-born Imam, Abdula Whalid, who led the recitation of the congregational prayers of the faithful, new worshippers kept coming through his welcoming, open doors. Numbers grew steadily by the week.

The throng of young Muslim men was increasing progressively, as the loudspeakers called the faithful to prayer. Worshippers were drawn from across Bradford and the surrounding towns to this new, independent, Saudi-funded mosque. They came to listen to the Imam's fiery sermons, which every Friday denounced and derided Western attitudes towards Islam. To cleanse their blasphemy, he advocated Sharia law be introduced into the areas of British cities; in some cases numerically dominated by ever growing Asian Muslim communities. Imam Abdula Whalid warned his rapt audience of the dangers of associating or integrating too far into the highly immoral, non-Muslim culture, which surrounded and constantly taunted them all.

Paradise would be closed to the weak-minded who rejected his teachings; he warned them. The very fires of eternal hell, he cautioned, awaited those whose faith and courage wavered in the struggle to promote Islam in this vile infidel land, riddled as it was with Christian un-believers. All around the world, he roared, innocent Muslim women and children were being slaughtered by the Americans and their British lackeys; the evil men who commanded their remote controlled drones wanted nothing but the destruction of Islam; their attacks proved beyond doubt they wished to grind the teachings of the blessed Prophet Mohammed into the very ground beneath their feet.

There was a line within his rhetoric, however, which the Imam never publicly crossed. He was no fool. He applied his hard-core, hate-filled sermons to smaller gatherings, targeting only the most vulnerable and obedient during closed and private sessions in the small flat he had rented above a local tobacconist. Its dingy rooms were ideal for what he wanted, it offered the privacy he needed, without putting himself under threat of arrest and deportation under the government's latest bundle of hastily implemented race-hate laws. He vetted his chosen ones carefully, rejecting those he deemed unworthy. His mission demanded caution. There were bound to be police informers among his growing congregation, he was convinced of it. They would inform on him for money if he spoke out too violently, or went too far. The irony of his situation, however, wasn't wasted on the radical Tunisian. He often laughed to himself in the country where he was free to publicly preach his subtle hatred under both the nose, and the cast-iron protection, of British law.

* * * * *

When the call came from distant Pakistan days earlier, he instantly recognised the phrase '*He who obeys the Messenger, has indeed obeyed Allah.*'

Imam Abdula Whalid and his radicalised disciples were ready. It was the signal he was waiting for from Zahira Kahn. The hidden message told him he had almost reached his secret mission's deadly endgame. The long months Whalid had endured, since claiming political asylum with the immigration authorities at Heathrow airport, had been well spent and fruitful.

Burdened with the enormous task of processing a growing bottleneck of more than half a million asylum seekers, as he plotted, Kahn knew according to the latest press coverage, the British Home Office was swamped. Many applications were bogus, but according to Home Office regulations, each recorded claim had to be judged on its own merits. With the mounting backlog, the British immigration authorities couldn't possibly scrutinize Whalid's application for at least twelve months or more. It allowed plenty of time to complete the real purpose for which Whalid had first entered the country, using an assumed name and an equally false Jordanian passport.

Like many from Pakistan, Khan had family ties with those living within the large local Asian community. He used the connection to facilitate part of his plan. It had been child's play for Zahira Khan to coerce several of his more radical kin, who were sympathisers to Al-Qaeda's cause anyway, to help Imam Whalid find somewhere to live, and assist him in setting up the new mosque off Vincent Street, in the back-streets of Bradford.

Perfectly legitimate money was available to the right people, donated by devout Saudi princes to further worldwide expansion of the Islamic faith. Supporters in high places and creative false accounting through numerous international bank accounts made things easy. Cash had been syphoned off and diverted by Zahira Khan's associates to fund his black operation. The Al-Qaeda facilitator quietly set aside sufficient funds, when his planning to avenge the death of Bin Laden was at an early stage of development. Refurbishing and converting a new place of worship would neatly establish Whalid's cover within the UK, satisfying both the overwhelmed authorities, and those who had given so generously to the cause of spreading the Prophet's sacred words around the globe.

The Tunisian cleric switched off the remaining lights and stepped outside into the wintry darkness of Greater Horton for the last time. He fumbled for his keys, reached up and locked the building's heavy main doors. He wouldn't be back, but wanted to keep to his routine, in case he was under surveillance. Turning up his raincoat's collar against the bitter cold, he headed towards his flat, where the chosen ones would gather for the last time that evening.

In a few short days, the first of his prodigies would be unleashed. Soon, he thought, they would cast a shadow of fear and suffering over a peaceful and unsuspecting London. Carnage and devastation would surely follow in the footsteps of his brainwashed group of the living dead.

Imam Abdula Whalid had only one true purpose in coming to the UK. His deadly mission, on the orders of Zahira Khan, was to recruit and train a handful of religious zealots; he had been given twelve months to turn them into mindless, obedient automatons who would follow his orders, and give their lives without question.

Abdula Whalid was triumphant. His chosen soldiers of Islam would soon end their pointless existence as martyrs, in a sea of fire and blood. The sinister agent of Zahira Khan's master plan was almost finished; it had taken a long time to bend their minds, but he was satisfied that he had achieved his ultimate goal with every one of them.

As the cleric approached the tobacconist, and the faded, nondescript door which led upstairs to his flat, Abdula Whalid smiled smugly to himself. In under a year, he created his own deadly weapons of mass destruction. Hidden within the grimy back streets of Bradford; he had fashioned a brainwashed cell of untraceable, fanatical and utterly ruthless suicide bombers.

# Chapter Thirteen

Three days later

Terminal Three – Heathrow Airport -10.04 am

'Take me to the London Hilton.'

Pat nodded in silence at the fare's gruff instructions. His latest passenger stepped back as Pat opened the luggage door well beside him. A chill wind blew through the grey concrete façade of the soulless taxi rank outside Terminal Three of London's premier airport: Heathrow. The accent and manner nailed the man immediately in Pat's mind. The American businessman hefted his suitcase and Pat slid it snugly onto the parcel shelf beside his driver's seat. Satisfied the case was secure; the paunchy, middle-aged American slammed the taxi door a little too hard for Pat's liking, and then climbed unsteadily into the back of the cab. Pat's nose wrinkled at the smell of booze, which suddenly assailed his nostrils.

Not feeling in the mood to initiate conversation with another pissed American businessman on such an overcast and dreary Monday morning, Pat stayed silent. Leaning to his left, he switched on the taxi meter. Having checked his mirrors, Pat pulled smoothly away from the rank, joining the flow of traffic moving towards the airport's exit. As he had done so many times in the past few years, Pat pointed the nose of his cab towards the M4 motorway. It should be easy enough, he thought; thirty minutes or so depending on the traffic, before reaching the prestigious Hilton hotel, off Park Lane in central London.

Pat's fare remained silent until they were cruising eastwards on the motorway. Suddenly, above the muffled roar of the cab's diesel engine, he said,

'The name's Pine buddy: Jim Pine from Fort Worth, Texas. How you doing today?'

Pat's eyes flicked up at the rear-view mirror. If the fare wanted to talk, it was part of his job description to make a standard reply,

'Pretty good, thanks. The name's Pat. How was your flight?'

The American's grin was a little lopsided,

'Yeah, pretty good thanks, Pat, but long and boring. Still, they served up some pretty mean whisky sours in business class.'

Pat smiled and nodded. He didn't really care what his fare's choice of breakfast was, somewhere high over the Atlantic, but there was no reason to upset the man. There was silence in the taxi for a moment, and then the American piped up again,

'I'm in the oil business…'

* * * * *

Pat dropped his fare at the front of the Hilton. The man's tip was generous. He offered to buy Pat a drink now they were best buddies, but Pat had declined,

'Not while I'm working, thanks Jim. The drink drive laws here are pretty severe.'

Jim Pine nodded with understanding; he scowled,

'Yeah, I guess… same as in the States.'

The American had helped himself to a nip or two from a hip-flask during the journey into London, but Pat didn't sit in judgement. It was one way to keep the cold out, and get over the jet-lag; he reasoned, suppressing a wry smile.

'Well, so long Pat, you're a great guy….'

With that, the American oilman turned, and unsteadily followed the uniformed bellhop, who was already disappearing into the hotel's plush foyer, carrying Jim Pine's heavy case towards reception.

At the end of the day, like so many others who rode his cab, the American was just another face in Pat's day, which he'd never see again. Dismissing the man from his mind, Pat swung the cab around, and headed to the back of the line of empty cabs, waiting for the next fare from the hotel. With eight cabs in front of him, Pat decided to take a chance, switch off his engine and see if the rank moved quickly. Sometimes it did, especially towards lunchtime; and then he'd be away again, perhaps back to Heathrow, or to some destination around central London.

Pat had finished reading his paper earlier, while he'd sat relaxing in the taxi park at Heathrow, waiting patiently for his turn to join one of the busy terminal ranks. The only thing which irritated Pat while he waited, were the loud voices of the *'faces'* who drove licensed cabs and worked exclusively from the airport. Two were laughing, openly boasting to each other of the money they had made from their first runs of the day. They were regarded by the majority of London cabbies as scavengers, with no qualms about breaking the strict rules of first come, first served; illegally brooming poorly paid local jobs without conscience onto other unwary drivers. Only interested in the lucrative London runs, they were highly unpopular with the rest of the taxi trade. Pat shrugged to himself; it was the way of life. There was low-life in every trade.

His paper read, and with nothing else to do, Pat settled down to watch the flow and ebb of visitors and guests entering the hotel. Like other prestigious up-market hotels in London, the Hilton was a cosmopolitan hub, a melting pot, where foreign businessmen did deals over lunch in the hotel's expensive restaurant, and sometimes minor visiting diplomats stayed when their own embassy's limited accommodation was full. Like all hotels in major capitals, some guests went off on tourist day trips during their stay. Occasionally, lovers met discreetly, to indulge in more intimate relations during their clandestine affairs.

Like all the other days of the year, there were people from all over the world, staying at the Hilton; a kaleidoscopic mixture of race, creed and colour. Naturally, no-one noticed another faceless Asian man, wearing a long parka overcoat enter the bustling marble-lined foyer. If anyone had taken an interest in the young man, which they didn't, they might have noticed that despite the chill wind, which blew outside, he was breathless and sweating as he walked past the rich and famous into the heart of the Hotel's busy concourse.

Unknown to the guests and visitors in the busy foyer, it wasn't the warmth of his coat which had overheated the young man, but the brisk walk of nearly quarter of a mile from Marble Arch tube station, and his anticipation of what was to be. He was burdened by a heavily laden suicide vest, packed with almost twenty kilos of high-explosives, covered by a thick layer of nails and ball bearings. The crystal filled pouches strapped to the bomber's body were linked, primed and ready. Inside his coat pocket, he nervously fingered the bomb's trigger.

Beads of sweat trickled down his forehead as Muktar Said Omar licked his lips nervously. Standing in this decadent temple of western culture, he devoutly believed that his actions were fully justified; they were not wrongful he had constantly been told, but righteous acts in the service of holy Jihad. Now was the moment he had waited for so patiently, since Abdula Whalid's special teachings had begun to reveal the unquestionable truth about the evil of the un-believers, their vile abhorrence of Islam and the blasphemy they spouted towards the teachings of the beloved Prophet.

Muktar's poisoned mind overflowed with pathological rage and hatred. How he despised them all. His eyes narrowed to hate-filled slits as he looked into the faces of the kafirs moving around him, blissfully unaware and intent on their business of the day. Now was his divine opportunity; his moment in history where he personally would make them pay for their insults to Islam. In a few seconds, the fanatical twenty-five-year-old would enter the golden gates of paradise as a martyred warrior, and sit forever at the feet of the blessed Prophet.

Taking one last look at his unsuspecting victims, the young bomber raised both his hands aloft. His right hand was filled with the vest's trigger; his left held the holy Koran. With eyes closed; his fingers began to curl around the detonating switch. In exultation, he opened his eyes, threw back his head and cried aloud,

'*Allah Akbar!...*'

Pat was daydreaming as the thunderous explosion blew out the front of the hotel's lobby. The world suddenly went to hell in a maelstrom of fire and smoke;. In a split-second, the peaceful lunchtime facade was gone. Pedestrians walking by were seared by the bomb's orange fireball, then picked up and hurled into the road by the hammer blow of the blast's powerful concussion. The chaotic scene around the hotel's entrance was concealed by thick billowing smoke; hysterical screams of terror and pain echoed through the swirling chaos. Blood splashed brightly among the smoking debris of the hotel's frontage, which in a single heartbeat was ripped out and pulverised by the explosion.

For a moment, like other shocked survivors, Pat sat stunned in his cab as his mind struggled to make sense of the horror. At the far end of the taxi rank, directly outside the burning reception area, the first two cabs were in flames.

Recovering his wits, ears still ringing from the explosion, he leapt from his cab and raced headlong towards the carnage of broken glass and shattered concrete in front of him.

Pat reached the end of the rank in moments and skidded to a halt at the very edge of the debris field. Raising his hand to shield his face from the heat, he stared into the burning hulks, which moments before, had been gleaming London taxis, waiting patiently for their next paying passengers. It was no good, Pat knew instantly; both drivers were gone. With a curse, Pat pushed a dazed traffic warden aside, and headed into what was left of the smoke-filled foyer.

Twisted wires hung jumbled and sparking from what was left of the ornate ceiling. The place reeked with the acrid stench of burnt explosives, brick dust and worst of all, the stench of human blood. They were smells which brought dark memories flooding back; they filled him instantly with revulsion. Pat had been here before. One dark rain-filled night in Londonderry, as a young infantry soldier long ago, he had seen the same destruction; the terrible, merciless effect of high-explosives and scything shrapnel on fragile human bodies. He felt his gorge rise as he stared through the swirling smoke at the blackened bodies which surrounded him. They lay still and scattered like broken dolls, in what was left of the devastated lobby. Desperately, Pat dashed from one corpse to another, searching for signs of life. In the centre of the smoking atrium, he found none. Suddenly, above the noise of the crackling fires around him, he heard something.

What sounded like a faint whimper reached his ringing ears. The sound came from roughly where the main reception counter had stood, until moments before. Pat picked his way through thick smoke, climbing quickly over smashed debris towards the noise. He guessed it had come from somewhere beneath a jagged sheet of fallen ceiling plaster. Frantically, Pat pulled the blackened rubbish aside. Beneath it lay a young woman. Her face was streaked with dirt and splattered with blood; her arm badly gashed. A long, twisted nail was embedded partway into her left shoulder above the main bleeding wound. Pat automatically set aside his shock. His training kicked in, as it had done so many times before. Stone-faced, he assessed the casualty, and prioritised her injuries as he had been taught to do. As he went to work, his busy mind forced aside the horror around him, which would certainly have overwhelmed a lesser man.

Airway, breathing and circulation, the mantra of all para-medics repeated over and over in his mind. There was blood trickling from her nose, and each of the girl's ears, which at best suggested ruptured eardrums, at worst, a fractured skull or even serious brain injury. The girl displayed no sign of fitting, so Pat hoped for the best and moved on with his examination. Blinking away the smoke which stung his eyes, Pat gently opened the girl's mouth. There were some dark blood clots in there, but not enough to choke her. With no apparent blockage to worry about, Pat looked for any faint rise and fall of her chest as he felt her neck, searching desperately for a pulse. At last, he found it. It was faint, fluttering like a butterfly's wings, but at least her heart was still beating. Pat put his ear to her mouth. Despite the tinnitus, he could hear she was breathing, although Pat didn't like the rattle rising up from her chest each time the next shallow breath trickled life-giving air into her lungs. Probably internal injuries, Pat decided grimly; broken ribs with a collapsed or punctured lung, but there was little he could do, except stabilise her as best he could, and keep the girl alive while he waited impatiently for the arrival of properly equipped medical help. The deep gash in her shoulder was Pat's main concern.

She was already in deep shock; Pat knew the grim reality of the girl's imminent prognosis. If the heavy bleeding continued, it would quickly cause her blood pressure to plummet to a critical level, stop her heart, and kill her.

Pat's mouth was dry; it tasted of bile and soot. The back of his throat was raw from inhaling dust and smoke, which hung around him like a shroud within the shattered foyer. He coughed as he pressed down on the jagged rip in her arm. Blood oozed between his fingers; his tight grip wasn't enough. Pat knew he had to do more to staunch the bleeding or he'd lose her. Lying behind the girl, half-buried in the rubble, was a piece of charred rag; a fragment of someone's clothing. Pat snatched it up, shook it free of dust and rammed it into the wound. Saving her life was his primary goal, infection, right now was a secondary concern. He must stop the blood loss, or she was going to slip away before help arrived. The girl moaned softly again at the powerful pressure he exerted on her open wound; Pat ignored her reaction. Something a medical instructor had said to him long ago in Hereford, flashed through his mind,

'*You've got to be alive to feel pain.*'

The blood loss slowed. With his spare hand, he reached for her neck and checked her pulse again. To his relief, he found it; fluttering, barely detectable, but still there.

Pat coughed again as he held on grimly. Looking away from the girl and peering through the gloom, he took stock of his surroundings. Clearly, the girl had been lucky. On duty at reception, standing behind the heavy solid counter, her legs and lower torso had been protected from the main force of the blast, and most of the flying shrapnel. More shielding had come from those who had been standing in front of her. Their bodies had taken the full force of the blast, and all of them were dead. Pat looked down and refocused his bloodshot eyes on the girl. Maybe, he thought, maybe he could make a difference and save at least one victim.

Ever since the intense IRA bombing campaigns in the '70s and '80s, terrorism had long been accepted as a threat to the capital. The fire, police and ambulance services remained coordinated and well-drilled in rapid response to deadly terror attacks.

Somewhere outside, he heard the mournful wail of a siren, quickly followed by others whose rise and fall grew in volume with every second that passed. St. Thomas and St. Mary's hospitals were closest, and Pat guessed it must be their ambulance crews that were now racing to help the injured survivors. Fire engines and the police, Pat knew, would be following close behind.

After more agonising seconds kneeling beside the girl, trapped among the torn and twisted bodies surrounding him, through the smoke, Pat saw blue lights flashing and movement outside. Someone came to his aid at last. With enormous relief, he spied the green and yellow day-glow jackets of the first paramedics clambering into the chaotic ground floor mess of the Hilton. More followed. Wearily, Pat cleared his throat of soot. He spat, and then shouted hoarsely,

*'Hey, you two! Get over here; I've got a live one!'*

\* \* \* \*

Standing alone outside Marble Arch underground station, un-noticed in the cosmopolitan bustle of startled shoppers around him, Abdula Whalid's pockmarked face slowly broke into a twisted smile. The detonation had been gratifyingly loud. It had echoed back and forth along the tree line bordering the edge of Hyde Park on the far side of Park Lane. The oily pall of black smoke, stretching up towards the heavens, was, he thought, a fitting epitaph to the first martyred warrior, Muktar Said Omar.

Ignoring the flashing blue lights and wailing sirens of the emergency vehicles hurtling down Park Lane, his crooked smile faded. He must go. It was time to meet again with the bomb-maker, and discuss their final preparations for tomorrows attack. Telephones might be monitored by the British, so only face to face discussions would do. Abdula Whalid turned, and casually descended the concrete steps towards Marble Arch's underground station. Reaching the bottom, lost in his own smug triumph, Abdula Whalid strode purposely through eddying groups of tourists and travellers, towards the sentinel line of automated ticket barriers.

## Chapter Fourteen

'Food…. *Eat!*'

To the deep background thrum of the ship's powerful engines, Brigadier Lethbridge stared gloomily from the hunk of bread, and the tin cup filled with oil-sheened water his captor placed beside him. It was a new face he hadn't seen before. How many was it been now? He tried to remember. Yes, it was six. They were Africans; a rag-tag bunch; this one was definitely the sixth he'd seen. Their clothes had changed since he first woke up. After the second day, their apparel had morphed from dirty tee-shirts and grubby shorts, to battered, ill-fitting jeans and jackets. Probably bought as a job lot is some filthy native bazaar, he thought grimly to himself. The men were all black and equally skinny; they wore their hair long and frizzy. He guessed they were either Somalis or Ethiopians. Either way, it didn't make much difference; his bonds remained tight, and each of the bastards had been well armed.

On the positive side, however, they seemed to have relaxed a little each day, probably lulled by his meek, downcast behaviour.

It was certainly colder today inside his steel prison; the temperature dropped significantly during the last few days of the voyage. It surely meant they must be out of the Mediterranean and sailing north up the coast of Spain, through the Bay of Biscay. Their ultimate destination was still unclear, but every turn of the ship's screws, at least for now, was taking him closer to home.

Maintaining his persona of a downcast, beaten man, Brigadier Lethbridge had weakly mimed a shiver and pleaded for a blanket when the weather began to change, but had received only a sneer from the tall one with a limp, on the third day. The Brigadier had sent a silent, sulphuric curse at the man's back, as his latest jailor swaggered from the container. The curse showed no ill effect on his captor however, and was probably physically impossible, but nevertheless, the thought cheered Lethbridge and forced him to raise a fleeting smile. As a prisoner, any victory, however trivial, was to his advantage. A positive attitude remained vital. Keeping morale high during captivity was another hidden victory. It was something important and invisible, which, despite his desperate situation, only he could let slip.

The Brigadier's nose wrinkled. The stench from the open latrine bucket wasn't any worse, but remained as bad as ever. Chained up as he was, it had to stay within arm's reach, to be of any use.

Brigadier Lethbridge forced the stink from his mind. He had survived pretty much worse conditions during his long career with Special Forces, but had to admit to himself; it was a long time ago. Lethbridge shifted his position uncomfortably and turned to look at the hunk of bread left by number six. He picked it up for a closer inspection. Using the chink of light beaming in from below the container's steel door, once again, he saw the stain of dark mould growing on one side. With a resigned sniff, he began picking out the worst of it before eating what was left. Every scrap of food gave him strength; his survival depended on it. The Brigadier knew that when the time came, he was definitely going to need it.

* * * * *

It was the following day after the outrage at the Hilton. Pat was called into the intelligence wing of his SAS HQ in Chelsea, for a de-briefing.

Pat had spent some time in the back of an ambulance at the scene, under the supervision of the para-medics, breathing pure oxygen through a plastic mask which helped purge the inhaled smoke from his lungs. While he was being treated, the last of the casualties had been removed to hospital, and the corpses taken to Westminster morgue, under the supervision of the Coroner's court officers who had been alerted to the fatalities by the police. All the major news companies had raced to the scene, and were busy filming and interviewing eyewitnesses. Pat had refused to be interviewed. He had had to resort to threats of extreme violence, much to his medic's amusement, when one pushy BBC reporter, at first, wouldn't take no for an answer.

As Pat walked into the de-briefing room, a young woman, Pat recognised as Cornelius' assistant was sitting cross-legged beside the analyst, seconded by MI6 to Shadow Squadron. Cornelius Wilde leapt to his feet. The concern in his voice was real,

'Jesus Pat, you look absolutely terrible!'

There were dark circles under Pat's eyes and no masking his fatigue. Pat nodded towards the girl, and then turned his attention back to the MI6 man,

'Yeah, thanks Cornelius. Pretty much sums up how I feel at the moment.'

Both men sat down on opposite sides of the small table; the only furniture in the room apart from a large mirror on one wall. Cornelius broke the silence,

'Did you get much sleep last night?'

Pat shook his head,

'No, not much,' he didn't mention the dreams, which had returned suddenly with a vengeance. He had awoken twice in the night, sheets twisted and soaked with sweat. He stared at the MI6 analyst for a moment in silence. The dreams remained Pat's problem, so he didn't mention them.

'Ok, so tell me exactly what you remember?'

Pat bowed his head,

'It's all in the police statement I gave yesterday.' He shrugged absently. 'Sorry mate, but I haven't remembered anything more.'

Cornelius slumped back in his chair. He had already read Pat's statement, and those of the blast's other survivors and bystanders. He'd been working all night to create a mental map of the events leading up to the explosion, but despite his best efforts, didn't have much to go on. Cornelius clasped his hands together and rested them on the table. Below them, was a thick sheaf of papers. Cornelius cleared his throat softly, and began,

'Oh well... Ok; so much for the idea of holding a de-brief. It was worth a try, I hoped there would be something extra... I might as well update you instead, on what we've got so far.'

Cornelius wiped his hand across his face. He wished he had some black coffee to keep his own fatigue at bay. A drink might help, but he put the thought to the back of his mind. He'd been dry for months, and wanted to keep it that way. It looked like his friend might benefit from a stiff drink too, but shunted the thought aside. He turned to his assistant and held up two fingers.

'Two black coffees please, Julie, if you'd be so kind?'

The girl smiled and stood up,

'Not a problem, I'll be as quick as I can. To be honest, Cornelius; you both look beat.'

Pat fought hard to suppress a smile. As Julie left, Cornelius began explaining what the Security Service and Special Branch had got so far,

'The hotel's lobby was fairly busy late yesterday morning, but thankfully, most guests had long finished breakfast and were either upstairs in their rooms, or had left for the day. Of the twenty-six bodies recovered; twelve were confirmed as staff members. Nine have been formally identified by the police as official paying guests, and all except one of the remainder have been identified as purely innocent visitors going to or leaving appointments at the hotel.'

Pat's head snapped up. His suspicions aroused, his dark eyes bored into the face of the man sitting opposite. Deliberately, he enquired,

'*All* except one?'

Cornelius nodded grimly, but his face gave nothing away,

'Ah yes, there was one who was unaccounted for, he's our odd man out.'

Pat's eyes narrowed,

'Go on…'

'What was found of his remains, according to the forensic team who combed the site following the explosion, suggests he was our culprit, and therefore, the attack was a suicide bombing; not initiated by someone carrying a suitcase bomb, but instead, the perpetrator was wearing an explosive vest, packed with home-made shrapnel. We're pretty sure that our assumption is correct you see, because there was nothing left of his body at all,' Cornelius removed his glasses, and carefully wiped each lens in turn with his handkerchief. Before replacing them, he added,

'We found fragmented pieces of two matching arms and legs amongst the debris, but I'm afraid our suspect's torso was completely vaporised by the blast.' Cornelius held up his glasses to the light. Satisfied they were clean; matter-of-factly, he continued,

'The clinching evidence was the behaviour of the blast wave. The bomber's head, you see, was found embedded in what was left of the ceiling.... All consistent, I'm afraid, with a suicide vest explosion.'

Pat nodded. He'd seen the aftermath of a suicide attack like this once before in Iraq. On the orders of a local warlord, after death threats to the man's wife and small children, the unfortunate perpetrator had detonated his padlocked explosive vest just outside an Iraqi police station. Considering it too dangerous, the Iraqi police hadn't bothered with a follow-up search for body parts. The bomber's head was found the following day by an army patrol, laying in an irrigation ditch almost a hundred metres from the police station. Pat remembered grimly.... He had been leading the patrol,

'What about the explosives?'

Cornelius opened his hands and leafed through the papers in front of him. He stopped suddenly, and read one page for a moment. His eyes danced with triumph.

'Ah, here we are. The forensics team has identified the explosives as non-military; almost certainly home-made. Their analysis says it looks different from the stuff they used on the 7/7 London Underground bombings, though... Apparently, it's got an acetone peroxide base, and has been used recently, according to our colleagues in the ISI, in Pakistan and also over the border in Afghanistan, but not until now, has it been used here in the UK.' Cornelius read on, 'It's unusual and pretty unstable, but a very powerful high-explosive when it's mixed correctly, especially detonated in a confined space.'

Pat nodded in silence. The devastation caused by homemade explosives inside a bus and three central London underground tube trains, during a wave of simultaneous suicide attacks back in July 2005, had been catastrophic. All but one of the fifty-two civilian fatalities were resident in London when they were caught by the powerful blasts. The victims were from a diverse range of backgrounds. Among those killed, he remembered, were several foreign-born British nationals, overseas exchange students and parents on their way to work. The rush-hour victims were a typical cross-section of London's cosmopolitan population. Tragically, there were also hundreds of other passengers seriously injured by the nail-filled rucksacks the bombers detonated inside the underground tunnels. Their horrific injuries were caused by the blast and hundreds of large 6-inch nails, tightly packed around each of the home-made rucksack bombs. Pat winced with bitterness at the memories,

'The same Muslim terrorist cell tried again with new bombers, two weeks later, didn't they?' he asked.

Cornelius nodded again,

'Yes, they did. There was another wave of attacks, when five more attempts were made to simultaneously detonate the same kind of home-made bombs in buses and underground trains around central London, on 21st July 2005.' Cornelius shuddered, 'we got lucky on that day, Pat, really lucky. The explosives they were trying to detonate had decayed. They used the same batch as 7/7, but thank God, with two weeks apart, the bloody stuff chemically broke down, and didn't go off.'

'The police tracked down and arrested the bombers that time, I remember,' declared Pat with a spark of triumph in his eye. Cornelius grinned,

'Yes, that's right. All five were subsequently caught and found guilty at the Old Bailey. Every one of them got life, with a minimum recommended sentence of forty years apiece.'

Pat shook his head as his eyes narrowed dangerously. The MI6 analyst felt a distinct chill suddenly creep down his spine as he noticed the murderous look in his friend's dark eyes. Pat growled,

'It's a real pity Shadow Squadron weren't around at the time. Trust me… given half a chance, we'd have saved the taxpayers a lot of money…'

Cornelius locked eyes with Pat, but said nothing. The chill was still there. It felt, in that instant as if he was looking into the merciless eyes of a hunting cobra. He implicitly believed every word the veteran SAS man sitting opposite him had just said. Cornelius felt distinctly uncomfortable. He had spent his career office-bound as an MI6 analyst; he'd long since accepted his lot as a backroom boy, who worked chair bound in the busy offices of MI6 headquarters on the south bank of the River Thames. He spent many years looking for subtle patterns in spy and terrorist movements and activities, constantly unravelling plots and evaluating and updating potential dangers to the United Kingdom. As a result, Cornelius had very little field experience. He knew, out there in the real world; violence stalked such men as Pat. It was an ever-present companion; invisible and unseen; lurking silently and hidden in the darkness of their shadows. Despite some politicians leaning towards a more liberal society in the UK, Cornelius decided, the country needed men, tempered in the fires of terror and chaos, who wouldn't hesitate to pull a trigger. Cornelius took a deep breath and forced himself to relax; glad to count Pat as a friend, and not an enemy. The analyst swallowed, cleared his throat, and stuttered,

'Yes, well…..'

His troubled thoughts shattered like a breaking mirror with a soft knock at the door. It opened and his assistant, Julie Wallace, swept in smiling. Clasping the handles tightly, she carried in two steaming mugs in one hand. She set them down in front of Pat and Cornelius. Both men nodded their thanks, dismissed her from their minds and continued. Pat spoke first,

'Have you identified the bomber yet?'

Cornelius shook his head,

'No, not yet, but there is a strong feeling over in Vauxhall that we have another homegrown clean-skin on our hands.'

Pat winced. It was common knowledge that the clean-skins who had carried out the 7/7 underground bombings had all slipped under the Security Service's radar, prior to their deadly attacks. Without knowing of their existence, Special Branch couldn't make pre-emptive arrests to de-rail the plot before it happened. The suicide bombers weren't hard-core international terrorists known to MI6; MI5 or the police. Instead, they were Asian Muslims, born in the United Kingdom. Without criminal records, apart from one, they came as a complete shock to Cornelius, and the other government departments involved in the nation's security.

His face glum, Pat changed tack,

'Do your people think this was a one-off, or will there be more attacks on London?'

Cornelius raised an eyebrow,

'Good question. Last time, when they hit the underground, apart from the bus in Tavistock Square, the attacks were simultaneous. With only one blast yesterday, it could mean this was one lone-wolf religious nut-job with a chip on his shoulder, who radicalised himself. Given the sophistication and the rarity of the explosives, unfortunately, that's unlikely. On the other hand, if it is a new suicide cell, they may have changed tactics, and are planning more random, individual attacks.' Cornelius spread his hands, 'the simple truth is, Pat, we won't know either way, until we catch them, or there is another blast…'

Pat's mood darkened; his gut instinct screamed serious trouble was brewing; he and the rest of Shadow Squadron might be in action sooner, rather than later,

'So honestly, Cornelius, have you got anything else to go on?'

Cornelius' worried face lightened slightly,'

'We'll identify the dead bomber soon enough, Pat. After that we can start to unravel the whole story.' Cornelius pursed his lips, and then continued, 'There is one other lead which Special Branch are looking into. It's tenuous, but definitely worth following up.' Cornelius shuffled the papers on the table before him. Lightening his expression with satisfaction, he extracted a grainy photograph, and handed it to Pat,

'This photo was extracted from the CCTV security footage, taken close to Marble Arch underground station, just seconds after the blast at the Hilton.'

Pat stared intently at the image of the man in the photo. Dressed in what looked like non-descript Asian garb, a small white circular cap on his head, and the distinctive frock coat, blouse under a very ordinary jacket, the slightly blurred image of the man's face would make positive identification difficult; but one thing was clear. The man was looking down Park Lane towards the Hilton. In that instant, passers-by were looking in the same direction; curiosity and shock registering on their faces at what must have been the sound of the explosion. Pat saw Cornelius' point instantly. In what might well be a sinister twist, the man in the centre of the photograph was the only person grinning...

'We're trying to identify this guy over at Vauxhall right now. Using the cameras, we backtracked the bomber's route to the station at Marble Arch. He was on the CCTV footage, emerging from the underground, crossing the top of Oxford Street and walking south down Park Lane.' Cornelius nodded towards the photo, 'That man had no direct involvement as far as we can see, but he appeared on the pavement just after the bomber left Marble Arch station. The video footage clearly shows he hung around for at least ten minutes waiting for the explosion, then almost immediately, turned on his heel and disappeared back down the steps leading to the underground tube network. Unfortunately, the station security cameras were offline for maintenance during the incident, so we lost him at that point. Special Branch and the Met are doing what they can. They are checking Oyster card records and interviewing station staff. They have also called in every inch of CCTV footage, from all over the entire underground network to try to find out, if they can, where he immerged.' Cornelius shook his head, 'but with two hundred and seventy odd stations to cover around Greater London, most of them with multiple exits, it's going to take time for the police to track him down,' he shrugged, 'if at all?'

Pat blew out his cheeks; it was clearly an enormous task, and would involve around the clock scrutiny by hundreds of police officers and their support staff. It could take days to get even an indication of where the man was going to, if they got lucky. To make matters worse, his association with the attack might be entirely innocent. Maybe, the only other lead they had to go on was pure coincidence; nothing more than a massive red-herring. Cornelius sighed, sensing his friend's frustration,

'We have no alternative; we just have to keep trawling through thousands of hours of video tapes, and hope someone gets lucky, and spots him…'

# Chapter Fifteen

At least one living creature still called the deserted streets of the wasteland home. Ready to pounce, a feral tabby cat crouched beneath the burnt-out hulk of an old Comma van which rested on its side, forlorn and long forgotten. The tip of the cat's tail flicked back and forth as ears twitching, the hungry animal's yellow eyes watched patiently. It stared from behind one of the blackened van's wheel arches, watching a jagged hole just a few yards away along the stained viaduct arch, on the east side of the empty street. The rent in the masonry concealed its squeaking prey; inside, was a crowded nest of fat scurrying rats.

Fifty feet away, in an old archway workshop, nestling under the railway viaduct which spanned the derelict area, deep within the grimy back streets of east London's Isle of Dogs, all was ready.

A Docklands Light Railway train, filled with commuters, rumbled slowly overhead across the ancient viaduct which linked Crossharbour and South Quay stations. The DLR train line was a southern gateway, carrying thousands of commuters every morning from their homes on the other side of the Thames, straight into the commercial heart of the City of London.

Abdula Whalid stood in silence, hidden from the train's passengers and the prying eyes of the police, behind the bolted doors of the ancient brick-arched garage, nestling sixty feet beneath the rumbling railway tracks. In the deserted cull-de-sack outside, the narrow cobbled street was strewn with decaying, sodden rubbish.

Awaiting re-development after years of neglect, the abandoned estate had fallen into ruin; the surrounding community of decent, hard-working people was long gone. Empty pubs, shops and warehouses displayed faded signs from another era. Deserted now, they had all once thrived, serving London's bustling docks. At this moment in time, echoing with the ghosts of times gone by, they reeked of nothing more than a forgotten epoch, the roaring heyday of the long-past Empire.

The interior of the occupied garage was illuminated by a single fluorescent strip light, which threw long shadows across the cold, gloomy interior and left the back of the garage in virtual darkness. There were other lights suspended from the high arch of the damp brick lined ceiling, but these had long since succumbed to lack of maintenance and stopped working.

A sleeping bag lay semi-hidden; rolled against a wall at the back of the garage. Close to the double doors at the front stood a portable gas burner. Several large cooking pots lay abandoned beside it. There were three finished suicide vests next to a collection of sacks and commercially available chemical containers. Several drums bore in bold red letters, a warning –

'*Caution! - Hydrogen Peroxide – Highly Corrosive.*'

The bomb-maker's equipment was rudimentary, but he wasn't at all concerned. He had used similar apparatus and chemicals, many times before in Pakistan and Afghanistan, to teach others how to create deadly IED's - Improvised Explosive Devices. Car-bombs, mines and suicide vests, it was all the same to the bomb-maker, as long as his chemical mixtures exploded, and slaughtered the sworn enemies of Al-Qaeda and Islam, he was content that he was faithfully serving the Holy Jihad.

The cold atmosphere mixed with a powerful stench of old engine oil, mouldering damp and drains. The last odour was strong and came from the back of the garage. The bomb-maker showed its source; an open manhole leading down to the sewers, which flowed via an outfall into the Thames. The iron cover was long gone, stolen by thieves who occasionally searched the estate looking for illicit scrap metal. The sound of running water came from somewhere below, but whatever its source; it was hidden from view in the obsidian blackness which plugged the hole, and concealed all but the first rungs of a rusting iron access ladder, which disappeared down into the reeking depths. The stench was powerful above the open manhole. It still filled the Tunisian's nose as he walked back and listened intently to the words of the

Pakistani bomb-maker from Peshwar, who had entered the country only a week previously, through Birmingham airport on a scheduled Pakistan Airlines flight from Islamabad.

The bomb-maker was travelling on his twin brother's passport. It was a perfect cover. His sibling was clean in the eyes of the ISI – Pakistan's equivalent to MI5, his holiday visa and passport raised no interest or warning flags when he departed from Islamabad, or when they were inspected by an immigration officer at arrivals within Birmingham airport. One of Zahira Khan's network in Bradford had willingly picked up the bomb-maker outside the terminal; driving him straight to London's East End, where he could begin his work.

The bomb-maker had proudly begun by displaying his labours. Opening the car's boot had revealed ten large plastic containers, filled to the brim with white crystals. Each fat container was linked to its neighbour by electrical wire, which disappeared inside each of them, via a small hole drilled into every container's plastic lid.

There was a third person in the garage, intently listening to the bomb-maker's narrative. A young bearded Asian man stood beside Abdula Whalid. Like the bogus cleric, he listened intently to the bomb-maker's commentary. Satisfied that both men understood his technical genius, the bomb-maker carefully closed the boot lid, and walked to the open driver's door. Leaning inside, he ignored the dog-eared London A-Z lying on the passenger seat, turned his head and said,

'When you approach your target, reach into the glove compartment and take out the electrical switch with the wires attached to it. Everything is linked to the car's battery, and operation is very easy…. When the time is upon you; simply flick the switch. In that moment brother, the bomb will send you speeding to paradise, and I hope, cast many kafirs down to hell.'

As the driver watched and listened, his eyes widened as he nodded his understanding. Like the car-bomb, he was ready. His lips moved silently, muttering the many names of God. As he listened to the bomb-maker, he fingered a string of rosewood prayer beads…

\* \* \* \* \*

In a secure underground briefing room below the Home Office, a mid-morning crisis meeting had been called by the Home Secretary.

The suicide bombing of the Hilton the day before had sent shockwaves through the intelligence community, charged with guarding the United Kingdom against terrorism. There had been no warning, and Sir Henry Teesle, the Home Secretary, wanted to know why. The heads of MI5, MI6, GCHQ and Special Branch shifted uncomfortably in their seats as Sir Henry demanded answers. Staring at each of them in turn over his half lens reading glasses, he exhaled his dissatisfaction loudly through his nose. Through gritted teeth he said with exasperation,

'Well now, gentlemen. Once again, British citizens and foreign nationals under our protection have been slaughtered in the capital by whom; I'm led to believe, were Muslim extremists. The P.M. is absolutely furious because the press are screaming for the government's blood over this affair. As usual, we have been accused of being weak and unprepared by Fleet Street. After seeing the headlines this morning, the P.M. has ordered me to begin an immediate investigation, to find out why we were caught napping again, and why Her Majesty's government, and we as a nation, are being embarrassed shortly before the G8 summit begins. As you all well know, the Prime Minister is hosting it here in London, in just a few days' time,'

The Home Secretary rested clenched fists on the table before him, and demanded,

'Well?'

Sir Alex McLean, head of the UK's overseas espionage service, MI6, elected as a spokesman after several discreet phone calls between the service chiefs prior to the meeting, looked up and broke the uncomfortable moment of silence which followed,

'Sir Henry, as you know, we have faced a sophisticated and growing threat from Al-Qaeda in recent years. Their tactics and methods have evolved almost as fast as we find ways to detect and counter them. In the past, their security was poor. Frankly, it leaked like a sieve, but like us, they have learned,' Sir Alex thought for a moment, choosing his words carefully, and then he continued, 'Because of the fragmented nature of terrorist cells linked to Al-Qaeda, many have been preempted by us due to infiltration, or informers run by our colleagues in MI5.' Sir Alex paused for a moment and nodded towards the head of MI5, who smiled his grateful acknowledgment. 'The majority of attacks planned in the UK, have been initiated by poorly trained, loosely associated fanatics. As a direct result, we have successfully managed to thwart any number of amateurish plots designed to cause mayhem and death in our country.' Sir Alex sighed, and then continued, 'admittedly not all, but the vast majority…. In the past few years, however, the Security Service, MI5 has detected growing professionalism among homegrown jihadists. This has, in no small way, been caused by a large number of young Muslim men born in the UK going overseas, particularly to the Middle East and Pakistan, for advanced terror training. We, as an intelligence community, have constantly warned the government of this new and highly dangerous slide, but as far as we are concerned, Home Secretary, our warnings have, for the most part anyway, fallen on deaf ears and been totally ignored…. There are no leaks involved with the current headlines, of course; Editors running the national newspapers are already aware of the situation. Personally, I think that is the real reason they are baying for government blood.'

The Home Secretary scowled. Damn the man, he thought angrily. He's another one laying a trap for me to take a fall over this in the national headlines.

Despite the MI6 chief's assertions, Sir Henry knew a well-placed leak from an un-named intelligence source, concerning his lack of attention to their collective warnings, or any positive action upon them, would not go well with the press, or the British public. A softly, softly approach had been agreed, months earlier in Cabinet, concerning these young men. Race relations were a constant problem, and the government didn't want to be viewed as racists by minority religious groups, particularly the Asian Muslim community. In an age of high-profile whistleblower, an anonymous email to the Times would be all it would take. Worse still, the Home Secretary suppressed a shudder; the fall-out of an email denouncing him to the Editor of the socialist Guardian or New Statesman could have catastrophic consequences to the future of his political career. The press and opposition would go for his jugular. The P.M. would naturally put the umbrella up, apportion one hundred percent blame to him as Home Secretary, and throw him to the wolves. He'd find himself languishing in the back benches immediately after an emergency Cabinet re-shuffle, and then, if he wasn't extremely careful, de-selection by his constituency office was a distinct possibility, should there be a full-blown scandal. Refusing to rise to the bait, the Home Secretary swallowed hard and growled,

'Go on…'

Not wishing to initiate the mud-slinging, knowing anyway, where the buck for UK security ultimately stopped, Sir Alex nodded politely,

'Thank you, Sir Henry. My people have also noticed that on occasion, recently, when a particularly complex and important operation has been implemented by Al-Qaeda, such as the 7/11 attacks on New York for example, they are willing to move high-ranking operatives in from their training camps, to support a new terrorist attack.'

'You think that happened in this case?' demanded the Home Secretary.

'According to our analysis of the explosive used, the chemical quality suggests it is a distinct possibility. We are of course currently looking into it.'

Unknown to the Home Secretary, or the senior intelligence officers at the meeting, Sir Alex was absolutely right. The bomb-maker's twin, dressed in his sibling's clothes, had been photographed by undercover ISI agents during the last few days, arriving and departing from the front entrance of the Martyr's House in Peshwar, a known meeting place of hard-core jihadi militants.

The Home Secretary frowned; he wasn't convinced at all,

'It seems highly unlikely that Al-Qaeda would risk the arrest of a key operator, for one suicide attack.'

Sir Alex nodded somberly,

'Yes Sir Henry, precisely right. If we are correct, that's what seriously concerns us.'

The Home Secretary's face seemed to turn a little grey, as the penny dropped,

'You mean you expect more attacks before the G8…?'

Before Sir Alex could reply, there was a sudden rapid knock on the conference room door. One of the Private Secretaries stepped into the room. He strode quickly towards the Home Secretary. Leaning forward, he whispered something urgently in Sir Henry's ear.

The Home Secretary complexion turned from grey to white as the Private Secretary hastily withdrew. Sir Henry Teesle fought to keep his voice under control, but it trembled nevertheless as he spoke,

'It seems your fears are well founded, Sir Alex. A massive car-bomb has just exploded outside Waterloo station…!'

# Chapter Sixteen

Pat headed straight back to his flat in Paddington after leaving Chelsea. He felt physically and mentally drained. Somehow, he didn't fancy plying London's streets in search for his next fare.

Throwing off his clothes, he stepped into the shower cubicle built into the corner of his bedroom. Pat hoped the powerful spray of hot water might help wash away the memory of the hotel lobby, and the dreams from last night, that went with it. The pounding water did help to relax him a little; he didn't hear the echoing boom that came from across the Thames. Rinsing off, Pat slid the cubicle door open and reached for a towel.

When he had finished towelling himself dry, he padded into his small kitchenette to brew some tea. Disappointment hung over him like a cloud, because the dreams had receded to almost nothing since leaving the regular SAS. True, he thought to himself, there had been plenty of action since, but something, somehow had banished the nightmares until the Hilton had almost exploded in his face. Still struggling to understand, Pat carried his steaming cup back to the bedroom.

From inside the jumble of clothes scattered on his bed, Pat heard his cell phone chirrup. It was an incoming text. Wondering who it was from, Pat dropped the towel and walked naked over to the bed. Rummaging through his discarded jacket and jeans, he found his cell, and flicked the cover open. His heart beat faster as he read the message. It simply said – '*Six Nation's Cup.*'

Meaningless to outsiders, it meant everything to Pat. It declared an amber warning, sent automatically from his HQ in Chelsea to every member of the Troop. It was a stand-by warning order, placing the entire SAS Shadow Squadron on one hour's notice to mobilise. Something had happened, thought Pat grimly, something very, very bad.

Pat acknowledged the text by sending a curt text – *Roger* - back to Chelsea. Snatching up his clothes, he dashed into the small living room and switched on the TV. Finding Sky's news channel, his tea forgotten, he started dressing as he listened to what the newsreader was saying.

'Reports are coming in of a massive explosion at Waterloo railway station, on the south bank of the River Thames…. Early indications are that there have been a number of casualties, but no figures have yet been released by the police.' The newsreader suddenly reached up to the earpiece in his ear… 'I'm told we are now taking you, live, to Hanna Wade, our reporter at Waterloo station…'

The TV picture changed. The head and shoulders of a young woman holding a microphone, sheltering beneath an umbrella appeared. She was looking down, adjusting her earpiece. Behind her, beyond a line of fluttering police incident tape, was a sea of stationary ambulances, fire engines and police cars, some still with blue lights flashing. Beyond the emergency vehicles, it was a scene from Armageddon, a smoking blur of devastation. The camera panned momentarily to the right and refocused as the cameraman prepared his equipment and set up his shot. Pat winced at what he saw. It was the mirror of so many middle-eastern blast scenes, which seemed to pepper overseas TV news reports daily.

The front of the station was a ruin, a swirling pall of black smoke rising above it. Firemen and ambulance crews were clambering over piles of shattered glass, station facade and fallen masonry. They had already begun their desperate search for survivors in the rubble. Several blooded civilians, shocked and dazed, were being helped away from the ruined station, towards the sanctuary of the waiting ambulances.

The camera panned quickly back to the young Sky correspondent. Clearly shocked at the enormity of what she had seen so far, Hanna Wade began her televised report…

'The situation here at Waterloo Station is one of utter devastation. Just before we came on air, an injured eyewitness told me he saw a car mount the pavement outside the station and drive straight through the plate-glass frontage. Seconds later, there was a blinding flash and a huge explosion inside the building...'

Pat stood watching, mouth open; appalled at what he saw. It was obviously a car-bomb, but it hadn't followed the pattern of the old days during the troubles in Northern Ireland, where car-bombs were parked up by terrorists who then fled the scene. During that campaign, the abandoned car-bomb was usually detonated using a timer, with or without a telephoned warning.

This time, it was all different. The car's driver had stayed in the vehicle, deliberately ramming the station front before setting off the huge bomb his car was carrying.

All this was way beyond coincidence; Pat thought angrily. Cornelius had his proof now; one thing was absolutely certain. This was beyond doubt, the second in a pre-planned wave of suicide bombings, targeting the heavily populated centre of London. Pat felt his stomach tighten. Right now, he'd give his pension to have the bastards in his gun-sights.

Pat's cell phone rang. He tore his eyes from the TV screen, and answered it. It was Spike, his voice sounded distinctly worried,

'Hi Pat, have you seen the news?'

Pat grinned to himself, relieved to hear a friendly voice, after the bloody carnage he had witnessed on the television screen,

'Yeah, Spike, I'm watching it on the TV now.... It looks pretty bloody awful.'

Spike replied, 'I'm watching it too... I got the text from Chelsea, but is there anything I can do right now?'

Pat ground his teeth with frustration. They had their military orders to stand-by; that was all they could do,

'Like it says on the tin, Spike... we stand still matey, and wait for orders...'

\* \* \* \* \*

Pat and millions of shocked United Kingdom citizens weren't the only ones watching the unfolding newscast. Sky beamed a constant news flow, syndicated via its own ring of satellites to other TV news channels around the globe.

In the remote Balochistan district of Pakistan, the Al Jazeera broadcaster was voicing over the scenes of devastation, transmitted live from the TV studios in London.

One man watched the unfolding scenes with particular interest. Zahira Khan stroked his beard and smiled to himself, as his eyes drank in the chaos. Very soon, he thought, it would be time to implement the next phase of his plan.

\* \* \* \* \*

As the sun began to set, Zahira Khan finished his prayers, and stood up. Rolling up his prayer mat, he placed it in the corner of the room.

The head of Al-Qaeda in Pakistan reached beneath his robe for his notebook and cell phone. Opening the notebook, he found the page he was looking for. The phone's display lit up as he began dialling the long number taken from the page in front of him. Khan waited as the international connection was made. There was a final click, and then on the crackling line, he heard the electronic, pre-recorded voice of the distant operator.

'You have reached the Metropolitan Police at New Scotland Yard. If you know the department you require, please say it clearly and slowly after the tone.'

The smile returned to Zahira Khan's face, as he licked his lips. The fools; it was all working perfectly, despite the hollow chirrups and whistles he could hear; Khan ignored them, his connection was made. After the beep, the Al-Qaeda man's eyes narrowed as he said slowly and clearly,

'Ah yes… I wish to talk to your secret policemen…you call them *Special Branch*.'

# Chapter Seventeen

The Home Secretary was ecstatic with the news. When he received the telephone call from Scotland Yard, informing him of a breakthrough concerning the suicide bombings, he had trouble disguising his relief from Commander Harry Roebottom, the tough, straight-talking Yorkshire policeman, who headed Britain's Special Branch.

'Yes Sir Henry, that's right, you heard me correctly. We have just received an anonymous tip-off concerning the whereabouts of the terrorist cell responsible for the bombings at the Hilton and Waterloo.'

With London holding its breath as it waited fearfully for the next attack, and the rising clamour in the press because of apparent inaction by the Home Office, Sir Henry knew his political career, in that moment when Roebottom repeated his news, was saved. If what the head of Special Branch had said was true, and Sir Henry wanted to believe it with all his heart, then further attacks would be stopped, and the culprits detained. If he took decisive action now, he would emerge as the champion of the hour. He'd be feted by history as the saviour of London. Sir Henry glanced at his watch. It had been only five hours since the blast at Waterloo. If what his security chiefs had told him earlier was correct, the next blast wouldn't be until sometime tomorrow. They had suggested the attacks might be a deliberate campaign of terror, to embarrass the government before the G8 summit. How could Britain expect to sit at the world's top table, if it couldn't secure its borders, or protect its own citizens? When or how exactly, the next attack would come, the security people couldn't predict. If they were right though about one blast every twenty-four hours, which gave him precious time to plan a proper response, before there was another outrage. Recovering his composure, he replied,

'I will inform the Prime Minister immediately, Commander.' Sir Henry thought for a moment and then added, 'I will require you in my office in one-hour… I am calling another meeting of the heads of all the security organisations, the police and…. um, yes…. as there have already been multiple fatalities, I want the military to sit in as well.'

* * * * *

An hour later, Commander Harry Roebottom had the floor,

'Gentlemen, at 18.33 this evening, a call was made to our offices at New Scotland Yard, with information concerning the recent wave of suicide bombings. The caller refused to give his name, but he gave us the location of the bomb factory where the devices are being made and stored.'

There were smiles and murmurs of relief from the gathered intelligence chiefs. The commander let their murmuring fade, and then continued,

'The caller only gave us a general area; that of the derelict warehouse district just south of the old East India docks on the Isle of Dogs. Overall, geographically, it's a big, U-shaped area, surrounded on three sides by the winding River Thames. At this time, the Isle of Dogs is pretty much abandoned, awaiting demolition and re-development.' The commander ran his hand over his chin, and then thoughtfully, he continued, 'Given the sensitive nature of this operation; I didn't want to over-react and instigate a full-blown ground search. It certainly would have alerted the terrorists if we flooded the area with uniformed officers, so instead, to avoid compromising the operation, I ordered up one of our police helicopters, call-sign India 99, to make a covert sweep at high altitude over the warehouse district, to see if they could find anything.'

Unable to contain himself, sitting on the edge of his seat, Sir Henry lent even further forward and spluttered,

'*Well?*'

Commander Roebottom suppressed a frown at the interruption. He could only imagine the pressure the Home Secretary must be under,

'India 99's first visual flyover, using binoculars revealed absolutely nothing. No sign of movement, and no sign of life anywhere…. There are no street lights in use down there anymore, and as it was already dark, the pilot ordered his observer to switch to infra-red, and they made a second sweep.'

Sir Henry interrupted again,

'Infra-red?'

The Special Branch chief was tempted to snap back, but he *was* talking to the Home Secretary; he reminded himself. Roebottom suppressed the urge to tell this bloody rude politician to shut up. Instead, he simply continued with his explanation,

'Yes Sir Henry. Police helicopters are fitted with passive infrared heat detectors. They can cover huge areas quickly, and often use the device in the dark to find missing persons and escaping criminals. The IR sensors are incredibly sensitive; the observer aboard India 99 sees both heat source and its pin-sharp shape on his screen aboard the helicopter. As a matter of fact, we've enjoyed considerable success using them in the last few years, to find houses in and around London which have been converted into illegal cannabis factories. The lights the criminals use to speed up plant growth, you see, give off enormous heat, which lights up the roof in infra-red. The chopper can see them from miles away,' the commander spread his hands, 'it's brilliant really, Home Secretary. In IR mode, our officers can see anything which is warmer than the surrounding area, even on the darkest nights.'

Sir Henry breathed out deeply,

'I see. Thank you Commander, please go on…'

Commander Roebottom nodded and continued,

'India 99's infra-red camera made a thorough search, from a height where the helicopter's rotor blades and main engine would be almost impossible to detect from the ground. The observer had nearly finished his sweep, when he reported one small hit on the detector. Now, bearing in mind that all the buildings should be empty and abandoned, there should not have been anything there to register a heat source… but there was. The operator found a distinct heat bloom coming from a spot underneath the Docklands Light railway. He couldn't be sure what was causing the heat, it was inside one of those old archway commercial units, but he was sure, because of its size and location, that it was man-made, and definitely coming from inside the building....'

Sir Henry leapt to his feet,

'Excellent Commander, we have them then! Now all we need is to formulate a plan to arrest them.'

Sir Alex, head of MI6 interrupted,

'Just a moment, Home Secretary, if I may?'

Irritated at the apparent attempt to rain on his parade, Sir Henry snapped back,

'Yes?'

'If the Commander is correct, and it's not a tramp sleeping rough, and we have indeed found them, may I remind everyone that we are dealing with a very dangerous suicide cell, whose members are sworn to, and are fully prepared to die for their cause. It occurs to me that arresting them like normal criminals might not be too easy. Perhaps...' Sir Alex glanced to his right, 'we could ask Brigadier Hunter for his military opinion?'

Deflated, Sir Henry sat down. Damn the man, he has a point, he thought angrily. He nodded towards the newly promoted SAS Director,

'Yes, yes, very well then. Perhaps you can enlighten us, Brigadier?'

Brigadier Hunter cleared his throat; he'd been warned about dealing with stressed politicians, by his predecessor. With a glint in his eye, outgoing Brigadier Lethbridge had told him over a private lunch at his club, to give them only the cold, hard facts. He had added with a grin that it was their political master's problem, exactly what to do about them.

'Well, Sir, it is my experience that if they are armed, or wearing a suicide vest, there isn't time to arrest them. If the vest is live, which we must assume it is, in these circumstances my men are trained to fire through the terrorist's brainstem, which will kill them instantly, and stop the wearer triggering his vest and causing an explosion. The trouble is that in the moment of breaking into this building, we must assume, to avoid missing anyone, that every terrorist is potentially wired up and ready to blow himself, and my men, to kingdom come.'

The Home Secretary spluttered incredulously,

'You mean, if I hand over this operation to the SAS, you recommend killing all of them?'

Unblinking, Brigadier Hunter's steely blue eyes narrowed as they returned Sir Henry's troubled stare,

'Yes, Home Secretary; that is exactly what I am saying. My initial assessment, given the circumstances and to avoid un-necessary deaths, is that we should assume arrest is impossible. We must kill them all in one fast, surgical strike.'

There was silence around the table. Apart from the Home Secretary, none of the others were directly constrained by his political shackles. Like a drowning man, Sir Henry looked from one chief to the next, hoping for a straw of salvation. His political future still hung in the balance, and his only option, knowing full-well how the ruthless SAS operated, was to agree to the Brigadier's assessment. By doing so, he'd effectively sign each of the terrorist's death warrants. There was a hint of pleading in the Home Secretary's voice,

'Surely there is another way…some other option, gentlemen? We have trained negotiators who can deal with these sort of situations, don't we?'

The silence continued; it was embarrassing and painful. Negotiators had their uses, but this wasn't a hostage crisis, not even close. Events had propelled them way past contacting the ruthless bombers to discuss the finer points of a peaceful resolution. Every man in the room, including Sir Henry, knew the cold hard truth contained within the Brigadier's chilling appraisal.

Sir Henry nodded at last. Reluctantly, he accepted the hard facts. They had only one opportunity on the table to halt the campaign of merciless bombing. By agreeing to the Brigadier's strategy, his position as Home Secretary was secured. He would have to deal with the political fall-out from the PC brigade in both Parliament and the Economic Union. God alone knew what the Strasbourg Court of Human Rights would make of it? There would be a howling outcry from the left-wing press afterwards. The New Statesman would, no doubt, claim a shoot-to-kill policy, but at least this way he hoped his decisive actions would be protected by the support of the P.M, the government and his own party. Clearing his throat, the Home Secretary came to a decision and said,

'Very well, gentlemen, we all know what must be done.' Sir Henry looked reluctantly towards the SAS Director, 'In principle, at least; I accept your advice Brigadier Hunter, but I must explain it to a specially convened sitting of the emergency COBRA committee before I can give you the final go-ahead. I am due to brief the committee in,' he glanced down at his watch, 'thirty minutes. Given the lack of viable alternatives, I expect their agreement but do not, under any circumstances, take arbitrary action until you hear directly from me…. Is that clear?'

The Brigadier nodded.

'In the meantime, please be aware that time is now of the essence. Your men must move fast, as soon as I get approval to hand over control of this situation to the military.'

Pushing his chair backwards, Brigadier Hunter stood up. Staring towards Sir Henry, he said coldly,

'With your permission, Home Secretary, I'll leave immediately. I have to get over to Chelsea quickly; plan the operation, and brief my men.'

Sir Henry held up his hand,

'Remember, I must have a final agreement from the COBRA committee,' he glanced at his watch, 'you will have their decision as soon as it is made, do you understand?'

Brigadier Hunter nodded again. He had answered Sir Henry's questions according to his predecessor's advice, but the meeting confirmed one fact he would carry with him throughout his tenure as SAS Director. It was now a solid fact that he didn't like squirming, mealy-mouthed politicians,

'Yes,' Brigadier Hunter said through clenched teeth, 'that's all perfectly clear, thank you, Home Secretary.'

# Chapter Eighteen

Pat was still awake and fully dressed when the next text came. Like his men, he had been tensely standing by, ready for the call. The new message raised Shadow Squadron to the highest level of mobilisation. It was brief; it simply read - *'Grand Slam.'*

Heart pounding at the go signal, he dropped everything and ran. Taking the internal stairs from his top-floor flat three at a time, he dashed down the narrow corridor and threw open the communal front door. Pat slammed it behind him and sprinted to his waiting cab, parked thankfully this time, just around the corner. Firing up the diesel engine with a roar in a cloud of black exhaust smoke, he slammed it into gear and sped towards Chelsea with his pulse still pounding in his ears.

There was no point advertising the cab's modifications to his neighbours. Pat waited until he'd swung onto the Harrow Road before hitting the lights and two-tones. He had wanted to try them out before, but had resisted the temptation. His orders were clear. The lights and horns were to be used only on receipt of a 'Grand Slam' 'go' order. The call to arms must be something to do with the bombings; Pat thought. He and his boys were obviously needed in a hurry.

The evening traffic seemed to melt away as he dropped off the Harrow road and cut down through Paddington's narrow side-streets towards Hyde Park. The distinctive rise and fall of emergency sirens were commonplace in central London, and the new horns and lights were working beautifully. Pat dropped a gear, and gunned the engine again. The cab surged forward as he jumped the lights and flew across the Bayswater Road into the Royal Park. Missing Marble Arch and Hyde Park Corner, it was a good shortcut under normal circumstances, but with sirens blaring and blue lights flashing, Pat almost felt as if he was driving laps around Silverstone's formula-one race track.

Keeping his eyes glued to the road ahead as he crossed the Serpentine Bridge, Pat found a moment to wonder about the mission again. Only one scenario came to mind; it had to be something to do with the suicide bombers. An image of the injured girl from the wreck of the Hilton lobby flashed into his thoughts. He'd phoned St Mary's hospital twice that day to ask after her, but both times, annoyingly, the intensive care ward only confirmed she was still alive, and remained on the critical list. Pat couldn't do any more for the girl; she was in good hands now, but given the chance; he thought savagely, he'd make those responsible pay for what they had done to her, and all the other innocent victims.

Pat slowed as he approached the Knightsbridge box junction lights. A policeman had heard him coming, and already stopped the traffic. Pat didn't see the quizzical look on the officer's face as his cab roared past the young officer. Hidden from view by Hyde Park barracks, the surprised policeman calmly expected a police car or ambulance would appear; not, in his wildest dreams, a speeding black London cab flashing blue lights, with sirens wailing.

Angled off down Brompton Road, the sparkling lights of the distant Harrods store were a fleeting blur; Pat's tyres screeched as he negotiated the Knightsbridge chicane into the top of Sloane Street. He shot past bemused open-mouthed pedestrians waiting for their chance to cross the busy road. An arm flew up; someone tried to hail him, but Pat ignored the would-be fare.

*Not this time mate*, he frowned, *I'm busy!*

Other vehicles pulled into the curb, eager to get out of the way of the echoing sirens. Just as well, Pat thought, because few would stand much chance in a high-speed collision with his speeding two-ton FX4 taxi.

In less than two minutes, Pat thought with a grin, he'd be at his SAS HQ within the Duke of York's barracks, finding out what was happening. His grin lingered. Pity, he thought as he screeched around Sloane Square past the Edwardian facade of the Royal Court Theatre; he could do with the lights and sirens when some punter hailed his cab and declared they were dreadfully late for a flight leaving Heathrow.

Standing inside, against the pitted wooden door, Abdula Whalid shivered within the abandoned garage. Reaching up to the cracked windowpane, he pulled down the cardboard which he had pinned there to shield the light and wiped away decades of grime and a damp layer of fresh condensation from the fractured glass. He searched the horizon of deserted buildings, looking for the first rays of light which would herald the coming dawn. Like broken teeth in the distance, he detected the slightest hint of a lighter sky, above the crooked outline of the distant buildings.

Abdula Whalid smiled mirthlessly. It was almost time to launch the most devastating attack yet on London. So far, they had attacked only the centre of London, but now it was time, like fishermen of the seas, to cast their net further. Pre-dawn prayers were finished, and the three remaining members of the suicide cell were huddled around the flaring gas burner which had been their only source of heat throughout the long, cold night. The bomb-maker was missing. He was at the back of the unit, rolled up in his sleeping bag snoring softly. It was him who had demanded the heater be left on. His body had not yet acclimatised to the chill night air of autumnal London, and he had become highly agitated when Abdula Whalid had ordered it switched off. How, he demanded angrily, could he fit and make final adjustments to the delicate suicide vests before they left, shaking with cold and using numb fingers that he couldn't feel?

Abdula Whalid reluctantly agreed. What harm could it do, he asked himself, to keep warm while they waited for the dawn? He needed the bomb-maker rested. One slip when he awoke and armed the vests, could have devastating results on the last phase of the operation.

His face impassive, Whalid replaced the cardboard covering the window and shuffled back towards the heat of the fire. It was almost time to wake the bomb-maker. Soon, he would order his disciples to put on their vests and outer coats. When the bomb-maker was satisfied that all was safely fitted and armed, Abdula Whalid would issue his men with the grenades the bomb-maker had also manufactured. The bogus cleric looked into the faces of the chosen ones. He detected no fear, but only eagerness in their expressions when he had briefed them just before pre-dawn prayers. As devout soldiers of Islam, they hungered and thirsted for martyrdom because he had spent months convincing them that was their pre-ordained path. Their part in the plot would send them straight to paradise, and all the rich rewards, which awaited them there.

Whalid's plan for the morning was as simple as it was deadly. They would leave the bomb-maker behind. Having washed thoroughly to remove any lingering traces of explosives from his body, he would dress in clean clothes, abandon the archway and then take the long walk to Canary Wharf underground station, where he would disappear into the crowded cosmopolitan throng of morning commuters, before making his tube connections to Heathrow airport, and an evening flight back to Islamabad, in Pakistan.

The others would be collected by one of Khan's trusted Bradford men, and driven north towards the bottom of the M1 motorway at Staple's Corner, where it touched the Edgware Road and North Circular ring road. Their target, Brent Cross shopping centre, was close by. His disciples of Jihad would be dropped off one by one, in the centre's vast underground car-park. From there, the three young men, wearing their concealed explosive vests and their pockets filled with deadly nail bombs, would make their separate way to different shopping levels within the complex. It was up to them to pick which shops, they simultaneously lit and threw their grenades into, when the time to launch the attack came. The civilian security personnel were unarmed, and should not pose a serious threat. Abdula Whalid had asked for guns, but these, he had been told, were unavailable.

As with the deadly mayhem in Nairobi's Westgate shopping Mall, he knew the terrified customers would run like rabbits. There were many Jews living around Brent Cross in the affluent suburbs of Golders Green and Hendon. Trapped and terrified, their deaths would be a bonus; Abdula Whalid thought slyly to himself, if they were unlucky enough to have picked today to go shopping with family or friends.

The chaos of each explosion would provide his martyrs with the smoke and mayhem needed to make their way from one crowded shop to the next. Under no circumstances, he had told them, were any of them to be taken alive. With their last bomb thrown, they were ordered to make their way to the nearest stairwell, which was bound to be crowded with panicked fleeing shoppers. That would be their penultimate act; they were commanded to run into the mass of hysterical, screaming men, women and children. Only then, in the black heart of chaos and terror, were they to press the switch and detonate their deadly suicide vests.

\* \* \* \* \*

Moments earlier, concealed in the darkness beneath a rusting sheet of corrugated iron, which lay abandoned on a patch of wasteland nearby, one of Pat's SAS troopers slowly moved his blackened hand to his throat mike. His face was similarly blackened; it blended perfectly within the dark shadows under the old iron sheet. Speaking softly, he whispered,

'Zero Alpha, this is Oscar Two; I've got light and movement in the target door. One Tango confirmed, over.'

In his earphone, above the background hiss of static, the trooper received a curt,

'Zero Alpha - Roger that, out.'

The rest of the Special Forces troop heard the message through their own individual earphones. The three Oscar call-signs were close-in observers, who had inched their way silently into concealed positions, from where they could watch the target. Using shadow and whatever other cover they encountered, the crawling troopers had taken their time, moving invisibly in the darkness, to get within an unobstructed visual range of the building.

The SAS radio net crackled again,

'Zero Alpha, this is Sierra One, I confirm the sighting, over.'

Call-sign Sierra One was Frankie Lane, one of Pat's two highly trained snipers. He lowered his blackened hand as he moved it cautiously away from his own throat mike. The crack-shot sniper had a commanding view of the target frontage but was standing well back from the second-floor window, inside an adjacent warehouse several hundred feet away. Pat's other sniper was in a similar building, concealed somewhere to Frankie's left. Between them, with the ground-level observers, they formed an inner cordon, establishing a deadly crossfire on the front of the terrorist's base, should a breakout occur.

Like an invisibility cloak, Frankie's body was enveloped by the inky-black interior on the musty storeroom where he stood. He couldn't be seen at all from outside, but the sniper could see perfectly the row of shabby archways opposite, the peeling doors of the garage and the railway signals set to red above them. Scheduled commuter trains were held safely further down both ends of the line. Loudspeakers on the trains and platforms declared a temporary signalling fault, and of course, made the usual apology to waiting passengers.

Frankie licked his lips as he bent down slowly, and retrieved his high-powered sniper rifle from the wooden floor. His orders were not to fire at fleeting targets before the attack went in. At this stage, his job, like the others, was to observe, and only provide fire support for the exposed watchers scattered below him, if things turned ugly, and their cover was blown.

Hidden from view, other heavily-armed Shadow Squadron troopers also moved stealthily into concealed positions of ambush. Now hidden and ready, they provided a ring of steel around the archway hideout. If the Tangos realised they were surrounded, and made an attempt to escape, it was the outer cordon's job to stop them slipping by. The troopers had accepted their stark orders grimly, without hesitation or reservation. Each of them saw the potential danger. Even one terrorist wearing a suicide vest escaping past their screen into the unsuspecting London rush-hour, was unthinkable.

Once final confirmation had come from the COBRA committee, giving the SAS the green light, the Brigadier's orders had been explicit and precise. Not a single terrorist was to be allowed to escape alive. If they did make a break for it, they were to be given no quarter and shot on sight. The Brigadier's logic made sense. If an SAS bullet struck a suicide vest, triggering its premature detonation; wearer aside, casualties would be kept to an absolute minimum in the deserted Isle of Dog's wasteland. Better there, he had emphasised earnestly, than an explosion on a busy thoroughfare, filled with passing traffic and unsuspecting civilian pedestrians.

Two streets away, Pat stared intently at the luminous dial of his watch. The second hand swept inexorably around the dial. Moments now, before he gave the order to move to their final assault position. Adrenaline made his heart beat faster. He turned his head towards the assault team huddled behind him, and whispered softly through his S10 respirator,

*'Twenty seconds…Stand-by…'*

Pat could feel his heart pumping under the black flameproof boiler suit, and his dragon-skin body armour. He hissed,

*'Ten seconds…'*

Behind him, Spike, Danny and the new boy, Jim Conrad tightened their grip on their weapons. Each man felt the same powerful kick of adrenaline surging into their bloodstreams. It was time. Ignoring his own elevated heartbeat, Pat raised his hand and gestured them forward;

*'Right lads… let's go.'*

# Chapter Nineteen

Hugging the lattice of opaque shadows, Pat motioned his small assault team forward.

It was agreed during the planning stage that using flash-bangs inside the garage was a very bad idea. The terrorist's home-made explosives were deemed too sensitive to throw in the usual disorientating concussion grenades before entry. If one landed close by, a premature detonation of stockpiled high-explosives might bring down the entire archway. Explosive entry; cutting a hole with a shaped frame charge through the rear or side walls was vetoed for the same reason. CS gas could be tossed in first, but nothing else.

Surrounded by the derelict shells of ancient two and three storey buildings, hugging the nearest wall, Pat led the way cautiously through the darkness along the empty pavement. The only sound the team could hear was their own rhythmic breathing and the faint hum of distant early-morning traffic, blissfully unaware of the drama unfolding on the Isle of Dogs; as vehicles moved through traffic jams into the City of London, almost half a mile away. Like the others, Pat was taking his time; he was 'ghost walking'.

It was a technique the British army had borrowed from their Chinese enemies during the Korean War. The modern SAS Regiment had no problem using a good lesson learnt long ago. With every slow and calculated step, each man placed his weight first on his out-step, and then slowly rolled the rubber sole of his boot flat onto the ground beneath it. If there was something under the boot which might make a sound when stepped on, using the slow and deliberate ghost technique, it was easily detected and avoided. It made progress painfully slow, but uncannily silent.

After several time-consuming, agonising minutes, Pat reached the first corner, held up his clenched fist, and stopped the team who were moving silently behind him. The three troopers automatically shrank back into the deeper shadows, hard against the wall beside them. Crouching in the darkness, each man silently swept their arcs with their weapons, as they were trained to do.

With a faded sign - 'The Jolly Sailor' - hanging above him, Pat slowly peered around the decaying wall of an old corner pub, but saw no movement ahead. Through the black hood which shrouded his respirator, his ears strained for the slightest sound which might alert him to something amiss, but nothing moved, nothing registered. Satisfied, he silently waved his men forward, leading them further into the darkness.

The next corner brought Pat and his men to the edge of the cull-de-sac where the terrorists were hidden. Pat heard Frankie Lane's voice whisper through his earpiece,

'Zero Charlie, this is Sierra One. I have you on visual. No more tango movement seen since my last....'

The assault team was too close now for a spoken reply. Pat gently pressed the send switch twice on his throat mike, passing on an audible double-click to acknowledge Frankie's update.

Pat turned and patted his MP5 sub-machine gun softly. It was the signal Danny and Jim Conrad had been waiting for. Slowly, silently, they both slid past Pat and Spike in single file, and headed towards their final assault positions outside the old garage doors.

Moving like ghosts, Pat and Spike gently thumbed their safety catches to the off position, and followed on, close behind.

\* \* \* \* \*

To warm them against the chill, Abdula Whalid rubbed his hands briskly together. He cocked his wrist and peered down at his watch. It was almost six. He reluctantly rose and moved away from the reassuring warmth of the burner, heading towards the back of the unit. It was time to wake the bomb-maker and begin final preparations, before the car arrived to take the martyrs north, towards the unsuspecting shopping complex. He stretched away his tiredness as he stood over the sleeping man. His leader would be pleased. It was going to be another very, very good day…

With a deafening bang, hammered by Danny and Jim's solid-shot twelve-bore projectiles, the archways outer door hinges suddenly imploded. The creaking door fell inwards in a swirl of gun smoke, hitting the garage's concrete floor with a crash, as two smoking canisters flew over them. Following immediately behind them, two phantom shapes jumped over the fallen doors. A shout came from one of the shapes, and they both opened fire with sub-machine guns.

Silhouetted by the burner's flame, startled and half raised; the three would-be suicide bombers face's momentarily registered shock and confusion. They abruptly flailed their arms wildly as the SAS bullets struck each of them in the neck. Unable to utter a sound, they dropped lifeless to the cold floor, like discarded rag-dolls.

In the gloom at the back of the garage, the deafening noise awoke the bomb-maker. In his waking confusion, he rubbed his eyes and said,

'What is…?'

Abdula Whalid had no time to explain; frantically, he screamed,

'*Save yourself, brother… The drain! Get into the drain!*'

As the last syllable escaped Abdula Whalid's lips, without warning, the dark phantoms turned towards him and fired again. Twin streams of 9mm bullets hit the bogus cleric between jaw and temple, killing him instantly. His spinning body flew over the panicked bomb-maker. Splattered with Whalid's blood and brains, the bomb-maker frantically scrabbled across the cold concrete floor towards the maw of the stinking drain. A split-second later, retching at the stench, he grasped the slippery iron ladder and heaved himself down into the sinister blackness of the ancient sewer.

Pat saw the movement, and emptied the rest of his magazine towards it. A fresh stream of bullets sparked and ricocheted around the drain's gaping mouth, but Pat knew it was too late.

'*Shit! One's got away,*' he cursed angrily, as Danny and Jim clambered over the blasted door, joining him and Spike inside.

The gunfire and echoes stopped. The four SAS men were enveloped only with eerie silence. Swirling gas and trails of gun smoke curled lazily from the ends of the two hot MP5 muzzles. Pat's mind raced when he spied the explosive vests and nail bombs.

'Danny, you and Jim check the bodies; make sure they're all dead. Then call it in on the radio,'

Danny nodded. He already knew what to do, should there be the faintest sign of life. With a sharp double click; Danny rapidly pumped the shotgun's reloading mechanism back and forth, chambering another solid twelve-gauge cartridge into its smoking breach,

'I'll take care of it, Pat.'

'Good! …. And don't touch anything. Let the bomb-disposal boys' deal with the vests.' Pat pointed first at the bloody mess of the three would-be suicide bombers lying spread-eagled on the floor, 'You've got three there,' Pat jerked his thumb over his shoulder, 'and there's one dead up at the back,' he turned sharply towards Spike, 'I'm pretty sure I saw another one.'

Spike nodded,

'Yeah, that's what I saw too. There was definitely a shape moving beside the one we shot, and then it just sort of, vanished?'

Pat pulled his reloaded MP5 back into his shoulder. He swung the barrel towards the gloom of the rear. He growled impatiently,

'Come on Spike, we've got to find the bastard and nail him, before he gets loose into the bloody rush-hour. *Lights on!*'

Spike nodded, drew his MP5 firmly back into his shoulder, and switched on the mini Maglite torch clipped beneath the barrel of his sub-machine gun. He swept the area ahead with its bright narrow beam, as he followed Pat into the garage's gloomy interior.

Pat cautiously approached the back wall. He swung his own MP5's barrel light towards the dead man lying against it. The thin white beam starkly illuminated the corpse. The man's head and face were pulped. Pat's second glance revealed the top of the Tango's skull was missing. Dismissing the dark puddle of blood splayed around it, Pat swung the gun torch back and forth, searching the piles of rubbish stacked against the back wall of the garage for the slightest trace of the missing fugitive; Spike did the same. Drawing a blank on his half of the search area, it was Spike who spotted the circular mouth of the open sewer duct. For once, their protective equipment worked against them. Their masks had filtered out the pungent smell of raw sewage. From inside his respirator, Spike yelled,

'Here Pat, I've found something!'

Having already finished his sweep, with a few quick paces, Pat stood beside Spike. Both men pointed their gun torches down into the depths of the vertical shaft. Pat hissed,

'That's it, Spike. That's where the bastards gone, that's an access point into an old sewer.' Pat stared at Spike for a moment, and then reluctantly shook his head, 'We'll have to go down there Spike; sorry mate, we've got no other choice.'

* * * *

Enveloped by the shaft's inky darkness, Spike breathed heavily into his respirator as he followed Pat down the confining, claustrophobic shaft. As his boot found the next rung, Spike gripped tightly at each of the ladder's ancient iron rungs in turn; each one felt covered with something slimy and decidedly unpleasant. Spike tried hard not to think about what the slippery coating might be, and suddenly appreciated a whole lot more, the black rubber gloves, fire-proof boiler suit and military grade S-10 respirator he was wearing.

Spike felt a surge of relief when his boots touched solid ground at the bottom of the ladder. Thankfully, he wiped his gloved hands on his boiler suit, disentangled his sling, and swung his MP5 away from his chest into the ready position.

Using the light attached to his weapon's barrel, Spike quickly took stock of his immediate surroundings. He found himself standing close beside his sergeant in a black tunnel, which, thankfully, was just tall enough to stand up in. His first impression was that the tunnel was at least as ancient as the corroded ladder. Spike swept his beam up in an arc across the dripping roof then back towards the ground. He was standing on a narrow walkway,lined with chipped, decaying brickwork. It disappeared off into the gloom in both directions, tight against one side of the tunnel's curved wall. Beside the brick pathway where they both stood, ran a deep, wide and slime-lined channel, filled with a rushing cauldron of dark and evil-looking water. Its turgid surface was littered with pieces of familiar bobbing debris. The old Victorian sewer flowed quickly past the two SAS men with a muffled roar, rushing downstream, ever deeper into the inky depths of the tunnel.

*'Christ!* Is that what I think it is?' Spike asked, his stomach churning as he stared at the contents of the fast-flowing stream, rushing just inches from his boot.

Pat allowed himself a grin at his trooper's discomfort,

'Yes, Spike…. That's exactly what you think it is… so mind where you put your feet.'

Pat quickly pulled their conversation back to reality,

'You go upstream, and I'll go down. Don't take any chances, Spike. If you see him, no warnings, just kill the bastard, OK?'

Spike nodded in silence, turned, and sweeping his light back and forth, began heading upstream in search of the missing terrorist.

# Chapter Twenty

As Pat and Spike began their lonely search inside the dripping confines of the ancient sewer, Cornelius was sitting comfortably at his desk on the other side of central London, at MI6 headquarters in Vauxhall.

The analyst absently rubbed his hand slowly over the stubble on his chin, as he continued his far-away stare at the sun's first rays creeping over the east London skyline. He hadn't been allowed into the danger zone on the Isle of Dogs, when the SAS received the baton from the COBRA committee to assume responsibility for raiding and eliminating the terrorist bomb factory. Instead, with something weighing heavily on his mind, he drove through the deserted streets to Vauxhall. He needed somewhere quiet, to sit alone, and think...

There was so little to go on, but years of experience untangling complex plots against the Realm had set that same, nagging irritation tickling in the back of his mind. His intuition had never let him down in the past; now it warned him of something, which was at best, a new potential problem. Saying things out loud sometimes helped to clarify the picture. Occasionally, when he was stuck, he found it smoothed the path to run an idea by a colleague, but Cornelius hadn't reached that point yet. He lent down and opened a desk drawer, extracting a small, handheld recording device. Checking the battery light was green; Cornelius switched it to record, and began to speak into the silence of his empty office,

'You know, there's something distinctly odd going on here. I know it's a jolly good result to get rid of these bombers…, but I don't know exactly what it is yet, but somehow, I've got the distinct feeling we're being led down the garden path.'

He switched off the machine and thought for a moment, then flicked the device back on,

'That's the trouble, though; I've nothing concrete to go on. It's just the vaguest feeling nagging at me. I've dropped the ball and overlooked something. Cornelius stretched and stared up at the ceiling. 'Let's see.... Brigadier Lethbridge has vanished without trace, and suddenly, days later, in the opening stages of a vicious bombing campaign; completely out of the blue we get an anonymous tip-off, from Pakistan, of all places, which leads us straight to the bomb factory?' Still frowning, Cornelius shook his head, 'No, in my experience there's something not quite right here... In my book, this has all been, somehow, just a bit too easy....'

With a click, Cornelius sighed and switched off the recorder. Was there a link between the Brigadiers kidnap, and the current bombing campaign? He shook his head with frustration. If he was right, there was always a key in these situations. Some common element which glued all the pieces together? Right now, though, sitting in the comfort of his quiet second-floor office within the MI6 headquarters building, he was damned if he could find it.

Cornelius rubbed his tired, bloodshot eyes and yawned. He hadn't slept a wink for the last thirty-six hours; he needed to go home to bed. He knew there was more to be done, so before he left the building and headed wearily for his flat in Bayswater, he sent an email to his assistant, to gather every file they had, on both the Brigadier's kidnap, and the recent bombings. He also requested Julie to collate a list of anything interesting and unsolved that Interpol was working on when she arrived later, and anything, which might be of interest that had come over the pond recently from the CIA.

There would be a lot of information to sift through, but Cornelius had a profound feeling, once he had got some desperately needed sleep, that Julie's efforts would be well worth her trouble.

* * * *

Safety-catch off, MP5 locked firmly in his shoulder, Pat slowly inched his way silently along the dripping pathway. Sense's alert and finger curled around his trigger; he'd moved downstream as quickly as he dared towards the tunnel's far end. It felt like he'd been in the darkness of the claustrophobic sewer for hours, but when he tore his eyes from the gloom ahead and glanced down at his watch, the luminous dial told him only fifteen minutes had passed since he had split from Spike. To estimate distance, Pat was counting his steps, but so far, had reached a count of only three hundred and fifty. The map Pat had studied before the assault, of the area surrounding the garage, showed at its closest point it was about five hundred metres from the nearest bank of the River Thames. The small button compass he carried had indicated he was still heading almost directly south, which meant, give or take; he had ten minutes and somewhere less than two-hundred metres of tunnel left to search, before he reached the sewer's outfall.

Pat reached a junction. Several pipes poked out of the opposite wall, each of them flowing into the main sewage channel beside him. Pat swept his Maglite into the broadest of them, but apart from a trickle of brown water, and a fat rat, which scurried away from the light with a squeak, it was completely empty.

As Pat ducked his head under a rusty support girder, suddenly, he heard something ahead and tensed. His heart beat faster as the noise of his breathing increased inside the respirator. He couldn't identify it, but it was definitely an unusual sound coming from further down the tunnel. He kept low, and inched his way forward. Pat cursed; he still couldn't identify the sound or separate it clearly from the gurgling roar of the sewage flowing past him. It sounded something like a cat mewing, but as he got closer, and his light cut further into the darkness, he saw something lying on the pathway ahead. Pat advanced with his gun sight zeroed in on the centre mass of whatever was lying in front of him. Suddenly, the shape moved. A hand and frightened face appeared. The man pleaded in a heavy Asian accent,

'*No, please. No shoot!...* I do nothing wrong. I fell; my leg break.'

Keeping the muzzle of his weapon trained on the man, Pat moved closer then stopped just short of his quarry. Eyes glittering, he snarled,

'Both hands where I can see them… *NOW!*'

Meekly, the bomb-maker complied, doing his best to hold both hands above his head. He was clearly hurting; his face and clothes were streaked with filth. He must have panicked and injured himself diving down into the manhole; Pat decided. He had only managed to drag himself this far. Pat's eyes narrowed,

'Tell me what the next target was, you bastard, and maybe I'll let you live.'

In broken English, the bomb-maker wailed forlornly,

'No, no… I kidnapped by those men. They forced me to stay. I swear!' he started to cry… 'I swear!'

Pat didn't believe a word and was in no mood for lies or play acting. Menacingly, he raised the muzzle of his MP5; switching his point of aim from the man's chest, to the very centre of the fugitive's forehead,

'Last chance mate…where was the attack going to be?'

The bomb-maker was terrified; he knew he was going to be killed if he remained silent a moment longer; he didn't want to die in this foul-smelling place. Dropping the shallow mask of zealous beliefs, with an ingratiating smile and rush of pure self-preservation, he bowed his head and stuttered,

'Brent Cross shopping…Yes, yes, all I know,'

Starkly illuminated by the pencil beam of his Mag light, Pat stared hard at the cowering fugitive lying shivering on the filthy pathway. Whoever he was; one thing was absolutely clear Pat thought angrily to himself; the bastard was up to his neck in more than the shit surrounding him.

Unbidden, swirling images of the broken girl, lying insensible and bleeding in the smoke-filled Hilton's lobby, and then scenes of chaos and destruction at London's shattered Waterloo station flooded Pat's mind. His eyes narrowed; blood ran ice-cold through his veins as he remembered. Surrounded by darkness, alone in the cramped confines of the dank sewer as judge, jury and perhaps executioner, it was time to decide the terrorist's fate.

Pat based his decision on his own code of justice, and the truth he had shared weeks earlier, with Spike and Danny about dealing with hard-core fanatics. In further mitigation, before the assault, he was given clear and specific rules of engagement.

With no witnesses to complicate matters, there was no conflict in Pat's mind. He had no idea what might lie beneath the injured man's coat. This thing lying before him was the last loose end, and he knew what must be done to tie it off. Behind the respirator, his face devoid of expression, SAS Sgt Pat Farrell stared coldly at the bomb-maker for a second, and then he pulled the trigger....

# Chapter Twenty-One

Aboard the Athena Express, Brigadier Lethbridge woke with a start. Instantly, he knew something had changed. Still hooded and shackled inside his steel cell, he stretched out with his senses. The truth dawned quickly; everything was silent; the ship's engines had stopped. He strained to hear anything, which might offer the slightest clue as to what was going on outside, but annoyingly, nothing registered.

As best as he could deduce; it had been nine days now, since he was kidnapped. Still no interrogation, and just enough food and water to keep him alive. It was obvious to him now that his captors were solely intent on delivering him somewhere. As the engines were shut down, perhaps they had finally reached their destination, he thought? With a resigned sigh, the Brigadier accepted that, one way or another, he'd know soon enough.

The minutes ticked by until suddenly, the silence was ripped apart by the familiar screech of the container's rusty hinges, as the steel door creaked and swung open. The Brigadier tensed; his heart pounded as daylight streamed into his lonely dungeon. Breathing hard, he braced himself for whatever the next few minutes would bring.

There was a murmur of muffled voices speaking rapidly outside, in a tongue he easily recognised as Arabic. Through the tiny gap in the hood's burlap material, Charles Lethbridge saw the blurred outline of several figures entering the container. Guttural commands were issued, and something was dragged in by two of the men. Roughly cast down, their burden landed with a thump and a high-pitched whimper beside him. The noise was definitely made by a female; the Brigadier decided. It was filled with a heartrending mixture of pain, pure unadulterated terror and abject despair. There were more sounds. This time, the metallic scrape of chains being dragged along the container's steel floor, followed by a short pause, and then the distinct click of a padlock being snapped shut.

Laughing cruelly at the girl's distress, her captors turned to leave. Not wishing to raise his captor's suspicions, the Brigadier remained still and quiet throughout the incursion, until the container door swung shut with its usual bang. Silence returned to his echoing cell. He ground his teeth; so frustrating, not to be able to see properly. Thwarted by the darkness and his temporary blindness, Lethbridge turned his head towards the whimpering girl, lying somewhere close beside him. There was a sudden and heavy vibration, which rumbled up from far below as the ship's engines were re-started. Putting aside the fact that the ship was getting underway again; he listened to the girl's terrified sobs for several moments while he desperately searched for the right thing to say, given their seemingly hopeless situation. He wanted to avoid frightening the poor thing anymore than she obviously already was. He cleared his throat softly. Discarding any formality, he made a stab at calming the traumatised girl. Talking quietly, in a voice he hoped would reassure her, forcing a smile behind his mask, he spoke gently into his own world of darkness,

'Hallo my dear, I'm Charlie. I'm a prisoner too, but don't worry; everything will be all right... Please don't cry... now come on, there's no need to be afraid anymore, because I absolutely promise I'm on your side and won't hurt you...'

For the first time in weeks, there were no guttural threats or sudden sharp slaps to quell her terrified sobs. The girl, whose face was cruelly scarred with teenage acne, heard only a softly-spoken, gentle voice, speaking to her in cultured English. Her expensive education in one of the finest young lady's academies in Switzerland left her fluent in French, English and Italian. The strange man's voice brought comfort, his soft West Country burr helped soothe her rapidly beating heart. The sobbing subsided slowly and then faded away to silence.

Brigadier Lethbridge smiled with satisfaction behind his hood. Good, he thought; it was working. Gently, he continued,

'Good girl, now that's much better, isn't it? I've told you I'm Charlie, so please tell me, what's your name?'

\* \* \* \* \*

Less than an hour after the attack was over, sitting in the Ops. Room at his SAS headquarters in Chelsea, Pat stared in turn at the photographs of the dead men, taken immediately after the Troop's highly successful assault of the East London garage. He dropped the last photo onto the table before him and looked up,

'So who exactly are these guys, Cornelius?'

The MI6 analyst frowned. He'd received a call which diverted him on his journey home. There was new and important information to analyse. Cornelius rubbed his tired eyes; sleep would have to wait.

'We have the identity of two of the dead,' he said. 'The other three, we believe, are young men…. Cornelius sighed, 'they're clean-skin suicide bombers. The head-shots have made visual recognition nigh-on impossible of course, but we hope to track them down soon. We think they hail from the Midlands, but Special Branch is investigating that right now,'

Cornelius lent forward and swallowed the last dregs of his black coffee as he sifted through the grisly colour pictures taken after the assault. The head of each of the bodies was a mess. He isolated two,

'These two, we have already traced through our own records, using their fingerprints,'

He held one image up,

'This is Abdula Whalid. He's Tunisian-born, but over here on a false Jordanian passport, which we found in a suitcase when the garage was searched immediately after the attack. He's the guy in the picture from Marble Arch you saw yesterday. According to border control and the immigration service, Whalid arrived in the UK about a year ago, and set up a Saudi-funded mosque in

Bradford. We are, for now anyway, assuming he recruited young local Asian Muslims, and radicalised them between his arrival twelve months ago, and now.'

Pat nodded. Too dark to see clearly, he hadn't known who it was he'd riddled with his MP5, seconds after making entry into the garage. Above the shoulders, the picture was a mess of brains and blood, but Pat was hardened to such sights, and was secretly pleased at his tight grouping. Thirty rounds of 9mm ball ammunition took a little over a second and a half to fire; their effect on human bone and muscle was devastating at close range. Pat understood why visual recognition was impossible, as Whalid's face was gone. With a casual, matter of fact sniff, Pat locked narrowed eyes with Cornelius, and enquired,

'So who is the other guy; the one I slotted down in the sewer?'

The frown on Cornelius' face evaporated. It was replaced with a hint of a satisfied smile,

'We've hit the jackpot with him, Pat. The Americans and Israelis are absolutely delighted that he's been tracked down and taken care of. This is Saleem Mohamed Alabi…'

It was Pat's turn to frown, 'So…?'

Cornelius' grin widened,

'Ah yes, sorry Pat. Saleem Mohamed Alabi is one of Al-Qaeda's most prolific bomb-makers. He was well known to the Pakistani ISI for his radical anti-western views, while he spent three years studying chemical engineering at the National University of Sciences and Technology in Islamabad, before they lost contact with him. He dropped out of circulation and disappeared, more than ten years ago. When we cross-checked with the CIA and Mossad, both confirmed his fingerprints to us. One of his partial thumb-prints was found on a fragment taken from a bomb's timing mechanism, which exploded in a Tel Aviv bus depot five years ago, and another trace was found on a bomb casing which exploded outside the U.S. embassy in Kenya several years ago,'

The grin faded from Cornelius' face. Suddenly, he looked grim,

'We've also tracked his handiwork during the Afghan campaign. Several unexploded IED's, recovered from roadside ambush points used his signature explosive mix, and one had an almost perfect index fingerprint on the bomb's detonator….'

Cornelius' head tilted slightly,

'It was odd though, because he suddenly, apparently, stopped making bombs and mines in Afghanistan. We believed, at the time, that he had either been killed, or, more likely, been withdrawn to Pakistan, to teach bomb-making at one of their Al-Qaeda training camps up in the mountains, on the border between Pakistan and Afghanistan.

Pat stared again at the photo of Alabi's body, lying spread-eagled on the slimy walkway beside the running sewer. One on his hands lay half-submerged in the eddying grey water. Most of Alabi's head was splattered; his blood and brains mixed with the green slime covering the curved brick wall behind his body. Pat felt renewed satisfaction at his snap decision to slot the bastard. The man's background was all the justification Pat needed, and as an ironic bonus, his actions gave payback of a sort, for all the innocent victims over the years, whose life Alabi had cut short. The boss had accepted his quick trigger finger, when Pat had told him the target had suddenly moved his hand towards his jacket. Still staring at the graphic photo from the sewer, Pat's eyebrows furrowed,

'So why bring him over here, and not one of his most capable students?... Doesn't make sense to waste a valuable asset on an operation like this, does it?"

Cornelius shook his head,

'That's the problem, Pat. It does make perfect sense to use your best explosives man when it's absolutely necessary in a top operation, but whoever it was who conceived the bombing campaign over in Pakistan, ordered him to the UK and then someone else, conveniently, shopped him and the rest of the terror cell to Special Branch.'

Cornelius rested his hands on the table, lifted his head and stared back at Pat. His thoughts beginning to pigeonhole the facts he already had; silent alarm bells were tripping all over the place in his whirring mind. Cornelius rubbed his chin and said uncomfortably,

'Something's definitely not right with this affair, Pat. There are crucial parts, which don't fit, and it's all, somehow, been just a bit too easy.'

Pat showed his surprise, as his face darkened,

'But this is still a terrific result, Cornelius… isn't it?'

Straightening and rubbing his hands together, Cornelius shrugged and said almost absently,

'I'm going over to Vauxhall to clear this with Control, and then do an intensive work-up and full analysis on this whole business, as soon as my assistant, Julie, arrives.' With a farewell nod, Cornelius turned and strode towards the door. As he reached for the door handle, he stopped abruptly and spun back to face Pat… There was something distinctly ominous in his voice, when Cornelius added,

'The more I think about this; it is all beginning to smell decidedly dodgy; The facts and information, such as they are before us, just don't make any logical sense to me, at all….'

# Chapter Twenty-Two

Dense sea fog billowed beneath leaden skies. At the waterline, the cold grey English Channel hissed past the ship's hull, as dawn broke somewhere on the hidden horizon. On the bridge of the Athena Express, the Somali Captain glanced down, away from the swirling fog cocooning his ship. He stared again at the readouts on the glowing panel before him. The vessel's GPS navigation system plotted his exact position on the edge of the crowded, fogbound shipping lanes at the southern tip of the North Sea. The solid Kent coastline, rent by the Thames' mighty estuary glowed ghostly green on one side of the radar screen. The Sheerness coastline and the mouth of the River Medway showed starkly on the glowing screen, as the ship sailed steadily past both. A combination of GPS and radar confirmed his ship was a mile from the shoreline, slowly passing the Isle of Grain's Liquefied Natural Gas Terminal on the southern bank of the broad Thames estuary, at the mouth of the Medway. The freighter's captain lent forward towards the main instrument panel and depressed one of the control buttons, linked directly to the engine room. Within moments, the rhythmic thrum of the ship's engines began to fade. A voice answered in Somali, from the speaker above the captain's head.

'Slow ahead, Captain.'

The Captain reached up and pressed the send button beside the speaker, *'Very well.'*

He half-turned to the thin-faced Arab standing silently behind him,

'I will increase speed again once we have turned and fully entered the main estuary,' he glanced up at the ship's chronometer, 'We are scheduled to reach our destination at Tilbury docks in approximately two hours.'

Expressionless, Youssef nodded.

Staring into the swirling fog outside, Youssef's cruel face broke into a thin smile of satisfaction. Zahira Khan would be pleased. Everything was still going exactly to his great plan. Avoiding French police patrols, and transferring the snivelling girl from the cellar where she had been held captive to a small boat waiting at the fishing port of Almar St. Clair had been tricky, but successful. Once safely aboard the small cutter, to his and his men's amusement, the short pre-dawn boat ride to the waiting freighter had made Mohammed violently sick, but nevertheless, the girl had been delivered safely, and was now beside the other prisoner, bound and locked securely in one of the cargo deck's nondescript shipping containers.

Taking one last look into the eddying fog, which still hid the ship's prow from both men's eyes, Youssef glanced down at his own watch and said,

'Before it begins, I must go below and gather my men. It is time for us to pray together, for the last time.'

\* \* \* \*

Cornelius nodded to the security guard standing inside the MI6 Vauxhall headquarters, as he strode across the reception foyer towards the waiting lift. Stepping in, he pressed his I.D. badge against the electronic eye at the top of the panel. When the light turned green, Cornelius thumbed the second-floor button. The doors closed with a gentle pneumatic hiss. Moments later, the lift slowed and the doors reopened. The analyst straightened his tie, stepping aside momentarily to allow two chattering secretaries to enter,

'Ladies,' he said with a smile, acknowledging their thanks.

Cornelius felt a fresh wave of fatigue flow over him as he reached his office door. His mouth was dry, and he could feel the onset of a headache. Feeling washed out and thoroughly wretched, he reached for the office's door handle and opened it. Julie was already there, shuffling a pile of papers, and settling them down on his desk. The stack was one of many which were scattered around the room. To an outsider, the files and papers looked chaotic, but Cornelius knew Julie understood his methods. The piles of paper awaiting his attention would be arranged in chronological order; fully cross-referenced under subject matter, date and source.

With a nod and tired smile, he said,

'Morning, Julie,' he raised his eyebrows in mock horror. 'My God, so much?'

Almost apologetically, Julie grinned back and said,

'Yes, I'm afraid so. I woke up early this morning and read your email on my phone. I decided to come in as soon as possible, and I've spent the last ninety minutes in the lower basement, trawling through the records department, searching out hard copies of everything that's come in over the past few weeks, which I thought might be of use.'

With a resigned sigh, Cornelius rubbed his hand over his tired eyes. He took off his jacket and hung it neatly over the back of his chair, before loosening his tie. Sometimes, he thought to himself; these damned in-depth analyses could take days of sifting, but having searched through and eliminated the dross; it was the only way he knew to find patterns and hopefully, some keys to unlock the puzzle from what remained. Accepting his fate, he rubbed his hand over his face again and said with a sigh,

'OK, let's get started,' he thought for a moment and added in a pleading voice, 'but before we start, I really, really need some strong black coffee, and a couple of aspirins…'

* * * *

Like the rest of the Troop after the operation, Pat felt deadbeat and utterly spent as the sun came up. After finally arriving back to his flat, he ignored the jumbled heap of fresh letters lying unsorted behind his communal street door. He ate some toast, stripped off and showered. Quickly towelling himself dry, he fell wearily into bed. After the adrenaline fuelled night, it was a massive relief to crawl under the duvet, close his eyes and gratefully clear his mind of everything.

Like most professional soldiers, used to snatching catnaps wherever and whenever possible, Pat was soon sound asleep. As he began to drift away, he knew the nightmares might return, but for once, he was too exhausted to care.

# Chapter Twenty-Three

Still hidden deep within the swirling fog, the Captain ordered – *All Stop* - to his engineer, who was waiting for orders down in the ship's cavernous engine room. Carried on the incoming tide, making cautious headway in the wide middle of the winding river, the Athena Express coasted silently on the broad stretch of water known as Gravesend Reach, adjacent to the ancient and historic commercial docks at Tilbury, on the Essex side of the River Thames.

From stem to stern, the four-man Arab cell and the Athena's Somali crew did their best to keep warm; they had been kept busy since the freighter passed the mouth of the Medway, several hours earlier. With Youssef leading them, they had used the time to make their devotions, and then went up on deck, piling diesel-soaked mattresses, tyres taken from the cargo hold, wooden chairs and broken packing cases into tall strategic heaps interspersed along the ship's main deck.

The Captain watched his radar screen and nodded to himself with satisfaction. This was as far as he dared to bring the freighter up the Thames, without raising the suspicions of the English. Satisfied with his current position, he depressed the ship's fog horn button once. A deep, booming blast from halfway up the funnel echoed away into the fog. He waited thirty seconds, and then pressed the button next to it, labelled – '*Emergency.*'

The ship's klaxon began to blare out its warning every three seconds. On the original foghorn blast, burning torches, hurled by the terrorists, arced smoking through the damp atmosphere onto each pile of combustible material. Flames licked around them for a few moments, then caught and quickly spread, until every pile was engulfed by roaring flames. Thick black smoke eddied up from the raging bonfires, mixing into the surrounding fog.

As the fires raged; still securely bound, Brigadier Lethbridge and the girl were stripped of their blindfolds and dragged from the container. Stumbling and wincing with the light, they were frog-marched at gunpoint to the nearest lifeboat, which, for the time being, remained inboard, suspended securely under two steel davit arms. The ship's other lifeboats were ready to be lowered into the water by waiting crewmen.

On the bridge, the Captain walked across to the ship-to-shore radio. He snatched up the handset, having previously dialled the radio into the marine emergency band - VHF radio channel one-six. Under maritime law, he knew it would be constantly monitored by the English coast guard; their unwitting help would grease the evacuation plan admirably. Depressing the send switch on the radio's handset, the Captain spoke. His voice high-pitched and edged with panic,

'*Mayday! Mayday!* This is freighter Athena Express. There is explosion on-board. Our Captain dead. We on fire and sinking. Someone, please, please help us!'

There was a short burst of static, and then a calm voice radiated from the speaker above the captain's head,

'Athena Express! Athena Express! This is the coastguard. Please state the full nature of your emergency, and your exact location. *Over.*'

Forcing more panic into his voice, the captain smiled momentarily as he depressed the send button once again,

'Help us! I am chief steward. Speak English good. We in bad fog. Fire and smoke everywhere, cannot see… helmsman say we close Tilbury.'

The status returned for several moments, before the coast guard operator replied,

'Thank you, Athena Express. Now I need you to stay very calm… I have you on our radar. You appear to be stationary in the middle of the channel at Gravesend Reach. Is that correct? *Over.*'

Trying to sound as if he was struggling now on the very edge of desperation, the Captain replied rapidly,

'Yes, yes. I think so...'

'Good. Thank you, Athena Express. We are sending help. Use your lifeboats if necessary, and get your crew well away from your ship.'

This was the order the Captain was waiting for; he knew it was coming. Coughing theatrically into the microphone, he added,

'Yes, yes. We no steerage, abandon ship now' keeping the send switch depressed; he coughed dramatically, 'Too much fire…*Hurry!*'

The Captain dropped the handset and walked off the bridge, outside onto the tiny wing of the observation deck. With the ship's emergency klaxon still booming out every three seconds, he waited for the next available gap in the deafening blasts, and then blew a whistle repeatedly.

The Somali crewmen understood the signal. Each of them, ordered to man a lifeboat, pressed its engine's starter button. Satisfied when they felt the vibrations, indicating the propeller was turning at minimum revolutions; each crewman left the ignition switched on, and the lifeboat's motor running, then climbed out and scrambled down onto the Athena Express' deck, before pressing the lifeboat's emergency launch button. All along the main deck, rusty steel davits squeaked and groaned as gears swung each of the boats out. Once the launch button was pressed, they were cycled to automatically lower the lifeboats towards the cold grey waters below.

As each lifeboat hit the water with a splash, the lowering hawsers were released. With engines already running, the lifeboats bobbed on the water for a moment and then began to chug slowly away in all directions from both sides of the ship, disappearing quickly into the enveloping fog.

\* \* \* \*

Long before the revenge operation began, from his lair in Pakistan, Zahira Khan had worked out each part of his plan with meticulous care. Considering this stage, he estimated it would take at least twenty minutes for help to arrive at the waterline of the abandoned Athena Express, if she stopped in the widest mid-channel stretch just before her phantom sinking began. Given the time of year, he'd carefully researched and recorded the Thames's estuary tides and weather patterns on the web, and gambled on the presence of pre-dawn sea fog. Even if it wasn't there, he reasoned, or lifted early, the fires would still be raging. In the half-light, thick, billowing smoke would shroud the ship and add to the confusion surrounding it.

Getting aboard, without gangways or rope ladders would take the rescuers at least another fifteen to twenty minutes. By the time the English fools realised that something was amiss, to confirm their suspicions, before taking action, they would have to track down and search each of the lifeboats for the missing crew. Altogether, his cunning plan would provide more than enough time to pass for the last lifeboat, stripped of its fluorescent marker panels and filled with his men and the two hostages, to make their escape upriver. Small boats might or might not show as tiny blips on the coastguard radar, he reasoned, but with empty lifeboats haphazardly escaping in all directions, and so many boats of all sizes, rushing to the rescue, one small cutter, close to the riverbank should easily slip away un-noticed, hidden from radar by background clutter, and from human view by swirling clouds of fog and dense palls of smoke, which should be enveloping the Athena Express.

# Chapter Twenty-Four

His eyes blurring with exhaustion, Cornelius glared at the pile of folders on his desk. He had spent two frustrating hours sifting through the papers and folders Julie had brought up from the record store earlier. Most, he judged had been routine, mundane intelligence reports from across the globe which Cornelius scanned quickly and discounted. As he cast each one aside, Julie picked it up and shifted the discarded file to the untidy stack on the other side of his office.

What remained might be of interest, if only, he thought angrily, he could find a common theme which linked them together. Sipping from his third, or was it the fourth cup of black coffee, the drained MI6 analyst began spreading out what remained until every inch of his desk was covered. With a sigh, he swallowed more aspirins before picking up one marked with a reference number and the legend - Brigadier Charles Lethbridge – Kidnap victim - Cyprus.

He had to start his analysis somewhere. Absently, he opened it, and began to read….

When he finished evaluating everything it contained, right to the last page, his eyebrows furrowed. There was certainly something missing in the report, something important, but through his haze of tiredness, he just couldn't remember what it might be. Dropping the file to his desk, Cornelius stood up and walked slowly to the window. Tired men make the biggest mistakes; he thought. He stretched, and rubbed his bloodshot eyes. Turning his back from London's panorama, spreading beyond the sparkling River Thames, he said wearily,

'It's no good, Julie; this is hopeless. I can't properly focus on anything I'm afraid; I've had it, so I'm going to go next door, pull two chairs together, and try to grab a couple of hours sleep.' Rubbing the back of his neck, he added, 'Start sifting through the files on my desk, and see if anything catches your eye…hmm, make a start with the Lethbridge file, will you?'

Julie nodded sympathetically. She laid aside the file she was studying, walked past her exhausted boss and sat down behind his desk. Without uttering another word, Cornelius opened the door and dragged himself wearily into the small connecting anti-room. Windowless, it wasn't much bigger than a broom-cupboard, but it was quiet, dark and would suit his purpose admirably.

Julie read through the Lethbridge file. Her eyebrows furrowed too, when she had finished it. She closed the file, but her quizzical look remained. Chewing her lip thoughtfully, she turned towards the computer keyboard, tapped in her password, and accessed the main MI6 intelligence database. The screen changed, and the computer's cursor winked silently inside the default reference number box. She typed in the file's number, and waited for the central server to search out the file. She tapped a pen idly on the desk while she waited. The screen abruptly changed again as the program found the kidnap file she was looking for. Dropping the pen, she began to study it.

When Julie reached the section containing the kidnapper's video, she felt her blood chill when she accessed it and watched it twice over; searching for anything they had missed. When it was finished, she continued staring at the last frame for a moment, until her eyes fell and she noticed a small blue shortcut had been added in one bottom corner of the page; marked: *Voice-print Ident. Inconclusive 40%.*

Opening the paper file again, Julie looked for the corresponding printout, but annoyingly, due no doubt to a filing miss-match, the voice-print analysis was missing. Clicking her tongue with irritation, she turned back to the screen, ran the cursor down to the shortcut and clicked on it. A new electronic file instantly appeared with a bearded Asian man's head and shoulders picture to one side. He looked quite harmless, but Julie immediately ignored her first impression. She was well aware that looks could be very deceiving in the dangerous world of international terrorism.

The legend at the top of the screen was not at all helpful. It logged only a 40% chance of accuracy, but no alternatives were listed.

The man's middle-aged face was bespectacled, almost avuncular. The picture had been taken outside and showed a bright, sunny day around him. Judging by the collection of untidy stalls and the dress of the men behind the target, it had almost certainly been covertly snapped in what looked like a typical Asian bazaar. The highlighted name of the file was Zahira Khan. Intrigued, she began to read the information beside the photograph. As a matter of routine, it had been passed to London by the Pakistani I.S.S. four months previously. Her mood darkened, the more she read of the Pakistani agency's suspicions concerning the man on the flickering screen, whose wife and children had been killed in a U.S. drone strike, several years earlier.

When she finished absorbing every scrap of the new intelligence, proving at least possibly, that this new player was behind the narration on the kidnap video, she printed out the file, and added the missing information to the folder in front of her. She glanced up at the wall clock, then back at the other files spread out around her. It would take several hours to wade through them all, but having already spotted a missing snippet of information in the Lethbridge file, she was confident it would be time well spent. She had learnt from Cornelius months ago, about the importance of seemingly trivial and obscure pieces of the intelligence jigsaw, which sometimes turned out to be the handle of a hidden key. Julie thought for a moment about waking her boss, but given the state he had worked himself into, decided she needed more time before disturbing him.

With doubt still nagging as to the relevance of this new face, this man called Zahira Khan. Julie thought for a moment and then picked up the telephone. She dialled an internal number up on the fourth floor, and spoke quickly when the connection was made,

'Hallo Morgan, it's Julie Wallace. Sorry to bother you, sweetie, but listen, I need to beg a favour. I've just flagged up a name I might be interested in, and need some background information from your people on the Pakistan desk…'

\* \* \* \* \*

Minutes after leaving the freighter, still guarded closely by his captors, Brigadier Lethbridge sat huddled at the bottom of the lifeboat. Beside him was the little Greek girl he now knew as Christina; only daughter of Christos Angelopoulos, the Greek billionaire. She had been kidnapped and held prisoner for about two weeks, under constant guard in a damp cellar. She didn't know where it was, but with gentle coaxing during their long hours together, the Brigadier had worked out that her prison must have been somewhere under a house in a remote village, close to her family's Châteaux in Normandy. Her captors were the same Arabs, who had taken her, and killed Claude, her bodyguard.

The Brigadier had no idea where they currently were. He'd tried to spy out a familiar reference point or landmark when they were frog-marched to the lifeboat, but to his dismay, the ship was enveloped in fog, and as a result he had gleaned nothing useful.

Able to see his immediate surroundings clearly now, devoid of that damned hood, the Brigadier glanced around his new floating prison. The lifeboat was roomy and modern, and despite still being in great danger, it felt so good to be away from the stinking container. The solid superstructure above his head looked to be strong fibreglass, and was probably sealed into the steel hull, to make the cutter watertight. Sitting on the floor, he couldn't see out of the portholes, so he gave up trying to define their location, and instead quietly turned his attention to his captors. He counted sixteen of them. There were four Arabs and a dozen shivering black Somalis. They clearly hadn't yet acclimatised to the cold atmosphere. Most of them were shivering because of the chill. One of his captors, who he hadn't seen before, was occasionally glancing at a map, as he steered the boat. The Brigadier recognised the faces of some of the Somalis, who had been his jailors during the voyage. Some were sitting, quietly mumbling to themselves as they fingered strings of prayer beads. Others, including the one with a limp, ignored him and jabbered excitedly to another of his own group.

One of the Arabs, whose hollow, pockmarked face reminded the Brigadier of a weasel, stared out of the nearest porthole in silence. He had a haunted look in his eyes, but carried an air of aloof authority with them too. Both the Arabs and Somalis deferred to him and gave him respectful space. He had leader written all over him, but what concerned the Brigadier most, however, was the weaponry each of the terrorists carried. Every man held a battle-scarred Chinese or Russian AK-47 assault-rifle, and they all wore at least one heavy ammunition bandolier across a shoulder. Bulges in their chest pockets suggested concealed grenades.

This was no ordinary gang of guerrilla fighters; he decided. They were intent on delivering their hostages to some pre-planned destination.

No, he thought; there was much more to this. It was unusual to have a cell comprised of two very distinctive ethnic groups that spoke different languages, but nevertheless, these men were clearly members of a well-resourced and highly organised terror cell. If he was right, their mission was becoming worryingly obvious. Judging by the heavy firepower and recent changes to Al-Qaeda terror tactics, these men were a dedicated assault group, and surely, he reasoned, must by now be getting close to making a deadly attack on some defenceless and unsuspecting civilian target.

*God help the poor bastards, whoever they are; Brigadier* Lethbridge thought grimly.

The Arab leader turned his attention away from the fog outside, and spoke in English to the freighter captain, who was now acting as the cutter's helmsman,

'How long before we reach the rendezvous?'

Keeping his eyes firmly on the fog shrouded waters ahead, the captain answered from the side of his mouth,

'Not long now,' he pointed at the blue ribbon marked on the map beside him, 'We are about… here!… You see how this great river twists and turns for miles before it reaches London.' Suddenly concerned, he shook his head, 'The tide is still with us, but now it is time to steer closer to the right-hand bank before we reach the next bend, or we could miss the jetty completely in this cursed fog.' The Arab nodded in silence. He saw no reason to argue; he knew nothing about boats, the flow of tides or unknown and unpredictable rivers.

Neither man saw the Brigadier tense when he heard the Somali mention London. Lethbridge silently ground his teeth with frustration. So the coming attack was meant for the capital, he thought angrily. A blood vessel throbbed dangerously on his forehead as he desperately tried to think of a way to alert the authorities. He sank dejectedly back against the boat's gently rolling hull. He knew it was hopeless. Brigadier Lethbridge's frustration grew exponentially, until he thought, he was going to explode. Surrounded by heavily-armed fanatics, and still trust up like a damned chicken, he knew there was absolutely nothing he could do to warn anyone.

# Chapter Twenty-Five

Julie almost finished wading through the files. As she initially feared, she found nothing concrete; absolutely nothing which leapt from the dry pages and rang alarm bells. It had proved a frustrating couple of hours, and not for the first time, she wondered at her boss's genius at unravelling intelligence mysteries which often, no-one else even knew existed. Although he had endured plenty of scorn from one or two colleagues, Cornelius had been right all along about the Al-Mahdi case. It was his insight and experience which had saved London from a deadly terrorist plot to incinerate the capital with a stolen nuclear bomb.

Lacking his intuition, but using what she had learned about Cornelius' vetting system, there were now only three folders left on the desk, which had even mildly flagged her interest. Individually, they all had something unanswered and indefinable, which made her lower them thoughtfully onto the small *keep* pile in front of her.

One had come from the Americans, and was linked to Zahira Khan. Months earlier, they had detected what appeared to be a terrorist summit meeting, hosted by Khan, up in the remote mountains on the Pakistan/Afghanistan border. Strangely, the CIA report also linked a previous GCHQ intercept, which picked up the name - Al-Amin. Julie's face flushed as she stared at the open file. Her friend working on the Pakistan desk upstairs had indicated growing belief between the ISI and MI6, that Khan was closely linked with both the Mumbai and more recent Kenyan terror attacks. If this was the man's forte, then could the meeting in the mountains have been about another attack, designated by the terrorists as Al-Amin?

Her heart beat a little faster; was there something there, after all? Taking a deep breath, she put the file down, and looked at the other two. One concerned the Lethbridge kidnapping, and once again, linked the name Zahira

Khan. The other, strangely, also concerned abduction. It was a blue Interpol file. Odd, she thought. Julie wondered why the European law enforcement agency had referred this particular criminal case to MI6? Intrigued, she opened the file and began to read.

\* \* \* \* \*

Still enveloped by fog, the muffled roar of the lifeboat's engine faded as the helmsman closed the throttle. One of the Somali deckhands was already waiting outside on the narrow prow. As the lifeboat gently bumped against the old concrete jetty, he threw a line to one of two Asian men who had been waiting. Grabbing the uncoiling rope, one of the men standing on the jetty knelt down and tied it firmly to a chipped and rusting bollard. At the other end of the lifeboat, a second Asian man, younger than the first, secured the stern rope to another of the mooring bollards.

The waiting men had been on the Quay since before dawn. In the darkness, it had been child's play to drive along the deserted approach track; having used bolt-cutters to crop the heavy chain securing the perimeter gate.

The old cement works were isolated from other riverside industry, and was long ago abandoned. Khan had used Google Earth to find it; it was perfect to get his men and their equipment ashore unobserved. He wanted somewhere close, but not too close to the target. Surprise was vital to his plan, and being seen unloading could easily have jeopardised success.

The older of the two men who had been waiting for the boat glanced around nervously, when he saw the lifeboat passenger's weapons. Glad to be back on land, Youssef stepped onto the solid jetty, and looked around him. The jetty was shaped like a T; its tail disappearing off into the fog towards, Youssef presumed the shore. Either side of the jetty, shallow waters lapped its barnacle encrusted legs, which even at high tide, kept it clear of the river's surface. Looking towards the hidden shoreline, just on the very edge of Youssef's vision, the water's ended and a thick green scum carpet of glutinous, glistening ooze replaced it. He turned to the older Asian, who had secured the boat's prow, and demanded,

'You know where to take us?'

The man smiled, 'Yes, brother; we know exactly where you want to go.'

The driver and his nephew were local men chosen by Zahira Khan on the recommendation of one of his agents living in London. They were part of a radical Muslim splinter group within the large Bangladeshi community settled in nearby Tower Hamlets. The ward was well-known to the Security Services as a hotbed of Muslim extremism and corruption. Only a few days before, although there was no suggestion he was involved in any way with terrorist activities, the local council's Bangladeshi-born Mayor had been placed under central government investigation, after an undercover BBC reporter had discovered possible evidence of block votes for cash irregularities, shortly after his election.

Satisfied, Youssef turned to his men, who were busy helping the hostages onto the jetty. Both prisoners were roughly forced to their knees, facing Youssef, who gave out new orders,

'One of you men, guard them. The rest of you, unload the packs and bring them with you,' he nodded towards the driver and his nephew, 'These men will lead you to their vehicle.' Youssef turned back to the Somali crewman who had stepped forward to guard the prisoners. The Arab's face was cold and expressionless. He looked down and locked his cruel eyes with the Brigadier's. In English, he hissed,

'If either kaffir tries to run, you know what to do…. *Kill them both.*'

\* \* \* \* \*

Julie closed the Interpol folder and silently shook her head. The only daughter of a man, who had almost as much money as God, had been brutally kidnapped, and yet no ransom demand had been received since she was taken? It simply made no sense. Why go to all that trouble, without getting millions of dollars in ransom to release her unharmed? Like the French police, Interpol was perplexed. Their own investigations exhausted, a copy of the file had been forwarded on, both to the Security Service and MI6, to see if a terrorist link could be found, but like other European intelligence agencies, they had drawn a blank.

The French police report said that the girl's bodyguard had been savagely murdered, but no DNA or fingerprints had been left behind by the kidnappers. Subsequent forensic examination of the body revealed that the man had his throat cut *after* being repeatedly shocked with a powerful Taser, which police investigators had recovered at the crime scene. Why, she wondered, would the kidnappers bother to kill a defenceless man, when he was already rendered completely helpless? Was he killed? she wondered. Perhaps to send someone a most brutal message? The father, possibly? But he had admitted nothing of it to the police.

The police report went on to say that the girl's father had been oddly evasive, bordering on uncooperative when they had questioned him about possible motives other than money, or enquired after enemies who might have kidnapped his daughter. Although he wasn't considered a suspect in the case, her father's behaviour had been considered strangely uncharacteristic for a man whose child had been so violently and ruthlessly abducted.

Julie Wallace closed the folder, and placed it on top of the Lethbridge file. To her, both kidnaps bore vague similarities. Crucially, neither has resulted in a ransom demand, and both victims had disappeared without trace. The level of violence was extreme in both kidnaps; Julie was convinced that the Brigadier's wife was very lucky to be alive.

After seeing the video, MI6 knew Lethbridge had been abducted by an Al-Qaeda linked terror group, and yet absolutely nothing was known of the girl's kidnappers. Why? Were they professional criminals or terrorists? She didn't know, but they had obviously gone to great lengths to hide their true identity. Not suspicious in a straightforward criminal kidnapping, of course, but why, she wondered, had the father been so evasive? Could it be that he actually knew a lot more than he admitted during questioning?

Lastly, what was Zahira Khan's connection with this, if any? According to her friend Morgan, he was wanted by both the Indian and Kenyan governments in connection with the two murderous assaults on Mumbai and the shopping centre in Kenya. Now, he might be involved in the kidnap of a senior retired British army officer.

Julie frowned. Was she about to make a fool of herself, and suggest these three folders somehow held the key which Cornelius had just begun looking for? She glanced up at the wall clock. Her boss had been sound asleep for almost two hours. He needed more, poor thing, but nevertheless, it was almost time to wake him. There were still ten minutes before the deadline was reached, so Julie stood up and put the coffee machine on to warm up so Cornelius could have some refreshments when he woke. With nothing else to do, and ten minutes to kill, she idly switched on the TV, to scan the latest on Sky's news channel.

What she heard and saw, from an outside broadcast reporter standing on a misty Quayside at Tilbury docks, sent her dashing into the adjoining anti-room, to wake Cornelius urgently…

# Chapter Twenty-Six

*'Uncle!'*

The young Asian was waving his arms frantically, as he sprinted back down the concrete jetty. Breathlessly, he skidded to a halt among the remaining crewmen of the Athena Express, next to his father's brother. Gasping, he said breathlessly,

'The van, uncle… It has a flat wheel.'

His uncle looked confused. Before he could say anything, his nephew said rapidly in Bengali,

'There is a big nail in the tyre, and it has gone flat. We must have picked it up when we drove down the track this morning…'

His uncle cursed. The derelict factory, they had passed in the pre-dawn darkness was littered with debris and broken glass. With the van's lights turned off to hide their passage, he had no choice but to stay on the track; it had been the only safe way he could find to navigate across the wasteland from the distant main road, and get their vehicle close enough to the jetty.

Youssef was bringing out the last heavy backpack from the lifeboat. Hearing the commotion, he glared at the younger Asian and snapped angrily in English,

'What is he saying? … What has gone wrong?'

Taking a deep breath, the boy's uncle answered quickly,

'It's nothing; a stupid misfortune. Not our fault; just a flat tyre.'

It was Youssef's turn to curse. His instructions were to get to the target as quickly as possible. A delay might bring discovery. He glared at the older man,

'Well fix it, *NOW!*' His hand dropped to the pistol-grip of his AK, 'I will make you pay if we don't leave quickly.'

The Asian saw the gesture; this man with the cold, dead eyes was serious. He knew his life was suddenly in real danger. As he turned and began to run up the jetty towards his vehicle, he shouted over his shoulder,

'It will take only minutes, brother. Don't worry; we will get it fixed quickly.'

\* \* \* \*

'*Cornelius! … Come on…WAKE UP!*'

Julie shook her boss roughly by his shoulder. The analyst stirred, and then grunted groggily,

'What? … What's the matter, what time is it?'

His frantic assistant shook her head. Excitement bubbling from every pore, she said,

'I've think I've found it, Cornelius. I think I've found the key…'

Cornelius blinked rapidly as he fought to claw his way back to full wakefulness. Swinging his legs from the second chair, he sat bolt upright and rubbed his tired eyes,

'What do you mean?… What on earth are you talking about?'

'Its ships, Cornelius. I think that's the key. Ships are the link between Lethbridge and the Angelopoulos kidnappings, and to Zahira Khan!'

Cornelius looked confused. Ominously, even in his dulled state, that name rang a bell,

'Zahira Khan? … how is he connected?'

Julie smiled triumphantly,

'I'm not positive of everything yet Cornelius, but what's the other thing the kidnapped Greek girl's billionaire father has access to, besides money?'

Cornelius shrugged as his weariness fell away, then the truth dawned. He could instantly see where this was going,

'Why yes… ships… *of course!*'

Julie nodded; words tumbled,

'*Yes, ships.* Zahira Khan is suspected of being up to his neck in those awful attacks on Mumbai and Nairobi. The Americans identified him hosting a meeting with Muslim terrorist leaders from all around the world some months ago, but the CIA never found out what the meeting was about.'

Cornelius nodded... 'Yes, that's right; I remember reading something about it... Go on.'

'There's been a stupid mix-up in our own files. It was *his* voice on the Lethbridge kidnap video, I'm almost certain of it, but that's not all... I was just watching the news before I woke you up. There was a report of a *Greek* registered freighter on fire and adrift near Tilbury on the Thames, but that wasn't what started me thinking though; it's what happened to the ship's crew.'

Cornelius looked confused again,

'What about them?'

Julie's expression changed from triumph to grave concern,

'When he was interviewed, the Harbour Master coordinating the rescue said he can't understand it, Cornelius. You see; when they found them in the fog, the lifeboats were all empty; the fires were bogus, and the crew has simply vanished into thin air.'

Cornelius leapt to his feet with a knot in the pit of his stomach. If his assistant was right, and she'd discovered the key, they could be facing something much, much worse than the recent wave of suicide bombings, and God knows, he thought morosely, they had been bad enough. His stomach churned again. This new terrorist operation had caught them off-guard, and might well be happening in real-time. The more Cornelius crunched the numbers, the more he felt it was beginning to sound both plausible and potentially very nasty. Striding past Julie towards the door, he said,

'Right.... You might have stumbled onto something that's worth checking,' it was Cornelius' turn to look worried. He rubbed his chin thoughtfully, and then hastily added, 'We'll go over everything you've got to make sure, and if it all still makes sense, I'd better run it straight up to the top floor, and seek an emergency audience with Control...'

\* \* \* \* \*

'So you see, Sir Alex, I think we've been double-bluffed. The recent bombings were a smokescreen, to lull us into a false sense of security. If this is a Zahira Khan operation, with his background, I suspect he's going for another full-on assault on a civilian target; probably striking in London.'

Sir Alex nodded. He knew Cornelius too well to dismiss his analyst's suspicions, but he needed more before declaring a full code red security alert to the Prime Minister's office. He stared at the dishevelled state of the man sitting before him and enquired,

'All right, it does sounds plausible, Cornelius, but what else have you got?'

The analyst groaned inwardly. It was always the same. Fearing a fiasco if he was wrong, C wanted tee's crossed, and i's dotted; belt and braces. Shaking his head, Cornelius said with growing desperation,

'This case stands on pure instinct, nothing else; I'm afraid. I've got nothing concrete to go on, C… just a bushel of mysteries surrounding outstanding cases which we have an interest in, and too many markers to ignore what I now firmly believe weaves them together into a very serious and imminent threat against the United Kingdom.'

Cornelius sighed deeply, and ground his teeth with frustration for a moment. Disbelief lingered on Control's face. Ignoring his lack of hard evidence, the analyst pushed on,

'The result of the voice-ident, after the message received at Scotland Yard from Pakistan, which betrayed the bombers, was not terribly clear. GCHQ said they couldn't be positive because of adverse atmospherics. It was something to do with sun-spot activity on the day; apparently it upset their sensitive monitoring equipment. When I spoke to him, the officer on duty at the time agreed, after listening to similar voice-prints that it certainly did *sound* like Zahira Khan's voice, but without full-blown electronic acoustical confirmation, which for purely technical reasons he couldn't give me, he would not commit himself and refused point-blank to put his reputation on the line by declaring a positive, formal identification.'

'Sir Alec nodded politely, and said,

'Yes, that doesn't help in the slightest, but tell me, why would Khan's identification on that particular tape be so important to your case?'

Cornelius leapt to his feet and rested his hands on Control's desk. With every ounce of emotion, his tired body could muster, he said.

'Because Zahira Khan is one ruthless bastard, Sir Alex, who throws away men's lives without a second thought, if he thinks it suits his purpose. If I'm right, he sacrificed one of his finest bomb-makers to convince us that the immediate threat was over, and that we'd won a victory. He's following that chapter immediately with his second and main attack. Khan is most likely behind the Mumbai and Nairobi attacks, where he sacrificed dozens of his loyal men in suicide assaults to spread pure terror. That's what he does…'

Still not fully convinced, Sir Alex was about to reply, when there was an urgent knock on the door. Flushed red in the face, his number two, David Fishburn burst in,

'Sorry C, but we've just had an urgent message from the City of London police. You need to see this.'

Without waiting for a reply, Fishburn strode over to the wall and switched on the large plasma TV screen. The news channel appeared. The scene was reminiscent of the 7/7 underground bombings, with emergency vehicles, blue lights flashing, silently hurtling past the reporter and his cameraman, heading into what ominously appeared to be the very centre of London's commercial heart.

Realising something huge was happening, Sir Alex spluttered,

'The sound David, for God's sake… turn it up!'

David Fishburn nodded, and fiddled for a moment with the TV's remote. With a grin of triumph, he suddenly declared,

*'Got it!'*

The reporter's voice was shaking. With the howl of numerous sirens rising and falling close by, the cameraman panned away from the rushing vehicles, to the reporter's ashen face. Breathlessly, he said,

'The police have launched a full-scale emergency operation, and have begun cordoning off the area, after a multiple shooting incident a few minutes ago. Early eyewitness reports indicate a group of heavily-armed gunmen arrived outside the NatWest tower and opened fire on civilian office workers outside, before storming the building.'

He put his finger up to the concealed earpiece he wore… 'I've just been told we can now take you live to the main entrance of the Natwest Tower.'

The picture on the wall changed. Crouching behind a parked car, one of ITN's roving reporters; his head bowed protectively, knelt on the ground. Like his cameraman, he was obviously reluctant to expose himself to the echoing gunfire which was coming from somewhere behind him. The reporter's expression betrayed both his rapid breathing and his pounding heart. He stared into the camera and ducked involuntarily at the sound of another sudden burst of machine-gun fire. Quickly composing himself, he said,

'The scene here is reminiscent of downtown Beirut… There are many dead on the street outside the NatWest Tower, and dozens more wounded….. Gunmen, presumed to be terrorists, whose sudden arrival coincided with the morning rush-hour, were delivered to the scene by a large van. As they arrived, they immediately jumped from the back of the vehicle and began throwing explosive devices or hand grenades, into passing groups of commuters on their way to work. Then the terrorists opened fire on innocent civilians with automatic weapons, as the commuters ran screaming for their lives,' he turned and risked a quick glance over the bonnet of the car behind him. Turning back to the camera, he said, 'I think the gunmen have now entered the main NatWest Tower.' He ducked again, 'but we can still hear shots coming from inside.'

The flow of further information tumbling from the reporter's lips was cut off abruptly. A police officer, missing his helmet and with bright blood splattered over his cheek and tunic appeared beside the newsman. He grabbed the reporter firmly by the lapel. Desperately dragging him away, the young policeman shouted,

'Get out! You've got to clear out right now! They could come back out again at any second!'

As Sir Alex and David Fishburn watched the TV screen, consumed with revulsion and horror; mouth suddenly dry, Cornelius croaked helplessly,

'God help us all; we've dropped the ball…. It's too late to stop them.'

Sir Alex had seen and heard enough. He tore his eyes away from the plasma screen on the wall and pressed the intercom connecting him to his secretary,

'Mrs Grey, put me through to the Prime Minister's office at No. 10… *quickly!*'

# Chapter Twenty-Seven

Pat was dreaming.

He groaned in his sleep as familiar images flooded in and out of the nightmare. His old friend Mad Chalky White's grinning face appeared. Another fade and they were both kneeling; crouching down behind a low sand dune in a desert, brewing tea. The sun was bright and hot; the horizon shimmered in the heat. Pat's Armalite rifle felt oddly warm to the touch; it suddenly got too hot to hold, and with a curse, Pat dropped it. Confused, he looked down at it for a moment, and then looked up at his mate. Mad Chalky's head snapped sideways suddenly, senses alert, eyes flashing, he whispered quietly,

'Listen, can you hear that?'

Pat nodded. It was the unmistakable growl of one of Saddam's battle tanks, rumbling along the road, miles behind the front line. It was closing on the cross-road they had been tasked by HQ to watch. Chalky raised his head and risked a quick glance towards the growing sound. He gave a commentary,

'Yeah, it's an Iraqi T72; It must be the Republican guard. With his familiar, lopsided grin he said, 'Come on Pat, let's go and zap it.'

Pat shook his head. He wasn't ready. He tried to pick up his Armalite, but it was glowing cherry red. Desperately, he cried,

'No Chalky! Wait, you daft bastard., Not yet; my rifle's fucked!'

But it was too late. In slow motion, whooping with delight, Mad Chalky disappeared over the brow of the dune, laughing and firing from the hip at the closing Russian-built tank. All that was left behind were the marks he had made as his desert boots scrambled over the hissing sand.

As the battle-tank turned; its turret began to swing towards their concealed O.P. To Pat's horror; Mad Chalky's wild spray of bullets had no effect. They sparked and bounced harmlessly off the tank's thick armour. Pat made one last attempt to pick up his rifle, but now it had dissolved into a smoking puddle of molten metal. Drawing his browning pistol and growling frantically, Pat charged up the dune after his friend. The tank was almost on them. Mad Chalky was changing his magazine when he was hit by a burst from the tank's machine-gun. Clutching his leg, Pat's friend collapsed in front of the steel monster. Frantic to do something to help Chalky, in a hopeless gesture, Pat aimed and fired off one round, and then, to his horror the pistol jammed. As he frantically struggled to clear the stoppage, the republican guard commander appeared standing on the turret, laughing and urging his driver forward.

Its engine roaring, the broad steel tracks of the forty-ton T72 screeched and squealed louder, picking up and throwing clouds of dust to its rear. The behemoth was driving straight at Chalky, who lay immobileand bleeding on the burning sand. There was nothing Pat could do; his arms and legs wouldn't move. Immobile, he stared at the closing tank with stomach-churning horror. Seconds later the screeching tracks reached Chalky, and...

'NO!...

With a groan, Pat sat up with his head in his hands. His phone was ringing on the bedside table. Daylight vaguely registered outside through a chink in his closed bedroom curtains. For a moment, he thought it was all part of the nightmare, but when eyes still shut, he willed the noise to stop; it continued to ring urgently; he realised he was awake. This was for real. Pat rubbed his hand across his face as he felt for and snatched up the cell phone with the other,

'Yeah, what?... who is it?' Pat demanded. The voice at the other end sounded familiar.

'Pat?'

'Yeah!'

'It's Stan, down at the orderly room. Look mate, sorry to wake you up, but there's been another big terrorist incident in London this morning. We've just been ordered by SAS Group in Whitehall to issue another Grand Slam. I had to phone you, because like the rest of Shadow Squadron, you didn't respond to the text, so I have to ring everyone instead.'

Pat glanced with one half-opened eye at his watch. He blinked away the initial blur. It was only just after nine; he groaned again; three hours sleep, tops. Still struggling to focus on the here and now, Pat said,

'Yeah, probably all still asleep… Wait a minute. Another Grand Slam?… Christ, Stan, what's happened?'

'It's bad Pat, really bad. Brigadier Hunter wants you all in here, ASAP.'

Pat nodded to himself with resignation. Shadow Squadron was needed again to protect London, and that was all there was to it,

'OK Stan, I'm awake. I'll get down to you as fast as I can….'

* * * *

Youssef's men easily completed their capture of the top floor of Tower 42, formally known as the NatWest Tower, in the City of London's commercial heart.

Opened in 1981; standing at over 183 metres (600 ft.) high, its unusual and iconic chevron construction had dominated the capital's skyline for over three decades. Ownership of the skyscraper had changed since it was first conceived and constructed, passing from the National Westminster bank to the South African born multi-millionaire businessman Nathan Kirsh in 2011. Now renamed by its new owner as Tower 42, within its forty-two operational floors, the building housed a multitude of 'A' grade companies, many of which were listed on the floor of the neighbouring London Stock Exchange, boasting annual company profits counted in many millions, and sometimes billions of pounds. Over more than thirty years, vast corporate fortunes had been earned within its glittering steel and glass façade, with huge bonuses paid to its most successful and astute CEO's, directors and financial dealers.

The tall building was still filling with unsuspecting employees, when the terrorists arrived. Youssef's orders were straightforward. Using the powerful weapons of subterfuge and surprise was at an end. He was to announce their arrival in the city by opening fire on anyone within range of their lethal weapons. Like the other murderous attacks Zahira Khan had executed in the past in India and Africa, no mercy was to be shown, to anyone.

As soon as his men leapt from their vehicle, they began hurling hand grenades and raking the crowded streets, shooting indiscriminately into knots of terrified passers-by, who until that moment, had been intent on nothing more dangerous than getting to their offices on time.

Youssef kept his men outside the Tower's entrance, firing on anyone still moving, for more than a minute. His thin face creased into a cruel smile as he viewed the results. There were crashed bullet-ridden vehicles, blood streaming in the gutters and bodies everywhere, mostly hit in the back as they tried to flee from the deafening high-velocity gunfire.

The Tower's startled security staff inside the ground floor reception area, hearing the shooting and explosions, immediately feared the worst and rushed to lock the tall glass doors, but to no avail. When one of the Somalis screamed that the doors had been secured against them, Youssef snarled,

'Well, shoot them open, curse you!'

With a long raking burst from the grinning Somali's AK, the toughened glass doors imploded, shattering into thousands of jagged pieces. With a guttural cry of triumph, the black terrorist accompanied by several other heavily-armed men with smoking guns, swaggered over the empty cartridge cases and then across the glittering shards of glass covering the atrium floor. Pausing only to change magazines, he was the first to cold-heartedly open fire on the terrified occupants he could still see, who was trapped, desperately trying to hide or escape from the ground floor horror of the charnel house, he and the others were intent on creating.

Deciding his men had announced their arrival sufficiently, fulfilling the murderous, headline grabbing entrance Zahira Khan's plan demanded, Youssef shouted at his remaining men to cease fire, reload and move inside the building. Suddenly, as echoes of gunfire faded, the silence of the blood-soaked streets were deafening.

Given the vastness of Tower 42, defending its entirety would be impossible for such a small group, but Khan's plan had allowed for that. They were ordered to seize the only level which he judged to be impregnable.

Dragging the two hostages with them, after ordering four of his Somalis to cover their next move and guard the shattered doors and foyer, Youssef and the rest of his cell, ignoring the bleeding bodies of their victims, moved across the blood-soaked atrium to the nearest central core elevator and stopped.

Youssef snapped his fingers and pointed towards the door behind the main reception desk, marked 'Security Office'.

His guards knew what the signal meant. With an excited whoop, one of them ran laughing to the door. It was locked, but he savagely kicked it open. The two unarmed security guards on duty inside, who constantly monitored the building's lifts, security and fire alarm systems had nowhere to run and stood no chance. Both men died in a roaring hail of bullets.

Youssef was satisfied; his control of the building, for now at least, was complete.

Burdened with their heavy backpacks, dragging the Brigadier and the terrified girl with them, at a signal from their leader, the main group entered the elevator. The stink of burnt cordite from their smoking guns, and the terrorist's acrid sweat filled the lift as it rocketed upwards.

The four atrium guards had been ordered to follow, as soon as the high-speed lift successfully delivered the others up the building's central core to level 42; situated at the very top of one of London's tallest and most prestigious buildings.

As small lights on the lift's console blinked, illuminating the passing of each floor, the Brigadier glared helplessly at his captors. He guessed they were nearing the terrorist's endgame, where only one logical conclusion held water. If he was right, he and the girl represented everything the hate-filled Al-Qaeda organisation detested. Both represented symbols of the might of the world's non-Muslim establishment. She was the commercial pawn, and he the military.

There could be but one reason behind assaulting this building, he thought angrily. Like 9/11, it had to be a suicide mission to make an announcement of intent, that absolutely no-one, anywhere, was safe from the murderous reach of Al-Qaeda. Their execution in the very heart of London, most likely broadcast live via the Internet into the homes of every fearful non-believer around the globe, would instil fresh terror, and dredge up memories of past Jihadist 'spectaculars'.

Beaming such stark images from the centre of one of the safest capitals in the world would be an enormous victory in the perverse minds of vile and utterly ruthless men who schemed and plotted in dark corners, using gratuitous violence in the furtherance of their twisted cause. If their plan worked, the message would rapidly spread around the globe, graphically demonstrating that despite the overwhelming military strength, the world was powerless to resist Al-Qaeda's ultimate victory. Having noted the bulky backpacks each of these bastards carried, the Brigadier suspected they might ultimately blow up Tower 42; all of them gladly accepting martyrdom and the promised reward of paradise. He was in no doubt that he was now involved in yet another deadly battle in the devil's web; the global war by radical Islamists against any who stood tall, and dared defy the evil of Al-Qaeda...

# Chapter Twenty-Eight

Relayed to Chelsea by Scotland Yard, the exterior CCTV images from around the entrances of Tower 42, portrayed slaughter in high-definition, stomach-churning detail. Running civilians fell suddenly like rag-dolls as bullets struck home, or disappeared in the smoke-filled explosion of grenades. Horrified and appalled, some of the toughest members of Shadow Squadron turned away from the screen. This was too much to bear, merciless murder on the usual peaceful streets of London. Pat and the rest of his men continued to watch with growing anger and disgust as the images changed from one camera to the next. The scenes where the same whichever camera was used, but the last clip was the very worst.

A heavily pregnant woman was lying shot in the legs in the gutter. One of the terrorists walked casually towards her. Raising his weapon, he laughed as he sprayed her where she lay…

'For fuck's sake, Pat, that's enough!…Switch the bloody thing off!'

Spike had half-risen from his seat. His face was flushed, but then, supercharged with raw emotion, so were all the others.

Pat threw the power switch on the projector; the images disappeared instantly,

'Sorry boys, but you needed to see who we are dealing with, and exactly what happened when those bastards started the attack.'

'Christ Pat, what a bloody mess,' it was Danny's turn. Sitting next to his best mate Spike, he was the first to turn away.

Pat nodded, 'Yes; you're right; that's exactly what it is. These murdering bastards caught us napping… literally, with a second-wave attack this morning,' his face grim; Pat shrugged, 'not our fault though. After last night's job, every security agency out there thought we were done and dusted.' Pat paused; he scanned his men's drawn faces. They looked haggard through lack of sleep, but there was more to be seen on their anguished faces. Pat could see past the masks of shock and grief. There was a cold, bitter anger glittering in their eyes. He hadn't ever seen the look before in the eyes of his Shadow Squadron soldiers; but he knew what it meant. His boys wanted revenge for the innocents who had been so cruelly cut down. Pat understood. As their leader, he'd tried his best to be detached and dispassionate as he'd watched, but Pat wasn't immune. With luck, he thought savagely, when clearance finally came, he'd give his boys every opportunity to deliver the payback they obviously hungered for.

Pat gave his men a few moments to settle and recover from the shock of what they had witnessed, before he continued,

'I've got another clip to show you, one which you all must see,'

There were groans, but Pat didn't wait. He selected another memory stick, plugged it in and switched on the projector once again,

'Scotland Yard picked up something of real interest from a camera angle you haven't seen yet, and believe me; you all need to watch this one really closely.'

Spike was halfway out of his seat again. Pat held up his hand to stifle another protest,

'Trust me guys, this is something you all *really* need to see.'

Pat ran the clip. Like an old silent movie, the flickering video showed the terrorists jumping from a large white van and opening fire in all directions. As the gunmen fanned out and cleared the shot, two civilians, a man and a young woman were dragged from the back of the van. Pat froze the clip and walked in front of the glowing screen. His features were bright in the shining light. Everyone noticed his eyes narrow, as Pat pointed towards the two civilians, standing frozen in the middle of the screen,

'These two are prisoners and have been deliberately brought along by the terrorists… as they exit the shot to the right, you'll see both have their hands tied behind their backs, but there's something else. Look closely at the man, as he turns his head…'

Pat walked out of the light and switched the video clip back on.

The Troop watched in silence, as both prisoners were shoved unsteadily by some of the gunmen, up the steps towards the Tower's entrance. Pat froze the video again, as the white-haired man, much taller than the girl, turned his head towards the camera.

Despite the soiled civilian tee-shirt and shorts the man was wearing, everyone in the Troop's briefing room instantly recognised the rugged, weather-beaten face. In the highly charged atmosphere of the briefing room, astonished by what he saw, Danny muttered to himself,

'*Fucking hell!*… it's the Brigadier!'

\* \* \* \*

After their initial briefing broke up, with the Troop already on standby, Pat sent his men away to begin checking and preparing their equipment.

Like all hostage release situations, Pat knew the key factor at this early stage was gathering as much information about the terrorists and their location. Armed with as much intelligence as possible, with the men from SAS Group, Pat could begin formulating a viable rescue plan.

One thing was painfully apparent, however. As the terrorists jumped from the van, Pat had counted at least sixteen of them. With only the same number of men in his Troop, Pat desperately needed a numerical edge because whatever happened, this was going to be a big operation, and currently, the numbers just didn't add up.

What he required were more men. To stand any chance of success, he needed numerical superiority; simply put, he needed reinforcements. To Pat's dismay, word had already come that the regular CRW SAS team, based in Hereford, despite their protests were being held as a strategic reserve. The Security Services, having been badly caught out and deeply embarrassed, reassessed the current threat levels based on recent events, as a matter of the utmost urgency. They came to the conclusion that there was a demonstrably high probability of a third wave suicide attack elsewhere in the UK, perhaps against a nuclear power station, or any one of the UK's busiest international airports, and the attack, if it came, could well be imminent.

As Pat drove to the initial planning conference at SAS Group in Whitehall, the answer to the manpower problem became all too clear. There were plenty of firearm-trained officers in the Met. Police, but due to their lack of specialist training, their role had to be one of containment, and definitely not final assault. The only other men available, he knew, sufficiently trained in aggressive Counter Revolutionary Warfare tactics, were their own reserve 21 SAS men from 'B' Squadron. Seven Troop where the obvious answer. They had only been recently stood down, when Pat's men in Chelsea rotated through, and once again assumed the mantle as London's covert shield against terrorism.

* * * *

On the forty-second floor, inside the old NatWest tower, the women's terrified screaming had stopped. Firing shots into the ceiling was enough to make them obedient.

The dazed and bewildered captives, who worked on the top floor, had been herded by his shouting gunmen into the main open-plan office, on the east side of the building. His men were under strict orders not to kill once they arrived on the top floor, unless specifically ordered to do so.

There were less captured than Youssef had originally hoped, perhaps thirty, but it was only when he and his men arrived, and burst onto the top floor like a tidal wave, that they saw the ladders and painting materials, and realised that major redecoration work was being undertaken, and just a skeleton workforce was currently present in the maze of corridors and offices which now surrounded them.

Forced at gunpoint to clear the middle of the main open-plan workspace of desks and chairs, the terrified men and women sat miserably in a shivering huddle in the centre of the wide room under guard. It was obvious to them all that this was a major terrorist attack, and their lives were in deadly peril. Some women sobbed quietly, with their fingers intertwined, and their hands held firmly on their heads.

Youssef had dispatched a handful of men to watch over their new prisoners, while others searched the other offices and placed their packs, laden with explosives, beside the floor's many lift doors and stairwells. Youssef ordered the explosives wired to a central point, where he could detonate them all simultaneously, if the kaffirs made the grave mistake of launching a rescue. The last explosive backpacks were carried into the vast open office where the whimpering captives were being held. His men were busy placing the final three packs in a deadly triangle around them. For now, he ordered his two original hostages to join them.

Youssef exalted as his men hurried to carry out his orders as the final part of Khan's great plan unfolded. As a Palestinian fighter, he felt gnawing disappointment they weren't in Tel Aviv, mounting an operation against Israel; but then the Jews were much more alert to such dangers. Far from his homeland, it had all been so easy to slip into this poorly guarded country and launch the sneak attack. His face creased with a contemptuous sneer, as he looked through one of the huge plate-glass windows, and gazed thoughtfully down at the grey roofs of London's commercial centre. What weak, stupid sheep these enemies of the true faith were, he thought. How safe and comfortable they must have felt in their pathetic little island, and how easily the fools had been deceived...

Youssef turned away from the spectacular view from the forty-second floor, and stared coldly at the huddle of prisoners still cowering in the middle of the room. Their fear pleased him, it was so clear to see.

Khan's plan called for the hated British government to know, as soon as the camera was set up and ready to make its initial broadcast; that should the kaffir dogs make the slightest attempt at rescue; their own miserable citizens would be the first to die...

\* \* \* \*

In Whitehall, Sir Henry Teesle, the Home Secretary, was at his wits end. Almost an hour earlier, confused reports had begun to filter into his outer office that there had been a serious shooting incident in the city. At first, it was rumoured to be a botched bank raid by a gang of armed raiders, but as police and television camera crews began to arrive on the blood-soaked streets around the old NatWest tower, wild rumour was quickly replaced by cold, hard fact. The news and situation changed considerably for the worse, as the Home Secretary watched the live outside broadcast on his office television. Before he could finish his report, the reporter had been dragged away by a blood-splattered policeman.

The Prime Minister's office had rung three times, demanding further clarification on what was happening in the City. The Home Secretary could only repeat what he had already gleaned from the TV screen. Thankfully, he could shortly get away from No. 10's demands. He was due to leave in under five minutes for a full briefing on the whole episode, from the Assistant Commissioner at the Gold Command incident room at Scotland Yard.

There was a knock on his door. One of Sir Henry's advisors stepped into his office and said,

'I've just been advised by the Security Service that they have identified one of the men believed to be leading the attack, Home Secretary. He is a Palestinian named Youssef Bin Ali. They said he's a commander in one of the Hamas death squads, and currently in the top-ten, on the Israeli's most-wanted list.'

The Home Secretary's heart sank. This new information made it another terrorist attack, when this morning's headlines, after being heavily manipulated by his Ministry's press office, were trumpeting his leadership and personal triumph against the suicide bombers.

Distracted by the Home Secretary's obvious discomfort, the aide turned to go, but stopped suddenly. Turning back to face Sir Henry, he said apologetically,

'Oh yes, sorry Home Secretary; I almost forgot. You're not going to believe this, but the terrorists have brought two missing kidnap victims with them... MI5 has identified them as Brigadier Charles Lethbridge, and the daughter of that Greek billionaire, Christos Angelopoulos.'

Before the Home Secretary could respond, his private telephone rang. Waving the aide away, struggling to absorb the full impact of this latest and most unwelcome twist, he cleared his throat and picked up the handset,

'Hallo?'

There was a moment's pause, and then a gruff, heavily accented voice enquired,

'Is this Sir Henry Teesle?'

Irritated, Sir Henry replied that it was.

'Ah, good. This is Christos Angelopoulos. I have just been informed that my daughter; Christina has been seen in London in the hands of terrorists, is that correct?'

Sir Henry spluttered,

'How on earth did you get this number?'

'Never mind that,' the Greek billionaire snapped angrily, 'my daughter is to be returned to me alive, Sir Henry. If she is not, I have some very powerful friends within the leadership of certain G8 member states, who owe me a great deal for their success,' the billionaire's tone darkened, 'I can assure you, Home Secretary; I will use my considerable influence over them to make sure the coming conference in London will become a political nightmare for you personally, and for your Prime Minister if Christina is not released safe and unharmed.'

There was a sudden click, and the line went dead. Open-mouthed, Sir Henry stared dumbfounded at the handset, before replacing it slowly onto its cradle. Before he could fully absorb this latest threat to his political career, there was a further knock on his office door. It was another of his aides,

'Ah, sorry to interrupt you Minister, but your car has arrived. It's waiting outside…'

# Chapter Twenty-Nine

Beneath the Ministry of Defence, the SAS anti-terrorist machine had already swung into action; their highly classified initial assessment based on the latest intelligence reports, had begun.

At the head of the table, surrounded by a dozen tough regular SAS men with years of experience in hostage rescue, Brigadier Hunter cleared his throat and opened the meeting,

'Gentlemen; at 08.34 hours this morning, a group of heavily-armed terrorists stormed the old NatWest Tower in the City, killing fifty-four civilians in the process. The London Ambulance Service has reported that another one hundred and thirty-six people are being treated in various central London hospitals, many of whom are on the critical list, with gunshot and shrapnel wounds sustained in the initial attack. The City of London police has now contained the area and successfully evacuated the building in question using their armed response units, reinforced by officers from the Met. Starting at the bottom, their teams have begun methodically clearing each floor in turn. The latest report I have seen said they have reached level fourteen. No terrorist has been engaged or captured so far. The terrorists are believed to have taken those working on the top-floor hostage, and have barricaded themselves in up there. The main lifts to the building's central core have been locked off by the bad guys, and are all stuck on level forty-two,'

The Brigadier thoughtfully wiped his palm across his mouth, and then he continued,

'The police negotiators are going to contact the terrorists shortly by telephone. We currently have no idea why they are here, or what their demands will be, but we do know for certain that my predecessor; Brigadier Lethbridge, is their prisoner on the top floor, as is the daughter of a Greek shipping magnate who was kidnapped in France a couple of weeks ago. What their reason for being there is, I have no idea… I have spoken with No. 10. Our orders are to prepare a deliberate action assault plan, in case negotiations fail and the terrorists begin executing hostages.' It was time to throw the meeting open, 'That's as much as I have presently… Pat; I believe you have something for us?'

Pat nodded, 'Yeah, thanks boss; I do. I'm assuming Shadow Squadron will lead the assault, but we need more men. I've taken a quick look at the floor plan of level forty-two, and it's bloody huge. There are four lifts, and I counted twelve entry points from the floor below, including the stairwells' and fire escapes. That means I've only got one man to cover each entrance if we assault… so it's simple, we need more men to do this job.'

The Brigadier nodded as he stared at Pat, the point had already crossed his mind. He raised an eyebrow and stared at Pat,

'Solutions?'

It was Pat's turn to nod, 'We need Seven Troop, but even then; we're still only going to have a two to one majority, and that's not enough.'

RSM Rover Walsh, who had almost finished his current secondment to SAS Group in London, chipped in when an idea suddenly occurred to him,

'Wait a minute, it's not a problem. We can scare up some bodies from here. We have a dozen or so regular SAS staff members and another handful of our own regular permanent staff instructors attached to your A & B Squadrons. We've all done our time on the CRW wing down in Hereford,' a steely glint of anticipation had crept into his eyes as he added, 'we may all be a wee bit rusty, but I know one thing for certain; every single one of our guys will volunteer like a shot; let's face it; we'd all give our pensions for the chance to slot the bastards...'

The other men around the table nodded and grinned eagerly. At a stroke, the serious issue of a manpower shortage was solved. With fifty or more crack SAS men now available, the numbers were beginning to make more sense. A three to one superiority in numbers carried with it a powerful tactical advantage during any assault. Brigadier Hunter grinned; the grizzled RSM was right,

'Good thinking, Rover. We'll plan accordingly... Now; we need to assimilate every scrap of information about the building, and the exact disposition of the terrorists and hostages. I've asked one of the lead architects who designed the place to come in; he's retired and living down in Southampton, but we're flying him up to London in an RAF helicopter.' Brigadier Hunter glanced at his watch, 'He should be here in about two hours. Now, the media have been using their own helicopters, at a safe distance of course, to try and film what's happening on the top floor. No-one has shot at them, so I'm guessing this is part of the terrorist's game plan. After their murderous arrival, clearly, they want as much publicity as they can get. The images are being beamed around the world live on the TV news channels, so I've requested, we have a feed from each of them brought in here. The Metropolitan Police are going to use one of their own helicopters to scan the place with their infra-red cameras. I want anything useful to us noted, and added to the intelligence pot....' The Brigadier turned his attention to the Two Troop's commander,

'Pat, as your Troop is in date at the moment, you *will* lead the assault, if and when we get the green light... I want you to link up with Rover, Taff and Mac. Start checking out the schematics of the Tower, and then begin working up an assault plan. As soon as you have the first draft of something viable, let me see it, will you? Once we have ironed out a workable plan, we can start rehearsing it. When that's all happening, I'll go and brief our political masters on the COBRA committee, on the military options and of course, our ultimate solution.'

Brigadier Hunter's features clouded momentarily as he stared into the fierce, eager faces of the piratical men sitting around the table. With a poorly hidden sigh, he added gravely, 'Gentlemen, like always, we need to be absolutely meticulous in our planning; we certainly can't run a quick smash and grab operation; this situation is far too complicated... Bear in mind, if negotiations fail and the police hand control to us, we must get this operation absolutely right, down to the smallest detail,'…his eyes narrowed with the truth of it as he added, 'I think you all know what I mean…' His eyes bored into each of the senior NCOs around the table in turn, 'if we get any of this wrong, it could well end up in a damned bloodbath!'

* * * *

On the forty-second floor of the old NatWest building, a telephone rang. Youssef had been expecting the call. Zahira Khan had told him long ago that the enemy would try to negotiate, while they bought time and schemed against them. Youssef's agenda and timescale were already pre-ordained, so he could play the kaffirs as he wished, but under no circumstances, Khan had ordered, was he to trust a word they said.

Youssef walked casually over to the jangling telephone and with a reassuring nod to his men, picked up the receiver,

'*Yes?*'

'Hallo, may I speak to Youssef Bin Ali, please?' The voice at the other end sounded polite and even. Youssef was momentarily startled that they knew his name, but he recovered instantly; it meant nothing and was of no import to his mission. With a sneer, he replied,

'This is Youssef, what do you want?'

The answer came quickly,

'My name is David Brand, from the Home Office. My government has asked me to contact you, to see if there is anything I can do to help you, and also to see what can be done to end this unfortunate incident peacefully? They want to know why you have come here?'

Youssef smiled. This man was a fool, working in a land of fools,

'We require nothing from you, or your government, Mr David. We will send our first broadcast shortly, and your questions will be answered then.'

Youssef hung up, and walked back to two of his Arab comrades who were setting up a small video camera in a side room, which, until now, had been the Equities Bond Corporation's CEO's office. One wall was draped with a broad black flag, which carried the embroidered image of a crossed AK47 and an Arab scimitar. Beneath it in two lines of gold-leaf Arabic script, was a chilling message. It read:

*The hour has come for the guilty to pay in blood for the murder of our beloved Osama Bin Laden*

*Our martyred leader calls to us from Paradise. His shade demands we seek an eye for an eye…*

Nodding with satisfaction at the improvised studio's backdrop, Youssef demanded,

'How long before we can send the first message?'

Mohammed looked up from the wiring adjustment he was making between the camera and a small portable laptop, laid on the floor several feet away. He said,

'Ten minutes, perhaps a little more? To make the first broadcast, I still need to make sure we have a strong and open Internet connection. I will check it as soon as I am finished here.'

Youssef raised a hand in acknowledgment. He was convinced by now he had the world's full attention, having explicitly forbidden his men to fire at the helicopters, which continued to hover in the distance. He needed them to stay exactly where they were. Youssef knew they would be filled with cameras and newsmen, eager to have their reports syndicated around the globe. His face creased into a thin smile of gratification at the thought. Manipulating and using the media was a fundamental part of Khan's plan. The fools would readily spread Al-Qaeda's message of invincibility and revenge. Youssef mused thoughtfully, wondering with awe at the subtlety of the plot. It cleverly used the world's commercial TV news channels, driven onward by their voracious appetite for ratings supremacy, and the latest headline grabbing stories.

\* \* \* \*

Shortly after the briefing broke up, leafing one at a time through the different floor plans covering Tower 42, Pat discovered some new and interesting aspects of the building's design. There were actually two more floors above level forty-two. Both were filled with huge air-conditioning machines, elevator lift engines and a complex mix of electrical and communications equipment. The other thing Pat noticed, was that below them, each floor layout was quite different, catering individually to the particular needs of the various corporate clients who rented the space. When he reached the blueprint of the fourteenth floor, he stopped with a quizzical look spreading across his face. Intrigued, Pat compared it with the schematic of the top floor, and then back again to the layout of the fourteenth. He let out a muffled whoop of triumph as he separated them both from the pile, and lay them side by side on the floor,

'Bingo! Take a look at this, fellas.' As startled heads swivelled in his direction, Pat grinned triumphantly, 'Look here; we've got a match. The fourteenth floor layout is almost exactly the same as the top one.'

Rover was first to peer over Pat's shoulder. He compared the two floor plans for himself,

'Blimey, yes, you're right… Well done, Pat, nice one.' Staring intently at both schematics, Rover went on, 'This looks like the perfect place to start rehearsing the boys, once we've sorted out the assault plan' Rover thought for a moment, and then he added, 'We'd better get over there straight away and do a thorough recce. If this pans out, once it's dark, I'll ask the Brigadier if we can move our entire operation up to the Tower's fourteenth floor.' He shrugged, 'After all, we'll have to put our guys somewhere, and right now, I'm buggered if I can think of anywhere better.'

* * * *

'The first broadcast from the terrorists came online at 12.07 hours.

Alerted of the transmission by GCHQ, Sir Alex had already watched it. The head of MI6 looked grave because of what he had seen and heard. Now, it was time for the Home Secretary to view it,

'We haven't released it to the press yet, Minister, but as it's live on the net, we have absolutely no control over who sees it anywhere around the world.

The Home Secretary looked drawn and tired. Almost reluctantly, he waved his hand in acknowledgment and nodded towards Sir Alex,

'Yes, of course. Run the video if you please.'

Sir Alex nodded to his assistant, who switched on the Ministers plasma screen. Stepping back, he pressed the Run button on the remote he held.

The screen flickered for a moment, and then the picture of three masked terrorists appeared. With one hand menacingly resting on the assault rifles strapped across their chests, they were standing in front of a black backcloth decorated with Arab writing. Kneeling in front of the terrorists, their heads slightly bowed was Brigadier Lethbridge and Christina Angelopoulos. Both had deep black circles under their eyes; their faces looked exhausted and spent.

The middle gunman took a half-step forward and spoke,

'We are the soldiers of Al-Qaeda, men of the Al-Amin Martyrs Brigade… Our purpose is to avenge the death of our leader Osama bin Mohammed bin Awad bin Laden, and to send a message to the world. We are willing to die. We welcome death fighting our holy crusade, our Jihad against all un-believers who oppose us.'

Behind the sinister black mask, Youssef smiled cruelly to himself before continuing,

'Tomorrow, at dawn, we will begin executing our hostages, starting with these two miserable wretches. One is a senior British army officer, the other, the daughter of a billionaire. You will see our graphic lesson, when we prove that no-one, anywhere, is safe from our vengeance….'

The girl kneeling in front of the gunmen slumped forward and began to sob. Youssef ignored her,

'When the last of our other thirty prisoners dies, one every hour, we will destroy the building, and take our rightful place in paradise, as martyrs.'

The screen went dead. The Minister's office was filled with silence for a moment, before Sir Henry shook his head. His shoulders stooped as he dropped his head into his hands and spluttered hopelessly,

'This is absolutely bloody outrageous! There's got to be some way to stop these monsters…

# Chapter Thirty

Level 14

Eight hours later

The initial walk-through's were done, and the third full-speed run-through of the assault was complete. Pat stared down at his stopwatch. He grimaced and shook his head,

It's no good, Rover; we are getting in quickly, but the boys aren't taking out the key terrorists fast enough.'

Rover nodded, 'Yeah; I see that,' he rubbed his chin, 'and to make matters worse; we've still got no idea who is holding the trigger for the explosives, or where he is.'

Both men looked distinctly concerned. Blowing the doors and getting in wouldn't be a problem, but in the few seconds of chaotic confusion that would follow, there was no guarantee that they could find, let alone neutralise the terrorist who was holding the central firing device for the explosives they assumed were rigged all around level 42. Pat stared thoughtfully at his old friend,

'We need to have a serious and urgent re-think, Rover. Let's go and check the top-floor plan again, and then have another chat with that architect bloke.'

\* \* \*\*

An hour later, as the SAS assault teams continued their rehearsals, in another more private part of level 14, Pat finished explaining to Brigadier Hunter the problem and hasty adjustment he and Rover had devised to fix their troubled attack plan,

'So you see, boss, if we do it this way, we get the edge we need and stand a much better chance of pulling the job off nice and slick, before the terrorists know what hit them… If it works, friendly casualties will be kept to an absolute minimum, and we won't all get ourselves blown to pieces.'

The Brigadier winced. What they proposed was risky, whichever way he looked at it, but Pat was right, with so little time in hand, there simply wasn't another viable option. Nothing was ever guaranteed on a mission like this, and all three men knew it. There were gaps in Pat's hastily arranged briefing; the Brigadier had questions,

'What about the press helicopters. We don't want them to see what we're up to, do we?'

Pat was ready for that, he answered quickly,

'No boss, you're right. We've got to ground them all before we start the first phase. If we put a couple of police helicopters into the same airspace when the press pull out, no-one should hear or see any difference in the darkness.'

The Brigadier nodded; it made sense. The last thing they wanted was for the terrorists to be tipped off that something was happening,

'All right, I'll get that organised through the Home Office. How many men will you need?'

Pat raised an eyebrow,

'I've given that a bit of thought. A small team would be best, the smaller the better, in fact, as we've got to do this really, really quietly. It's my idea, so I'll lead it of course, and…' his face wore a trace of an ironic smile, 'I have just the two men in mind,' Pat's smile widened, 'both of them definitely owe me one…. it was something they did a couple of weeks ago.'

Brigadier Hunter nodded silently without delving any deeper. When dealing with his tough, incorrigible SAS soldiers, it was sometimes definitely better not to ask…

\* \* \* \*

'*What!...You're fucking joking!*' exclaimed Danny, when Pat explained the change to the plan.

Spike was standing beside his friend open-mouthed, as Pat calmly broke the news,

'Naturally, I can't order you to do this, boys. It's strictly a volunteer mission…

Recovering from his shock, Danny piped up,

'Bloody hell! It sounds more like a suicide mission… Why us then, Pat?

Pat stared hard at them both,

'No Danny, don't worry, you see I'm going as well, and it's definitely not a one-way job, trust me.' His expression softened. 'As to why you two, there're three reasons, boys. Firstly, you two are the best close-range snap-shooters in the Troop.'

Both Danny and Spike nodded as they remembered. What Pat said was true. They had only recently shared a case of beer when the Troop had run a qualifying snap-shoot competition on a high-tech electronic range close to Imber village on Salisbury Plain, using both their MP5 sub-machine guns and back-up browning pistols. Each pair of troopers, cautiously covering each other, had moved through a specially designed urban close-quarter battle range, engaging random man-shaped targets, which appeared suddenly, from behind mocked-up windows and doorways without warning. Magazines were pre-doctored to deliberately cause random weapon stoppages. When a jam happened unexpectedly, back-up pistols had to be quick-drawn and fired instead.

The competition was the culmination, during the last training day at the end of an intense work-up week, before Two Troop picked up the baton once again for London's anti-terrorist cover, seamlessly replacing 'B' Squadron's Seven Troop when their tour of duty ended.

At the time, both Danny and Spike made the most of their high-scoring victory; they'd spent the journey back to London bragging of their quick reactions and uncanny, almost supernatural expertise. At the time, Danny and Spike had both thought it hilarious, repeatedly boasting of their top scores and generally annoying the hell out of the rest of the Troop. Now, they realised, there was a price to pay for their success and excessive bragging. With resignation, both Danny and Spike acknowledged their official top-gun status in Two Troop.

Their sergeant knew he had won the first round, but he had to get their full support. He had no intention of ordering anyone to follow him in; he didn't work that way. His expression changed; Pat looked very serious when Spike said quizzically,

'You said there were three reasons?'

It was Pat's turn to grin; it was time for an injection of old-fashioned, sergeant-style payback,

'Yep. Number two is because I never forget anything, and you two buggers still owe me…'

Both young troopers' expressions changed; they looked instantly confused. Pat ignored their bewilderment. He said something, which immediately explained point number two. Both young troopers winced when he explained,

'Remember your little prank at Chobham, lads?' Pat's face morphed suddenly into a dark scowl,

*'Because I bloody well do!'*

Spike and Danny looked sheepish. Troop sergeants, like God, didn't always take cash as payment.

'Lastly and most seriously, I've worked pretty closely with you two here, and in Africa… I've seen how well you both work under pressure, so listen carefully. What we're going to do is absolutely vital to the success of the whole mission… Look… The truth is, lads, this is going to be bloody difficult to pull off, and I want the two of you guarding my back when we go in.'

Danny and Spike stared at their sergeant, looking both sheepish and flattered. This was the ultimate accolade from one SAS man to another. Putting his life in their hands meant something special to both troopers. It was the ultimate praise from the man they would follow anywhere.

Spike grinned; so did Danny. There was almost nothing more to say. The two troopers locked eyes for a moment in understanding. They nodded to each other before Spike responded for both of them,

OK, Pat, fair enough… *we're in.*'

# Chapter Thirty-One

Following a stormy late-night COBRA meeting in Whitehall, the siege was formally handed over to the SAS. Negotiations had got nowhere, and the Cabinet Ministers knew the clock was counting down towards the first executions, which would begin in the full glare of the worldwide media, in just a few short hours. The death of more British citizens was unanimously considered absolutely unacceptable by the COBRA committee Ministers. Their final decision was made after the Police Commissioner had reluctantly accepted that his officers were powerless to stop the terrorists, and that the only viable option left on the table to avoid another massacre, was to risk everything and authorise the use of deadly force by the SAS.

The go-ahead was issued to Brigadier Hunter. When he arrived back at the Tower, a final briefing was called for the entire SAS assault group at 01.00 hours. The Brigadier had fifty-two SAS soldiers sitting in front of him. Two and Seven Troop were all there, plus an amalgam Twenty-Two Troop made up from a hotchpotch of regular SAS instructors and staff members. There was an eager look on all the men's faces who sat in silence, listening intently as Brigadier Hunter cleared his throat and began,

'Gentlemen, I have just returned from a final COBRA meeting in Whitehall. The government has authorised our assault on Level Forty-Two. They have decreed that they are not prepared to wait until the executions begin, and we have therefore been cleared to breach and assault before the terrorists start butchering any more civilians on British soil….'

There were muffled growls of approval from his audience. To a man, they had been waiting for the order, and now, at last; it came. Brigadier Hunter held up his hand to quell further disturbances. Background noise quickly abated, and he continued,

'Our assault is scheduled to begin at 04.30-hours, local time. I'm perfectly happy that you've done well during the rehearsal's, lads, and that you all know your jobs. When we are finished here, all three Troops will move, on foot via the stairwells, up to the Forming Up Point on level forty. Fifteen minutes before zero hour, each group will move to your final assault positions, and start laying charges on the access points. The three-pronged assault will be initiated by a burst of automatic gunfire from within level forty-two.... OK, before we get down to specifics, are there any questions?'

Someone at the back raised a hand,

'How are we getting someone inside beforehand, boss?'

Brigadier Hunter nodded,

'Good question Taff... Right, listen in.... This is what we're going to do....'

\* \* \* \* \*

The Polish War Memorial is a monument erected to remember the contribution of brave airmen from Poland, who helped the allied cause fighting the Nazis during the Second World War. Just beyond the memorial, the only remaining operational Royal Air Force base on the edge of suburban London – RAF Northolt – nestles between Uxbridge and Greenford, close beside the arterial A40 dual-carriageway, which flows directly into the centre of the capital's heart.

Under the glare of the high ceiling arc lights, Pat, Spike and Danny were standing inside the echoing confines of a small and otherwise deserted aircraft hangar, out on the remote edge of the airfield, far from the prying eyes of those not involved in the secret SAS operation. Outside in the darkness, a hastily stripped-down Augusta Bell helicopter from the RAF's 32 Squadron sat waiting in the darkness. On the Heli-pad, the Augusta's crew had finished their pre-flight checks and were sitting strapped inside the aircraft, waiting for their passengers, and permission from the control tower to start their engines.

Pat finished smearing black camouflage cream over his face and hands. He passed the tube to Spike,'

'Don't forget the back of your neck.'

Pat, Spike and Danny were almost ready. They finished packing their gear and tightening down the last straps. All three were now concentrating on the final part of their preparations, ensuring shiny faces were blackened, weapons were cocked and ready and equipment was firmly attached to their harness rigs, but remained within easy reach.

They had driven at high speed through the night west along the A40, leaving sleeping London behind, less than an hour ago. Pat winced at the tight nip of the biting strap under his crotch. He looked up at his two companions and said,

'Come on, you two, cheer up...'

Pat's cell phone rang. He listened intently to the caller, and then hung up and turned to his two troopers,

'OK, listen in; latest update. The plod's helicopter hasn't detected any sign of movement with their infra-red trackers, so the roof still looks clear. All the security keys to the top machine floors are accounted for.' Pat patted one of his chest pockets, 'so with any luck; the bad guys missed a trick, and we've got the only set of keys for both roof access and the machine floors.

Despite the latest update, serious pre-jump nerves were affecting Danny. He'd never shaken them off since earning his SAS parachute wings at jumps school at Brize Norton. He shook his head, his face filled with foreboding,

'It's no good, Pat. I must be completely barmy to have volunteered for this op. You know jumps frighten the living daylights out of me, especially at night.'

Pat grinned. He understood Danny's concerns; he had never been a fan of parachuting either. He shrugged,

'Don't worry about it, Danny. The Regiments been involved in odd situations before, where parachuting in was the only option. Remember back in the early seventies? Sailing from New York to Southampton, the QE2 liner received a telephoned bomb-threat and a big ransom demand. London took the situation very seriously and contacted Hereford. A combined SAS and SBS bomb-disposal team parachuted into the water beside the liner, in the middle of the Atlantic.' He shrugged, 'One of the team wasn't para-trained, and had to learn what to do on the flight in. It all turned out to be a hoax as it happens, but jumping was the only means to an end.' Pat grinned reassuringly, 'Stop flapping, Danny. It's just another mode of transport. You know it's the only way to get onto the roof of the Tower un-noticed…' Pat glanced at his watch, he was done with reassuring, 'come on, it's time to go. We take off in five minutes.'

As the three men left the hanger and walked towards the blacked-out aircraft, Spike chipped in as the pilot switched on the helicopter's engines. To the accompanying roar and whoosh of the rotor blades, with a broad smirk Spike shouted into his buddy's ear,

'Stop worrying about it, mate. You know as well as I do, whatever happens; the ground will break your fall.'

Weighed down under the burden of his equipment, parachutes and weapons, Danny glared back at his grinning ex-paratrooper mate and yelled miserably,

'Bollocks!'

Despite the noise of the helicopter, Pat heard the exchange. He grinned to himself, but remained silent. He'd had a bad parachuting experience up in the Shetland Islands the previous year, and heartily agreed with Danny. Parachuting, he decided, can seriously damage your health.

\* \* \* \* \*

It was quiet on level forty-two. The lights remained on. The traumatised office workers who had been captured hours before remained crowded together, sitting miserably in the middle of the cleared office. They huddled with each other, exhausted. A few lucky ones slept fitfully, but most found no solace in sleep.

As they would be the first to die as dawn broke, Brigadier Lethbridge and Christina had been separated from the others. Both had been dragged away, and left tied-up and blindfolded in a separate anti-room.

To ensure security, Youssef had arranged guards to stay awake outside in the main office area with the big group of hostages, while the remainder of his men rested after barricading the access doors. One of his Arabs, Mohammed, had been given possession of the trigger, wired to the explosives suspended around the portion of the building they currently occupied. Mohammed's orders were simple; at the first sign of attempted rescue, he was to destroy the entire floor. To Youssef's poisoned mind, it would still be a victory; after all, he decided, that was how Jihad worked. When his man pressed the switch, in that one blinding moment, Mohammed would send the hostages and would-be rescuers to hell, and he and his Muslim martyrs to their just and deserved recompense in paradise.

Unknown to the terrorists as they rested at the top of the building; the heavily armed SAS assault teams had begun to move. They advanced in long single files like ghosts, beginning their journey up multiple stairwells, heading towards pre-ordained forming up points on the fortieth floor.

It would prove a punishing climb for the SAS men, but even burdened with weapons, night-goggles, and body armour, clad in stuffy flameproof boiler suits; it was nothing the men weren't used to. Altogether, they would have to ascend almost four-hundred feet of concrete steps, but the thought didn't faze any one of them. The climb meant nothing compared to the tough speed-march training they did regularly over the rugged Brecon Beacon Mountains in South Wales. To a man, they relished both the challenge and the promised reward of hard-core payback, when the signal finally came to launch the attack….

* * * * *

Isolated and alone in the small side room, Brigadier Lethbridge whispered softly to his terrified companion. He did his best to reassure the poor girl, although he could tell his soothing, gentle words were having little effect; they did nothing to stifle her muffled sobs. Having heard of their fate when morning came, she was convinced she was going to die. The Brigadier secretly admitted to himself that it was a distinct possibility, but he guessed an assault must be imminent when the men he had only recently relinquished were unleashed. He'd been involved in the planning of too many rescue and assault missions during the long years as Special Forces Director, to conclude otherwise. His blindfold felt lose; his captors paid him little attention any more. They seemed to think he was nothing but a terrified and compliant mouse. The Brigadier smiled grimly to himself. His role-playing worked better than expected. It was the terrorist's first serious mistake, and he'd prove it to them when the moment came, if he got half a chance. Brigadier Lethbridge gave up his reassurances and rested his head against the wall behind him. Slowly, he began to rub his head up and down against the plaster, slowly working the blindfold off his head.

* * * * *

When the Augusta took off from Northolt, loaded down with its cargo of three SAS men, the pilot immediately began adding power to the collective and rapidly gained altitude, as he swung the helicopter's nose east towards the capital's commercial heart. Using night-vision goggles, he looked below occasionally as they continued to climb, closely following the silver trail of the A40 carriageway, which snaked away before them and faded into the darkness.

When planning for the assault was underway, the Augusta's engine note was deemed to be closest to the media's aircraft it would replace. The sound of a heavier military helicopter might alert the terrorists, so the smaller Augusta was chosen. The RAF was quickly contacted, and their co-operation was eagerly given. Pat and the other planners were aware of the importance of getting everything right, down to the minutiae of the smallest detail. This operation, they all knew, hinged on detail; it would be the difference between total disaster and absolute success.

The Augusta had been in the air for less than fifteen minutes, when the co pilot glanced over his shoulder into the back of the blacked-out aircraft, where his shadowy passengers sat in silence. He marvelled at their cool nerve.

Catching Pat's eye, the co-pilot held up two fingers. Pat held up his own hand in acknowledgment; it was the pre-arranged signal he had been waiting for. He alerted Spike and Danny by tapping them both on the knee, and then pointed towards the aircraft's side door. Both troopers nodded their understanding and moved awkwardly towards their sergeant as he grasped the door's handle, pulled hard and slid it open.

The sudden rush of cold air from the hissing slipstream, and the much louder roar of the Augusta's engine were almost overpowering inside the cramped passenger cabin. The tension was suddenly palpable within the compartment. Grasping the side-rail tightly, Pat thrust his head outside the aircraft and stared down past the landing skids at the twinkling lights of London's sprawl, far below. He could see little detail, except a brilliant lattice of urban streetlights. Pat and his men didn't deploy their own night goggles yet; wearing bulky vision aids before they landed would invite entanglement and a broken neck, or at best having them ripped from their heads by the rushing slipstream.

The plan was to make just one pass over the top of the old NatWest tower from five thousand feet. It was judged high enough to diffuse the engine's roar from far below, but thanks to meticulous planning, allowed for the Tower's great height of nearly a thousand feet. Dispatching from the helicopter with four thousand feet in hand still allowed just enough time for the SAS men's steerable parachutes to deploy fully, and safely slow their descent towards the tall building's wide, and thankfully, flat roof.

Sitting on the metal floor, his boots resting heavily outside on the aircraft landing skids, Pat's hand remained tightly grasping the handrail. His other rested on the metal D-ring fed through his harness, which would release his chute straight after he jumped. Crouched behind him, Danny and Spike followed Pat's example. Fumbling blindly in the darkness for the D-ring after leaving the aircraft and free-falling at relatively low altitude where every split second counted, was a very, very bad idea.

It had been tempting to order the pilot to hover when the time came for the SAS men to exit the aircraft, but there was a danger from the down wash created by the spinning rotor blades. The powerful down draught could potentially deform a rapidly deploying parachute, and made the option of a high-speed fly-by and clean exit, was considered by Pat and the others, a much safer bet.

His face and body buffeted by the freezing slipstream, Pat was alerted to a one-minute exit when a small light suddenly winked red beside him on the doorway's frame. His troopers saw it too; Spike was OK with it, but Danny's face looked distinctly pale. For him, deafened by the screaming slipstream and growling roar of the engine, the last few moments inside an aircraft were always the worst part of a jump, but each time, overcoming his trembling terror was part of Danny's ultimate buzz. With a growing knot in his stomach and heart racing, Danny licked his dry lips. He tensed and braced his body as best he could, as he prepared to hurl himself after his best mate and sergeant, into the black and sinister void outside.

As the SAS men prepared, the pilot and co-pilot ignored them. They were concentrating intently on the looming cloud bank ahead, and the rolling panorama below. As Kings Cross and St. Pancras railway termini flashed beneath them, the altimeter needle at last flickered steady on five thousand feet. Only a couple of miles away, the unmistakable outline of the tall NatWest tower loomed ghostly white in their night goggles. The tower's roof strobes rhythmically blinked into the night, silently warning of imminent high-rise danger ahead.

On a nod from the pilot, the co-pilot tore his eyes from the hypnotic flashing lights. He flicked his night-goggles up and calmly reached towards a particular switch on the instrument panel above his head. With fingers hovering beside it, he turned towards his captain and waited. Allowing for the northerly crosswind which had sprung up just before Kings Cross, any second now, the pilot would order him to extinguish the red standby light in the back. When it suddenly changed to green, it would instantly send their tough-looking passengers hurtling into the frigid abyss outside.

# Chapter Thirty-Two

Sitting with his back to the wall, Mohammed thought he heard a noise somewhere far above. He wasn't sure if it was the faint whirr of an aircraft, but paid it no mind; it was obviously too far away to be of any importance. With a sneer on his face, he stared coldly at the terrified hostages grouped before him. How simple it would be to send them all to hell; he thought savagely. He looked away from the terrified kafirs and idly regarded the bulky switch in his right hand, and the thin copper wire trailing from it to the ring of deadly explosive charges laid around the room. He smiled to himself. How proud he was, having been given the honour by Youssef, of keeping the trigger safe and ready. He was trusted above the others with their true insurance against attack. Youssef said he must stay awake and alert. He also said the un-believers wouldn't dare attack while he held it. Mohammed regarded the trigger device more closely, and the ring-pull dangling from it. Idly, Mohammed slipped his finger into the ring, and then quickly withdrew it; he remembered his orders and knew it was right to keep the safety-pin firmly in place, to avoid a mistake. He understood Youssef's wisdom when he had ordered it kept where it was. Mohammed smiled smugly to himself as a thrill coursed through him. He held in his hand, the greatest glory of all. It was he who had been trusted to pull the pin and squeeze hard when the time came. By his own hand, he marvelled that the honour of it all. It was him; a simple nobody from a small, run-down refugee camp in Gaza, who would have the glory of killing them all…

In the dark cloudy skies above the City, the Augusta's pilot was almost over the Tower. His aircraft bucked; the crosswind was tricky, but now, he judged was the moment. He glanced at his co-pilot and nodded. The switch clicked over.

In the passenger compartment, red light suddenly flashed to green. Without hesitation, Pat drew himself back, pushed hard with every ounce of strength and launched himself from the aircraft. It was vital to throw his body into the clear air, away from of the danger of the helicopter's landing skids. Pat's stomach heaved as with arms and legs spread wide, he dropped like a stone, feeling the powerful roar and a rush of cold air on his face. A heartbeat behind him, Spike hurled himself out after his sergeant, quickly followed by Danny.

As Pat began to accelerate into the darkness, he yanked hard on his ripcord. The helicopter sped away through the darkness as Spike and Danny dropped behind him and did the same.

Danny always jumped with his eyes tightly shut. He felt the sickening lurch of his body falling. To stabilise himself as he fell, Danny assumed the classic free-fall position, and ripped hard on his own D-ring. His chute began to deploy, slowing his descent and instantly filling with air with a muffled and welcome crack. This might be an unusual deployment, but in parachuting, the flight drills are always the same. Danny's eyes snapped open, and his training took over. He automatically threw his head back to check his canopy. To his relief, he was safely suspended below the steerable oblong wing which had deployed perfectly. Satisfied he was flying a good chute; Danny dropped his head and quickly scanned the immediate area around him. He was happy; the dark sky around him was empty. With no danger of a midair collision with the others, Danny opened his legs and looked downwards.

In the darkness several hundred feet below, sliding silently across the City's lights towards the Tower, Danny saw the unmistakable silhouette of Spike's chute. Below that, was another rectangular canopy. It was time to forget them and the last of his pre-jump nerves, and concentrate on assessing his own drift. Danny forced himself to relax as he fixed his eyes on the strobe lights below, to gauge which way he was drifting. He realised quickly that the crosswind was dragging him off course. He reached up and pulled down hard on one of the steering toggles, turning his chute slightly, compensating early before he wandered irretrievably off track.

Below his two troopers, floating almost serenely through the silent night, Pat had his eyes glued on the middle of the Tower's roof. There were two huge horizontal air-conditioning fans mounted on one side of it. Pat knew he must ignore them and steer clear, because where he eventually landed, the other two would follow. To allow as much space as possible, Pat was aiming to land on the very centre of the broad roof. Spike was supposed to come down a few feet on the left and Danny on his right. At least, that was the plan; Pat thought grimly, as he cursed the swirling wind and pulled down hard again on one of his steering toggles.

During pre-planning, intelligence photographs had revealed the central landing area was the only section of the wide roof clear of danger. Hazards lurked almost everywhere else. Landing on any of the many obstructions in the dark was unthinkable. There were large microwave communications dishes mounted next to one of the fans. On the other side, besides the tall masts of a high-tech signal array, surmounted with the flashing strobes, was a solid wedge-shaped structure containing the access door and stairwell they must use to access the first of the maintenance floors beneath. Pat had to land in the middle of the roof, or there were going to be problems.

Spike was struggling to follow the line of Pat's decent. In order to help Danny stay on track, it was vital he maintained his direction above and behind the stack leader. An old hand at free-fall, the current decent held no demons for the ex-paratrooper, but as middlemen in the rapidly descending stack, he knew he must stay focused on Pat's parachute floating below, and follow it exactly so Danny could stay tightly in line with them both.

Pat guessed he had less than five hundred feet of clear air left beneath him, but as usual, it was proving almost impossible to judge height accurately in the dark. It didn't help that the wind kept picking up, buffeting him harder the lower he descended towards the roof. Pat quickly gave up making delicate adjustments; he was pulling down hard on both toggles, constantly trying to keep his chute under control and stay on course. Hanging tight in his harness, Pat was now fully turned and steering directly into the wind, but to his horror, as he descended, he realised he was being forced inexorably towards the huge spinning fans.

Spike felt the gusting wind beginning to batter him too, as he watched Pat being blown off the target. He couldn't do anything to help, but Spike had more height, and therefore, more time to overcompensate and avoid disaster.

Above them both, Danny had a grandstand view of the unfolding drama below. He quickly followed Spike's example of compensating his own drifting flight path.

With less than one hundred feet above the Tower, Pat struggled frantically with the steering controls of his dangerously flapping canopy. If he relaxed and under-steered for a split-second, he'd be chopped to pieces by the spinning blades, but if he over-steered, he could well be blown off the roof altogether. Pat knew panic would kill him as sure as the whirring fans. He fought to clear his mind. He had only one slim chance to avoid disaster, and at best, it was highly dangerous.

Fifty feet now, Pat's hand groped for the left-hand Capewell. It was the quick-release device sown into his harness, which would release one-half of the suspension cords separating him and the chute.

Twenty feet now, he was drifting slowly over the middle of the fans.

'*Wait!*' he thought desperately, '*Not Yet!*

The wind dropped suddenly. Pat was less than ten feet from the outer sweep of the fan, drifting the last few feet towards the narrow strip between the hissing tips of the air-con blades and the abyss beyond the edge of the Tower's roof.

'*NOW!*'

Pat pulled the Capewell hard and his chute collapsed, losing its integrity instantly. Dumping all the trapped air it held, the canopy flapped vertically like a torn ship's sail as Pat dropped beneath it. In the two seconds he had left before he hit the narrow strip of roof separating him from an eight-hundred foot sheer drop, he pulled his legs together, bent them slightly and jammed his clenched fists over his face, with elbows tucked hard into his chest.

Pat hit the flat, stony asphalt roof hard, feet-first with a splash, but he'd been lucky. His exact timing, tight landing position and not least his Kevlar helmet was all that saved him from death or serious injury.

His collapsed chute fluttered down silently around him.

Still slightly dazed from the concussion of his helmet hitting the roof as he rolled, Pat shook his head, then realising the danger, desperately snatched at the collapsed chute before it refilled with air and cascaded down the side of the building. Kneeling in a puddle of stagnant water trapped on the roof's wet asphalt, he pulled at the tangle of para-cord rigging lines, harness and canopy. It took only seconds to gather it all together and when he'd finished Pat knelt on it as he tried his best to slow his ragged breathing and hammering heartbeat. In the middle of the roof beyond the fans, he was relieved to see first Spike, and then Danny flare their chutes at the last moment and make perfect landings in the centre of the roof, exactly where they should be. After Pat gave them a reassuring wave, both troopers began shucking off their harnesses; quickly gathering and bundling their chutes into tight balls, as they were trained to do.

Danny was closest, and reached his sergeant first. He saw how close Pat was to the edge of the blades. With a gulp, he hissed his concern into the darkness,

*'Blimey, you OK, Pat?'*

Pat didn't feel much like conversation as he stood up. He replied in a low whisper,

*'Yeah,yeah....peachy… I'm fine!'*

As Pat retrieved his pack and weapons from the tangle of his discarded harness, his mind whirled. No bones broken, but there'd be plenty of bruises. It might be a means to an end; he thought bitterly, but the truth was painfully clear. Through clenched teeth, he muttered savagely to himself in the darkness,

*'Jesus, I fucking hate parachuting!'*

# Chapter Thirty-Three

To the background whirr of the spinning blades, Danny gently drenched oil onto each of the two hinges of the steel access door. Either side of him, Pat and Spike swept the roof with their night goggles and the muzzles of their guns. Pat wasn't too worried about being bumped by the enemy on the roof. Like the famous Iranian Embassy siege in 1980, if there had been anyone up there, they would have known it by now.

Danny knelt and dripped the last hinge with oil. Satisfied there would be no agonising squeak when the door was gently pulled open, he stood up. Pat reached into his pocket, withdrew security's master key, liberated from the ground floor office, and passed it to Danny. Pouring oil over it, Danny cautiously inserted it into the top lock. He waited a moment for the oil to spread inside the mechanism and then turned the key slowly. He was rewarded with a faint click. Satisfied it was unlocked; Danny soundlessly withdrew the key, re-oiled it and gently inserted it into the second lock at the bottom of the steel door. He tentatively turned the key, but almost immediately felt resistance.

Danny swore softly and increased his grip. He turned the key again, this time using more force. The lock suddenly gave under the increased pressure, and the key turned with a much louder click. Still running on adrenaline, senses on the highest alert, all three SAS men ducked involuntarily. Pat scowled at Danny, who shrugged apologetically. Pat put his ear to the steel door and listened, but heard nothing from inside. There would be no flash-bangs hurled in; this must be a strictly covert, silent entry. Grasping the handle, Pat checked to see his men were ready. Satisfied when they both nodded, he stood to one side and slowly pulled it open, revealing an empty stairwell descending into darkness. With a nod to the others, Pat went first, taking great care with each step as he crept down each concrete step in turn. At the bottom of the well, was another solid fire door.

After Danny had prepared the hinges and unlocked it, the door swung silently open. Danny darted quickly into the right as Spike went left. There was no other movement inside, only the hum of machinery, filling the wide chamber. Pat followed them in. It was pitch black in the windowless, air-con machine room, but the men's helmet mounted night-vision goggles bathed everything in a cold green glow, making even the smallest detail visible.

Pat swept his arm forward to signal his troopers to begin their search. It was imperative to secure the machine room first, and confirm that there were no surprises. Among the jungle of heavy machinery, engines and control panels, a lone gunman could hide, or a booby trap might be set.

Pat waited patiently for the trooper's sweep to finish. When they both returned and signalled all clear, he reached up to his throat mike and whispered,

'*Alpha One, this is Charlie One. First level secure. Over.*'

The reply from the assault HQ far below came quickly and crackled softly in his earpiece,

'*Roger that, Out.*'

Pat pointed towards the steel security door leading to the stairwell and next floor below. He motioned Spike and Danny to follow him. They were getting closer now. It was imperative to take their time, and move absolutely soundlessly. Despite the hum of the huge air-conditioners, inadvertently brushing against an abandoned coffee cup left on the edge of a control console would have disastrous effects on the operation's outcome when it hit the floor with a loud splintering crash. Sub-machine guns pulled tightly into their shoulders, the SAS men ghost walked slowly to the door, keeping well clear of any obstructions.

Danny began his practiced routine of oiling the hinges. Pat listened for several minutes with his ear to the door. Again, he heard nothing to warn of ambush or discovery.

As they prepared to enter, it seemed to Pat that the lack of booby traps meant the terrorists had assumed there was no threat from above and hadn't bothered to, or perhaps couldn't, enter either of the machinery levels, but whatever the truth was, he was taking nothing for granted and maintained his guard against sudden ambush.

The next deserted floor contained the elevator cable drums and their powerful winding engines. Below them, concealed elevator shafts disappeared down into the dizzying darkness. The lift mechanisms were silent and unmoving, ever since the police had created a cordon and sealed off the tower from the outside world.

The SAS men continued their sweep, rolling their feet, keeping their breathing shallow and even. Danny silently oiled hinges as they came to each new door. Machinery still hummed from above. The electrical supply remained on. It was a facet of the assault plan and would be another weapon, of a sort, when the time came.

The sweep was almost complete. In the last partitioned section, on the other side of the building, Level forty-three housed four huge metal water tanks, which provided a high pressure gravity feed of clean fresh water to the entire tower. Pat's eyes narrowed as he scanned the ghostly green glow around him. He glanced down at his watch. It was just after 3. 30am. Time was getting short and dawn would break in seventy-five minutes. Pat had been following their progress using a small floor plan. He tapped the map and nodded to himself. This was the area, among the water tanks, where they must begin the search.

If the initial intelligence picture and his discussions with the architect were accurate, and Pat prayed they were, somewhere just below them was the unsuspecting terrorists, their recently retired Brigadier who was scheduled to die in just over an hour, and thirty-odd thoroughly miserable and absolutely terrified civilian hostages who would share the same fate if Pat, and his two troopers failed.

Pat reached for his throat mike again. They were too close to the enemy now for words. Pat rapidly depressed the send switch five times and received five clicks in his earpiece by return, acknowledging his message that HQ understood the second level had been fully searched and secured.

Gently tapping his MP5, Pat got Spike and Danny's attention. He pointed first to his eye, then down at the floor. His men understood their sergeant's hand signals. It was time to begin…

Spike knelt down, carefully placed his sub-machine gun on the floor and opened the small pack attached to his hip. Like ghosts, Pat and Danny searched out the floor's electrical access panels, which were clearly marked on Pat's utility diagram. Spike stayed where he was and began quietly assembling various stainless-steel items together. It didn't take long. His practiced hands quickly held a fully functional medical endoscope. At one end of the device, at the tip of its thin, long and highly flexible shaft was a mini-camera, no thicker than a fat knitting needle. At the other end, Spike attached a small, compact viewing screen. Assembly complete, he switched off the LED light beside the endoscope's camera and then panned the camera around the darkened room. Without an inbuilt image intensifier, the screen remained black until the camera swept the tall glass windows. Spike smiled with satisfaction as pinpricks of the city's lights scudded suddenly across the tiny screen. The lack of an infra-red addition to the device was a nuisance; there was an updated version coming to Special Forces, but that hadn't even begun trials yet. With only the standard medical version available, it was another reason why it had been arranged that both power and the lights downstairs would remain switched on.

Pat crept back to Spike, and tapped him lightly on the shoulder. Spike half-turned and gave his sergeant the thumbs-up. Pat nodded and beckoned Spike to follow him over to where Danny was crouched, waiting beside a newly exposed small oblong hole in the floor. While Spike had prepared the endoscope, Danny and Pat had located the first likely access panel and silently removed its cover.

Pat pointed into the hole; Spike understood. Using his night goggles, Spike leant forward and peered cautiously into it. There was a maze of pipes and electrical wires concealed under the floor where he knelt. The wires were tied in bunches, suspended above the next level's false ceiling; Spike ignored the transit wires. He was intent on searching through them for the point where the nearest light fitting was, and where its power cables disappeared through the ceiling below. He quickly located the closest one. Pulling himself back from the hole, he reached to one side and picked up the endoscope. Very deliberately, Spike lay down flat again, with his chest on the lip of the open-access panel. He took a couple of deep breaths and slowly lowered the device into the hole. Spike carefully guided the camera tip towards the port where the power cables disappeared vertically into the false ceiling. When he reached the point, hardly daring to breathe, he gently lowered the tip of the camera into the generous space left behind decades earlier by the original construction workers, which would allow future upgrades to the building's lighting systems, during the long projected lifetime of the groundbreaking NatWest Tower.

Spike looked up and shook his head at Pat. All he had seen was empty floor space.

It was Pat's turn to curse silently. Scattered around level forty-three, he and Danny had located five other access panels to remove and explore, but time was moving inexorably, and beginning to run out. Moving quietly was a slow business, and ate hungrily into the time they had left before the executions began, but the SAS men had no choice, to remain undetected they had to take things agonisingly slowly.

Pat had to take his best guess at the most likely access panel, which would expose the position of the man holding the trigger. He chose one of the furthest from the stairwells and elevators. It made sense; he thought. The terrorists would, no doubt, be expecting an all-out assault, and it was logical to be as far from a possible breach as they could get. Pat pointed to where he wanted Spike to go next.

As Spike began to lower the camera into the next port almost beside an exterior wall, he offered up a silent prayer they would get lucky this time. Chewing his lip with concentration, he steered the camera into the next electrical expansion port above the light fitting. As the camera screen flared, Spike stared at the image below and swallowed hard. He pulled back almost immediately. Spike spun towards Pat. Heart pumping with excitement; Spike lifted his hand to his shoulder. He clenched his fist and rested it for a moment on the top of his shoulder, then he quickly opened his fingers and spread just three back onto the top of the same shoulder. Pat and Danny understood the signal instantly. Indicating rank by silent hand signal was a basic soldiering skill. NCOs wore rank on their arm; officers wore rank on their shoulders. A fist and three fingers specifically represented only one type of officer. Spike's hand signal was a real bombshell to the other two SAS men. It could mean only one thing… he'd found Brigadier Lethbridge.

Spike hadn't finished. Keeping his goggles fixed on Pat, he held up two fingers, and then gave a thumb down, as he rapidly shook his head. Pat understood. The signal meant the brigadier plus one, with no terrorists in the room. Pat guessed the other person with the Brigadier must surely be the little Greek girl.

During his final briefing, Pat and his men were told that they must save the girl at all costs; these were orders passed down, straight from the top. Pat wasn't impressed. He didn't give such a priority a second thought during a rescue mission; there wasn't time. He'd try to save everyone, without specific and completely un-necessary instructions, direct from some remote politician who was sitting in safety, miles from any possible danger.

Crouched in the darkness, Pat quickly re-thought his plan. His mind made up, he pointed to the next likely access panel. Spike nodded, and moved off silently to begin his search afresh. Pat lingered. He was worried and had to think fast. If they managed to nail the trigger man, the explosives would be neutralised as the assault went in, but there was a very real danger that in the confusion, one of the terrorists might break away and execute the brigadier, and the girl before the assault team could stop him. Pat couldn't risk it by abandoning them; but there was always a danger that the terrorists would choose the next few minutes to check on their most prized hostages, but it was a risk Pat had to take. There was only one thing Pat could do.

He lay down flat beside the open floor panel and rolling onto his side, drew his pistol from its thigh holster and laid it beside him. Reaching into his pocket, he took out the small clasp knife he habitually carried, and placed it beside the Browning. He looked up. Spike and Danny were engrossed at the next port. Pat stood up and began searching. He struck lucky. He picked up a small roll of discarded electrical wire and walked cautiously back to the panel above the brigadier and the girl. Kneeling again, he tied the Browning and the knife together, and then lay down once again.

Pat leaned into the well under the floor and reached for the nearest polystyrene panel from the false ceiling. He licked his lips as his fingernails found its edge. Very slowly and quietly, hardly daring to breathe, Pat manoeuvred up one side just a few inches, gently easing it away from its supporting aluminium framework. He could see the top of the brigadier's head. Pat opened the panel a little wider. He felt his heart pounding as he carefully lifted the panel clear of its supporting frame, and gently placed it to one side. There was still no movement from either hostage. The girl's head was resting on the brigadier's shoulder; she seemed asleep. Pat cursed silently; he must get their attention somehow, without alerting the terrorists. He reached across and lightly scratched his fingers across the discarded plastic panel.

Brigadier Lethbridge stiffened at the faint noise above him. He looked up, and saw Pat's blackened face staring down at him, with his finger pressed to his lips. Lethbridge couldn't hold back a savage grin. Relief flooded him; he instantly knew the SAS were coming.

Pat felt for the bundle he'd tied to the wire. He carefully swung it into the opening he'd made. The Brigadier saw the pistol and nodded enthusiastically. The girl stirred. Brigadier Lethbridge shushed her to silence and nodded upwards. She gasped when she saw Pat grinning down at her. Pat began lowering the swinging pistol and knife to a point just behind the brigadier's back.

It took precious seconds for the Brigadier to grope blindly for the bundle and begin unravelling Pat's knot. His fingers were numb and stiff. After minutes, which seemed like hours, at least, Pat felt the wire go slack. Brigadier

Lethbridge nodded up at Pat, as his eyes narrowed. His drawn face creased as the wolfish grin returned.

As Pat withdrew the wire, Danny crept over to him; he too was grinning in triumph; obviously, he'd found something. Danny made a fist and pumped his thumb up and down, to confirm they had found the trigger-man. He pointed back towards Spike. Pat nodded and checked his watch. They had less than forty-five minutes before daybreak. He stared back into the well for the last time. Pointing to his watch, he opened and closed his fist twice. The assault teams would have been in place for some time now, patiently waiting for Pat's signal. They wouldn't move until they got it. The Brigadier understood Pat's new gesture; the assault would begin in ten minutes. Pat gave him a last thumbs-up, and then carefully replaced the panel. Satisfied everything was back in place as it had been before, he slowly heaved himself to his feet.

# Chapter Thirty-Four

Following Danny, Pat crept slowly over to where Spike lay, and knelt down beside him. Spike looked up, and repeated Danny's gesture with his thumb tapping the top of his fist. He pointed into the open inspection port and nodded his head. Pat nodded back to confirm his understanding. The assault would begin from here, but he must give the SAS assault teams their final standby. Pat reached up to his throat-mike and clicked ten times, paused for a second and then clicked another ten. Moments passed with just the faint crackle of static in his earpiece. Suddenly, he received the same ten clicks to confirm HQ understood. Ten minutes, and counting...

Two floors below, the message was silently passed to each SAS man in turn. Respirators were quietly withdrawn from hip pouches and slipped over blackened faces, and night-goggles refitted. Flash-bang stun grenades were withdrawn from pouches, and CS gas bombs were readied. Frame charges the teams would use to gain entry had already been propped against the doors. Only the bare minimum of plastic explosive was used in their preparation, the doors must go in, but there were civilians inside.


On level forty-two, one of the Somali guards yawned and stretched. He glanced up at the clock on the wall. His orders were to wake Youssef thirty minutes before dawn. The Arab leader wanted everything ready with the camera switched on and the Internet link live, before the first beheading began.

The exhausted hostages sitting huddled in the middle of the wide office floor, cast furtive glances towards the stretching Somali, their dark-circled eyes filled with dread. The guard knew he had five minutes before he must wake his leader. He licked his lips eagerly as he glared savagely down at the fearful hostages. Slowly, he raised his AK to terrify them further. There were frightened whimpers from among the huddle. A cruel grin erupted across his face as he saw them ripple; shrinking away from him, trying to make themselves small and un-noticed. He continued to sweep his weapon's muzzle across them, as if decided which one cowing prisoner to shoot first. Breathing deeply, he exalted. What power he had been given over them, he could smell their rank, abject fear…

Pat stared at the endoscope screen closely. Spike was right. Almost directly below, on the brightly lit forty-second floor, one of the terrorists was sitting with his back against the wall. Beside him, Pat could clearly see a dark trailing wire. In the Tango's hand, he held what must be the trigger. Pat glanced at his watch. Two minutes. He carefully lifted the endoscope away, and passed it slowly back to Spike with a confirming nod. Pat removed his night goggles and replaced the device with his respirator. Spike and Danny did the same.

Pat decided it right that he took the shot. He didn't doubt for a second that either of his men was capable of making it, but ultimately, Pat knew it was his responsibility. He'd got them this far, and everything hinged on killing the trigger-man. If the man's brain stem was cut instantly by Pat's bullets, the nerve connections between brain and central nervous system in his spine would be severed. Unless he was exactly on target, the trigger-man's body would spasm in its death throes, his hands twitching into a spontaneous reflex of a muscle tightening grip. he knew if he missed by a millimetre, there would be a cataclysmic explosion.

Pat glanced again at his watch. One minute to go. He heard movement and muffled voices below. The tone was calm; Pat didn't think they'd been rumbled. Ignoring the sounds, he hissed softly at Spike. The trooper understood. He lent past his sergeant and groped for the ceiling tile directly below. When his fingers found it, they traced their way to the nearest edge. Confident he could easily lift the tile away from the suspended framework; Spike gently hissed back at Pat.

Lifting his MP5 into his shoulder, Pat pointed the sub-machine gun's muzzle down into a vertical position. He felt it lightly touch the tile. Pat pulled himself up a few inches so that Spike could lift the plastic sheet clear. Very, very softly, he whispered to the man lying close beside him,

'Now!'

Spike tensed momentarily. Gently, very slowly, he began to pull the ceiling tile up and away from the frame. Inch by inch, as the gap widened, Pat saw the top of the trigger-man's head, almost directly below him. His finger slowly curled around the MP5 trigger as his eyes narrowed to slits inside his respirator. Taking careful aim, he gently took up the trigger's slack, squeezed and fired….

To the terrified hostages sitting on the floor, everything seemed to happen at once. One moment they collectively felt a huge surge of relief as the black terrorist stopped the torture of threatening them with his gun. As he turned away to wake his leader, there was a deafening staccato burst of machine-gun fire from above. Sitting over by the wall, some of the hostages saw one of the terrorist's head explode in a spray of blood and brains. The lights went out, and before any of their captors could react, there were blinding flashes and thunderous explosions all around the terrified civilians, quickly followed by more, even brighter and louder bangs. Deafened and dazzled by the stun grenades, none of the occupants saw or heard the hissing CS tear gas grenades flying into the wide room. It all seemed to happen in a heartbeat. There were terrified screams, and gruff shouted orders bellowed through the dark,

'STAY DOWN!… STAY DOWN!', and then more rapid machine-gun fire.

In the darkness and swirling tear gas, illuminated only by bright flashes of SAS gunfire, the coughing terrorists were gripped by feral panic. This was not the promised paradise; these were the burning fires of hell. One moment they were invincible lords and masters in their impregnable castle in the sky; the next, they were being riddled with bullets and slaughtered like goats.

Unable to see in the dark, several Somalis' fired blindly as they staggered haphazardly backwards away from the gunfire and chaos. They stood out starkly in the SAS men's night goggles; perfect targets, they were machine-gunned and cut down with ruthless efficiency. Every man in the assault teams had watched the CCTV footage when the terrorists had first arrived; they were in no mood to show the slightest hint of mercy to the fleeing murders outlined squarely in their iron gun sights.

One Somali broke away, followed by another. Both managed only a few paces before they were hit by multiple streams of flying lead. Long bursts of hot 9mm bullets hit them simultaneously in the chest; one dropped to the floor like a stone; the other spun crazily through a shattered exterior plate-glass wall; the riddled body disappeared into the cold abyss outside.

Youssef and his two remaining Arabs had been sleeping in an adjoining office with the video camera and Internet equipment. The explosions and gunfire woke them. They frantically groped and scrabbled around in the confusion of darkness for their discarded weapons.

Realising his mission suddenly lay in ruins, and his defence was in tatters, Youssef screamed at them,

*'Get to Mohammed, you must fire our explosives… kill them all!'*

As he shouted, one of his men groped blindly for the door handle. He found it, stood up and opened it just a crack. The gunfire was getting closer and louder. Muzzle flashes sparked like distant lightning in the empty corridor outside.

'I… I see nothing, Youssef, only darkness,' he hissed desperately,

Youssef fumed. The Kafir dogs had tricked them, but he swore to himself; he would be revenged. He hissed back at his man standing by the door,

'Mohammed was outside somewhere to the right. Follow the wall until you find him. If he is dead, find the trigger and send them all to hell.'

Stunned by the ferocious onslaught which had still only been running for seconds, momentarily forgetting his fanaticism, the man by the door hesitated,

'You… you want me to go out… *there?'*

With shrieking screams echoing and vicious raking bursts of gunfire hammering out of sight all around them, Youssef spat towards the chink of dimly lit doorway and raised his AK,

'Go now, or by the Prophet, I will kill you myself!'

Taking a tighter grip on his own AK, Youssef's accomplice believed him; he knew this was no idle threat. He grunted something and reluctantly slipped through the open door. As he disappeared, something else occurred to Youssef. His eyes glittering dangerously, he snarled at the outline of the remaining man beside him,

'Come; we will take our revenge on the unbelievers. If that fool fails, at least we can kill the English dog, and that little Greek whore…'

# Chapter Thirty-Five

In the deserted conference room, holding the Browning pistol, Brigadier Lethbridge crouched down under the long mahogany table which dominated it. Beneath the table, resting against one of its thick ornately carved legs, Christina stared fearful back at him, and whispered,

'What will happen to us, Charlie?'

Keeping his voice low and his eyes on the door, the brigadier smiled reassuringly,

'Nothing will happen, Christina. We will be saved soon. Then you can go back to your father, safe and well.'

Beneath a mop of dirty, unkempt hair, the teenager managed a half smile across her tear-stained face. She trusted this kind man; he had been her only friend for the last few days, and she didn't know what she would have done without his support and reassurance. Shivering, she eyed the big ugly gun in the brigadier's hand nervously,

'Will you kill the bad men, Charlie?'

The brigadier's eyes wrinkled into a gentle smile,

'I hope it won't come to that Christina, but I will use it if I have to.'

The girl nodded in silence. Brigadier Lethbridge had moved her from the tiny room where they had been held. The thin door splintered outwards when he put his broad shoulder to it, as soon as he heard the first gunfire and explosions. Being trapped in a confined space was not the best place to be when the SAS made an assault. Fearing a breakaway by some of the terrorists, particularly their weasel-faced leader, the brigadier had quickly led the petrified girl along the dark echoing corridor, and ducked into the conference room where he hoped he could hide her. He was about to say more to reassure the frightened girl, when he heard the door burst open. Keeping his head below the level of the polished table top, the brigadier's finger flew to his lips. Christina's eyes were wide with fear, but she obeyed and remained silent.

Brigadier Lethbridge had hoped to hear an English accent, but to his dismay, all he heard was rapidly spoken Arabic,

'Search the room, they can't have gone far.'

It was all the warning, he needed. Lethbridge felt his hand tighten around the butt of the Browning. In the darkness, it was difficult to see much, but he saw the blur of a man's legs walking cautiously down one side of the table towards where they were hiding. In the brigadier's mind, there was only one thing he could do...

Snapping up into a half-crouch, Brigadier Lethbridge raised the pistol in a two-handed grip, aimed at the visible centre of the grey mass moving towards him and rapidly fired two shots. There was a scream, followed almost immediately by the sound of a body falling limply to the ground, and the clatter of a weapon landing beside it. Swinging the pistol to his right, Lethbridge loosed off two more rounds towards the door, where he spied a more indistinct second shape.

Youssef had snarled with fury when he found the splintered door and the captive's room empty. The volume of gunfire around the building had diminished considerably in the last few moments, as the SAS searched the rooms and corridors, firing long raking bursts as they mopped up the last of the Somalis. Knowing that time was running out, and their attackers would be on him any moment, Youssef immediately began searching the dark, deserted rooms along the corridor. When Ali opened the third door, Youssef ordered him in. There were sudden flashes from a gun as two shots rang out. Ali was hit. Two more shots came from the other end of the room. The first missed his head by inches, the second smashed into the wooden butt of the AK he held across his chest, sending it spinning from his hands.

With a curse, the Hamas commander stumbled backwards, tripped and fell heavily into the empty corridor outside. As he tried to stand up, his head snapped involuntarily to one side; he heard something. It was voices shouting orders in English. He desperately glanced around for an avenue of escape, as there was a fresh burst of gunfire, much louder than before. More orders echoed from the hidden end of the corridor; they were louder too. Beams of light suddenly splashed against the far wall as dark, darting shadows eddied and mixed among them. His breathing ragged, Youssef wiped his hand across his dry lips. Without a weapon in his hand, there was only one way left to gain his rightful place in paradise. Reaching into his jacket pocket, he withdrew the grenade he had been saving just in case things went wrong. At least, he thought; he could still use it to kill.

Youssef's finger curled around the grenade's safety ring, attached to its pin. His eyes narrowed as he chewed on his bottom lip while he waited. The voices were clearer now; they were just around the corner, almost into the corridor where he stood. He tensed. Still gripping the grenade tightly, he pulled the pin out sharply with an audible click. He was concentrating so hard, he failed to see movement beside him until it was too late. Having left the pistol with the girl, unarmed. Brigadier Lethbridge launched himself towards the terrorist, his shoulder slamming Youssef heavily against the opposite wall. The impact knocked the grenade from the terrorist leader's hand. Fizzing loudly, it bounced backwards and came to rest behind a solid planter mounted against the far glass wall. Moments later, the grenade exploded in a cloud of black smoke with a deafening crash and bright sheet of flame.

Brigadier Lethbridge was first to his feet. Rage and hatred of the leader of men who had murdered his wife overcame him. He landed a savage, vicious punch against the side of Youssef's head, which sent the terrorist sprawling down the dark, carpeted corridor towards the smoke and shattered glass wall. Dazed by the blow, Youssef didn't have time to fend off the rain of blows which followed. In the gloom, he felt powerful hands gripping his collar. Dragging him upright, Lethbridge lifted the terrorist clean off his feet, and held him just inches from his furious face. His attacker's wild eyes were bright with mad, uncontrolled hatred. Youssef didn't understand what was happening, his prisoner was a beaten mouse…

Flecks of spittle spraying from his mouth, the Englishman snarled,

'This is for my wife, *you bastard!*'

Suddenly, his eyes flicked away from the terrorist, towards the gaping maw of the shattered glass wall. The madman grinned. In that moment, Youssef realised what was about to happen. He screamed in terror at something he was powerless to stop. Struggling frantically, he felt himself swung to one side and then launched into the cold night air. Still screaming shrilly, he felt the terrifying lurch of powerlessness and falling, as he began plummeting towards the concrete, over eight-hundred feet below…

Lethbridge was on his knees, when the SAS men reached him. Pat, Danny and Spike had climbed down, and joined the assault team as they made a final sweep for surviving terrorists. The grenade had exploded moments before they rounded the last corner. They had watched in silence during the few moments it had taken for their ex-brigadier to deal with Youssef.

Looking up, Lethbridge saw he was surrounded by his own kind at last; the tough SAS. Breathing heavily, he growled,

'Unforgivable… lost my temper, I'm afraid…' he shook his head, 'my poor wife; you see?'

Behind his respirator, Pat grinned, and said,

'No boss, you don't understand… Mrs Lethbridge is alive and well… she's downstairs.'

The brigadier face changed from sorrow to confusion,

What?… What's that you say?'

Two troopers were half-carrying Christina from the adjacent room as Pat gently rested his gloved hand on his ex-boss's shoulder. Reassuringly, he said quietly,

'She's still a bit banged up from when they kidnapped you,' Pat snorted suddenly at the memory, 'but honest, boss, if we'd let her, she'd have come in tooled up with the boys, to rescue you…'

THE END

# Epilogue

When the SAS returned to their base in Chelsea, equipment was quickly stowed away, and weapons cleaned. When everything was done, every man naturally gravitated to the bar. It wasn't formal, or pretty, but it was a tradition to celebrate a victory. Ten cases of champagne had arrived from a grateful Prime Minister, and beer flowed. As bottles and glasses were emptied, the smiling brigadier was loudly cheered, and naturally, once again, became the Regiment's guest of honour, once, that is, he had been privately and happily reunited with his loving wife, Edith.

Like everyone else, Pat drank too much. He was sitting comfortably in a corner with a crowd of his own men. Spike had found his voice, and was singing a bawdy ballad, about two prostitutes, a bag of carrots and an ostrich feather. There were hoots of laughter around him from the tough men listening to each outrageous verse, but Danny didn't seem to be joining in. Pat noticed, lowered his glass and said quietly,

'What's up, Danny?'

Danny slowly placed his own glass down on the table and stared hard at his sergeant. Making his mind up to speak his mind, with a sigh, he said,'

'We beat the living shit out of those bastards today, Pat, but it's not over, is it?'

Knowing the truth of it, Pat momentarily matched both Danny's mood and his expression of deep concern. He shrugged with resignation, and shook his head,

'No mate, not even close to being over. I wish it wasn't true, but to be honest; I think over here in the UK, this is just the beginning….'

Also by David Black

# The Great Satan

Shadow Squadron #1

Introducing SAS Sgt Pat Farrell and the men of the Special Forces Shadow Squadron.

In The Great Satan, the first of his compelling new Shadow Squadron series, author David Black has produced his own fictional nightmare scenario: What if the Iraqi weapons that were said to be dismantled in the late 1990s included the ultimate WMD? And what if the deposing of Saddam Hussein left one of his most ruthless military leaders still at large, and actively seeking a customer for Iraq's only nuclear bomb?

Published on Amazon in Kindle Format & Paperback.

http://www.david-black.co.uk

Also by David Black

# Dark Empire

Shadow Squadron #2

In the second of the thrilling SAS Shadow Squadron series, Sgt. Pat Farrell and his men are back in action, in DARK EMPIRE.

Pat and his reserve SAS Troop are on a training mission in Kenya, when they are suddenly ordered into the heart of Africa, on what should be a straightforward humanitarian rescue mission.

Unfortunately, nothing is straightforward on the Dark Continent. Pat and his men quickly find themselves trapped, deep inside the primitive, war-ravaged Congo. Hunted by Congolese government forces and a savage legion of drug-crazed guerrillas, things don't always go to plan...even for the SAS!

Published on Amazon in Kindle Format & Paperback.

http://www.david-black.co.uk

Also by David Black

# Playing for England

What drives a man, even to want to join the reserve SAS? - The famous British Special Forces Regiment whose selection process boasts more than a 90% failure rate.

David Black's book - Playing for England gives the reader a fascinating first-hand insight into the rigours of the selection and training process of those few men who earn the privilege of wearing the SAS Regiment's sandy beret and winged dagger cap badge.

Published on Amazon in Kindle Format & Paperback.

http://www.david-black.co.uk

Also by David Black

# EAGLES of the DAMNED

It was autumn in the year AD 9. The summer campaigning season was over. Centurion Rufus and his battle-hardened century were part of three mighty Roman Legions returning to the safety of their winter quarters beside the River Rhine. Like their commanding General, the Centurion and his men suspected nothing. Little did they know, but the entire Germania province was about to explode...

Lured into a cunning trap, three of Rome's mighty Legions were systematically and ruthlessly annihilated, during seventy-two hours of unimaginable terror and unrelenting butchery. They were mercilessly slaughtered within the Teutoburg, a vast tract of dark and forbidding forest on the northernmost rim of the Roman Empire.

Little could they have imagined, before they were brutally cut down, their fate had been irrevocably sealed, years earlier, by their own flawed system of provincial governance, and a rabid traitor's overwhelming thirst for vengeance. But how could such a military catastrophe have ever happened to such a well-trained and superbly equipped army? This is their story...

Published on Amazon in Kindle Format & Paperback.

http://www.david-black.co.uk

Also by David Black

# Siege of Faith

The Chronicles of Sir Richard Starkey #1

Far to the East across the sparkling waters of the great Mediterranean Sea, the formidable Ottoman Empire was secretly planning to add to centuries of expansion. Soon, they would begin the invasion and conquest of Christian Europe.

But first, their all-powerful Sultan, Suleiman the Magnificent knew he must destroy the last Christian bastion which stood in the way of his glorious destiny of conquest. The Maltese stronghold... garrisoned and defended by the noble and devout warrior monks of the Knights of St. John of Jerusalem...

A powerful story of heroism, love and betrayal set against the backdrop of the cruel and terrible siege of Malta which raged through the long hot summer of 1565. The great Caliph unleashed a massive invasion force of 40,000 fanatical Muslim troops, intent on conquering Malta before invading poorly defended Christian Europe. A heretic English Knight - Sir Richard Starkey becomes embroiled in the bloody five month siege which ensued; Europe's elite nobility cast chivalry aside, no quarter asked or mercy given as rivers of Muslim and Christian blood flowed...

Published on Amazon in Kindle Format & Paperback.

http://www.david-black.co.uk

Also by David Black

# Inca Sun

Chronicles of Sir Richard Starkey #2

Sir Richard and his giant servant Quinn begin their next great adventure, aboard the Privateer 'The Intrepid', in the treacherous waters off the Caribbean and South America coastline. Their heretic English Queen Elizabeth I had secretly commanded Sir Richard to prowl the high seas in search of King Phillip II of Spain's fabulously wealthy treasure convoys. They sail from the New World for Spain laden with gold and silver ripped from the Conquistador's mines in Peru and Mexico; dug from the dark earth by their cruelly treated Inca and Mayan slaves.

What Richard doesn't know, when he accepts his latest Royal commission, is that his arch nemesis - Don Rodrigo Salvador Torrez has become Governor of King Phillip's Mexican province of Veracruz.

One thing is certain, mere gold cannot pay the debt of honour that exists between the two men, since their first encounter on Malta during the great siege. The only currency, which will settle the terrible debt will be the loser's noble lifeblood....

Published on Amazon in Kindle Format & Paperback.

http://www.david-black.co.uk

Printed in Great Britain
by Amazon